Sign up for our newsletter to hear
about new and upcoming releases.

www.ylva-publishing.com

Other Books by Emily O'Beirne

Here's the Thing

Points of Departure

A Story of Now Series:

A Story of Now
The Sum of These Things

Future Leaders Series:

Future Leaders of Nowhere
All the Ways to Here (coming autumn 2017)

future leaders of nowhere

Emily O'Beirne

~ ~ ~

For all the girls who didn't think they could, you *can*. For all the girls who didn't get the respect they deserved, you should have. For all the girls who just wanted to see girls like them kick butt and fall in love on their screens, you did deserve better.

For all the girls who want their story told, let's start by telling them to each other.

For LB, who I am trying teach all of the above.

Part One: Finn

CHAPTER 1

As the bus veers onto the narrow bitumen road, Finn turns up her music, blocking out the noise so she can take in her new surroundings. Not that there's much to take in. The beige uniformity of the suburbs gave way to green about an hour ago, and the view has been an interminable, rainy sameness since. Wet, green paddocks stretch out on either side as far as she can see, and the horizon is a grassy nothingness, dotted with cows or sheep or some other kind of four-legged burger filler. This part wasn't in the brochure.

She actually likes nature, but the thought of being trapped this far from anywhere for weeks with no phones or laptops or best friend? Not so much. She wasn't sure about it when she packed her bags. And she's definitely not sure now that she's staring down the barrel of this no-man's-land reality.

Next to her, Amy grunts and snuffles. Her blue-streaked hair falls over Finn's shoulder. Finn pulls out her phone and sneaks a snap of her open-mouthed slumber. Amy's not going to love it, but Finn might need some leverage to keep her in line.

They are two of the seven kids her school has deemed sufficiently overachieving to cart off to this month-long camp. Trailing them on the highway is a caravan of minibuses packed with other schools' high performers. All total strangers. And for the zillionth time since leaving, Finn wishes her best friend, Dan, was with her instead of only Amy, who is fun and hilarious but hovers closer to long-term buddy/lab partner than friend. But Dan wasn't chosen. A fact he's proud of.

In the last half an hour, the hills start to close in, and trees huddle on the shoulder of the road, filtering the light a dull grey green. Bitumen fades to gravel, and they enter bona fide bush. Finn presses her face to the cold glass. Even in here, with the claustrophobic stink of stale sandwiches, worn upholstery, and too many kids in one space pressed up close, she can imagine the smell of wet dirt and the peppery eucalyptus. At least there's that to look forward to.

And, of course, there's the break from the ugly chafe of things she'd prefer to ignore. Like bad life choices. Like the constant tension at home. Her parents couldn't get her out the door fast enough. She hopes they fight long and loud and get it all out of their systems. Maybe then the hard ball of guilt in Finn's stomach will finally dissolve. She doubts it, though. You can't leave your conscience behind, can you?

She yanks her headphones from her ears as the bus turns through a set of wooden gates, and the words *Live, learn, lead* shake their finger at her from a wooden arch.

She plucks at Amy's sleeve. "Hey, we're here."

CHAPTER 2

The first speaker wears a crisp navy suit. It screeches wank against the cracked linoleum and institutional green chic of the dining hall. It's as cold and damp in here as it is outside, and it smells like a thousand meaty meals cooked. Finn wonders if she should finally make that jump to vegetarianism while she's here.

The suit monologues like he's giving some kind of corporate TED talk, and Finn takes the moment to finally get a look at her group. What a bunch of randoms they are. She doesn't know much about them besides names. It's been her job as intermediate school captain to know people's names. There's Amy. Then there's Craig, as wide as he is tall. She sits next to him in maths sometimes—total numbers whizz and a giant smart ass. The good kind. He's the kind of guy who makes even the tough guys not afraid to laugh. The kind even teachers like. But she can only put vague social statuses and academic specialities to the other four. And she can't even do some stealth social media research. Another downside to this weird social experiment of a camp: restricted technology. She's going in blind.

The suit talking at them is some kind of CEO who dabbles in politics. His company is one of the big guns Finn's dad always writes about, whose factories in some Second or Third World country are still pouring toxic crap into the atmosphere while he tries to jump on board the climate-change train. Right now he's ranting about how occasions like this camp are just tests for tomorrow, how kids need to challenge themselves and to think outside the box. It's all kinds of self-help, life-coaching, psychobabble. Like they all need a lesson in stating the obvious.

"Anyway, I wish you luck," he says. "Tomorrow the particular challenges you face will be laid out for you, and it's going to be exciting. Think of it as the most challenging role-play game you've ever experienced in your life."

Finn's played precisely none, so that should be easy.

"It will test your ability to work together, to think laterally and deeply, and to apply real-world situations to your fictional one," the man says in this hushed-but-excited tone, as if he's trying to chip away at the patent lack of enthusiasm his speech has invoked.

"I know exactly how to survive," Craig mutters next to her. "By not doing this *Lord of the Flies* crap."

Finn smothers a laugh as Mr Pinstripe winds up his speech. His beatific smile invites them to take a moment with his wisdom, but all he gets is a dismissive scattering of applause.

The moment he retreats, the camp director, Gus, a be-plaided hipster with requisite beard and man-bun, bounces out of his seat. He looks right out of place here in the middle of nowhere. She'd bet good money that he ducks back to Melbourne for an appointment with the barber and a local microbrew every chance he gets.

"Okay," he says. "Tomorrow we introduce you to the project and to your future digs, but first you need to pick your team leaders. We don't care who you choose or how you choose—no violence please, though—but you must have your leader selected and ready for tomorrow, when you'll receive your assignments." His grin turns slightly evil. "And just to make the job of selecting one a little quicker, nobody eats until you've decided."

A groan echoes around the hall. Finn can't smother a sigh either. It's been a long time since the hurried honey toast in the car this morning.

"Okay, so Finn's our leader." Amy says it like it's a no-brainer.

Craig nods. "Yeah, you do it, Harlow. School captain default."

Finn stares at them. They're all supposed to be future leaders. Shouldn't they *all* want the job? "Shouldn't we vote?"

"We already voted you intermediate school captain, didn't we?" Amy raises an eyebrow. "What? You need *more* validation?"

Finn shoots her a look, but Amy ignores it. "You know you want to do it."

Trust Amy to throw her under the bus. She once tried to pin an incident involving Ivan Kale, revenge, and a Bunsen burner on her in Year 9.

"I didn't vote Finn for captain."

Heads turn.

It's Brian something-or-other. All lank and basketball shoe. He folds his arms over his chest. "I wanted Steve Dorsen."

"Well lucky for us nobody else wanted that stooge," Craig says. "*And* that girl-brains beat your sorry jock-boy patriarchy for once. That boy's scraping the bottom of the brain-cell barrel."

Finn holds up her hand. "Hey, no fighting. I'm totally happy for someone else to be leader."

A guy called Jessie leans forward and shoots her a grin. "See, now you have to do it. No one else is going to tell us not to fight."

Finn has no idea whether he's mocking her or not.

"And you're good at this stuff," a girl called Hana adds.

Brian frowns. "But why does she get to—"

"Tell me, do you want to throw *your* hand in, or do you just want to complain?" Jessie asks. "Because we can vote on this if you want. You against Finn." He says it like it's a threat. Like everyone already knows Brian has no hope of winning.

"I don't want to be leader," Brian mutters. "I don't even want to be here."

Finn's starting to wonder if any of them want to.

"Then what's your problem if Finn's in charge? No one else wants to do it." He turns to the others. "Do they?"

They all sit back like someone lit a fire in the middle of the table. There's a long, pointed silence.

Finn shakes her head. Wow. Just wow. "Um, I just want to throw out there that I don't remember saying I wanted to do it either."

No one pays any attention.

"Okay, people, enough crap. I'm starving." Amy sits up. "Hands up if you're happy for Finn to lead."

Everyone's hand goes up. Even Brian's, eventually.

It still stuns Finn when people choose her for things. Dan says it's because she's the good kind of bossy, because she makes decisions and gets things done without being a total dictator. He says she's figured out this adult thing way before everyone else. Finn definitely doesn't feel like that. Not lately. And this job? Does she even want this job, in charge of whatever this high school edition of *Survivor* she's landed herself in? "So, do *I* get a say in whether I do it?"

"Nope. You do not," Amy says. "Because now we get to eat."

Jessie gives her another small lip curl of a smile. She wonders what he's here for. Lit or Philosophy is her guess. He looks nerdy but kind of indie, too, with his skinny jeans and floppy hair.

Around them, some groups are exploding into raucous rounds of laughter, slapping tabletops. Another group's sitting in total, glum silence, as if they've had enough of each other already. They are going to have a fun month. She spies Mr Manopoulos, their teacher representative, on the other side of the room, dwarfed by the regular-sized teachers around him. Everyone at school calls him "The Hulk", because he's tiny and skinny and looks like he hasn't eaten in a year.

Gus drums loudly on a table. "Okay! Can the leader of each group please stand up?"

Why does Finn get the feeling she's going to live to regret this?

He makes a show of appraising them, arms across his chest. "Out of interest, hands up any of you who put *themselves* forward for leader?"

Only two people raise their hands. One's a solid guy with thick, dark curls. He's got this slight smirk, and she can't tell if it's his mood right now or a case of resting smug face. The second is the only other girl besides Finn who's standing. Pretty and intense, with an impeccable, dark ponytail and a sharp, scrutinising stare.

"So, why did you volunteer?" Gus asks her.

"Because no one else was willing."

Finn smiles. At least she's not the only one with woefully lazy teammates.

"Self-sacrifice, I see." Gus points at the guy. "You?"

The cocky one with the curls grins. "Power. I like it."

"What a dick," Amy mutters. Finn can always count on Amy to say what everyone's thinking. Personally, Finn usually likes to cut people slack until she knows them, but his response definitely lurched toward the red end of the douche meter.

"An opportunist. Interesting." Gus opens his arms wide. "Now tell me, chosen ones, what kind of leader do you plan on being? Because I know everyone *loves* getting this kind of question at short notice." He chuckles at his own joke and points at a lanky guy at the table next to Finn's. "You?"

The kid turns red. "A good one?"

"Well, for your group's sake, I hope so."

People laugh, and Finn feels a rush of pity for the kid.

Gus turns his pointed finger at Finn. "You, with the blonde bob. What about you?"

Scrambling, Finn channels her school captain speech. "I guess I'll just try my best to represent everyone and their needs."

"Good luck with that," Gus jokes. "First rule of politics: you can't please everyone." He turns away, and the smirking guy smirks harder.

Why the hell did she agree to this? Oh, wait, that's right. She didn't. Finn shoots her group a dirty look, but no one's looking.

Gus is pointing at the other girl now. "You? What kind of leader do you plan to be?"

The girl raises her chin a little. "That depends."

"On?"

"On the task," she says simply. "Until I know what we're doing, how can I know how I am going to lead?"

Gus looks impressed. "Adaptive. I like it."

That was the smart answer. Finn looks at her, curious, but the girl's expression doesn't shift from neutral as she sits down at a table full of girls.

"Okay, one last task before dinner…"

Craig moans. "What? To starve us into submission?"

"The leaders need to pick a deputy. Now, the other members of the group have no say in this at all. The leader chooses. Choose wisely, though, because this person will step in for you in the unlikely case of injury or illness. And they will also take over in the event of a no-confidence vote." He rubs his hand together. "Spicy, huh?"

Amy shakes her head. "This guy is *way* too into whatever this is."

"Does anyone else feel like we're in some weird social experiment?" Jessie asks.

"Yeah, we're probably the guinea pigs for his sociology PhD or something," Hana says. "Look out for hidden cameras."

When Finn sits down, Amy's already firing up her best threatening look. "If you choose me, I will kill you. I mean it. I will wait until you least expect it, and I will exact revenge. Think of those tools in our dissection kits at school. Think how sharp—"

"Dude, stop. I'm not going to choose you."

Amy pouts. "Well, now I'm a little hurt."

Finn rolls her eyes.

"Joke. As if. I'm eternally grateful. Now choose someone. I'm dying of starvation here."

Everyone is pointedly *not* looking at Finn. The only person who meets her eye is Jessie. But he shakes his head.

Please, she mouths at him.

Finally, he gives her a grudging nod.

"Jessie's deputy." She mouths a grateful *thank you* at him. He gives her an *of course* smile. She's going to like this guy, she can tell.

"Great, let's eat," Brian grumbles.

"Why do I get the feeling that wasn't a choice based entirely on his potential leadership qualities?" Amy mutters.

"Shut up."

CHAPTER 3

The hardest part in the morning is remembering where she is. Then it all comes back. A cabin in the middle of nowhere. Fun. Finn huddles in the synthetic embrace of her sleeping bag, going about the gradual business of waking. Or, as her mother would say, avoiding the day.

It must be early, because no one is stirring, inside or out. At home, there'd be cars idling and neighbours slamming doors and the rumble of the 91 a block away on High Street. Instead, there's only a small, unruly chorus of mutters and shuffles. She blinks at the slats of the bunk above, where Amy is probably still sleeping like a sane person, and checks her watch. They've still got half an hour. But it's too late. The sleep window has closed.

Outside, the world is radiant. Sunshine ploughs through the trees, sending speckled light over the ugly brick cabin blocks. A complete, stark contrast from the gloom of yesterday. The air is brittle, though, and she zips her coat to her chin before skipping quietly down the wooden steps.

The only sounds in this sunstruck world are urgent, melodic magpie song and the rush of wind through the trees. She could get used to this. A series of cabins just like her own wind past before the path comes to an end at a small stretch of grass, surrounded by a stand of wizened peppercorn trees and a picnic area. She turns, and a new path meanders for a while. It borders some scrubby bushes and then stops at a fence overlooking another huge stretch of grass. A sports field. She clambers onto the fence, jams her hands into her pockets, and enjoys the bliss that is sunlight on her face.

On the other side of the field are more cabins. Fibro and decrepit, they are sadder than the ones on this side. Nearby, though, is an austere, double-storied brick house with a stretch of verandah running around both the top and bottom floors. She wonders who it belongs to. On the other side, the world slants downward to where a clump of willow trees lean, sweeping the grass with their branches. There must be water down there somewhere.

It's hard to believe this will be her world for a month. Four whole weeks.

"Why, good morning, fearless leader."

She blinks into the brightness. It's Jessie, sweat stains blooming from his underarms to the hem of his T-shirt.

"Hello, reluctant deputy. I didn't pick you for a runner."

He stretches his leg against the bottom of the fence. "Ah, but you were thinking about me. That's good news."

Flirting this early? Seriously? She shakes her head. "Don't flatter yourself."

He vaults up onto the fence. "So if you didn't pick me for a runner, what did you pick me for?"

"Wow, you really like to talk about *you*, don't you?"

He just smiles. "So, let me guess. You picked me for maths genius? Because of the Asian?"

"No. I pegged you for Lit, Philosophy, that kind of thing. A bit of Dostoyevsky and Bukowski. Maybe some Nietzsche thrown in. Well-thumbed copy of *On the Road*, maybe?"

"That's rough. And, while I do enjoy the oeuvres of all these authors you've pinned on me, I'm actually a total history kid. Which is why I'm at geek boot camp."

"Close enough. So, what do you think this game is going to be like?"

"Not a clue," he says.

"Me either." They feast on the sun while the cold air makes clouds of their breath. She fights the urge to look at him, to take stock of him properly, because she's scared he'll take it the wrong way. Or maybe the right way.

"Actually, I think that might be your literature buff over there." He points.

It's the leader girl, strolling across the oval, a book clutched in her hand. "She kinda ran circles around you all last night," he says.

"Yeah."

"But with those legs it wouldn't be hard." He stares across the field.

"I *was* kind of put on the spot."

"So was she."

"Hey, whose side are you on? Go see if Ms Legs wants you on her team if you like."

He just grins. Unruffled seems to be his setting. "Don't be like that. You chose me for your deputy, remember?"

"Only because you were the only one dumb enough to make eye contact."

"True." He swats at a persistent fly. "But I'm *your* fool deputy. And I happen to be stupidly loyal, so you're stuck with me now. Besides, between us we've got pretty great pins."

She kicks out her short legs. "I'll give you one thing—you really are a fool." Not many guys could pull off this kind of flirt-banter without being highly annoying. It helps that she can tell he doesn't believe any of the things he's saying, either.

"Told you." He launches himself off the fence and lands lightly on the grass. "I better get back before one of my bunkies finds my after-run food stash."

"And find a shower too. You smell like a wildebeest."

"Yeah, yeah. See you later, boss lady." He turns and strides away, whistling softly.

Finn should go, too, but she doesn't want to leave this pocket of peace and sunshine just yet. Or face this day full of unknowns. So instead she locks her eyes on the one thing moving on her horizon. The girl's arms swing gently at her sides as she walks. And when she reaches the dead centre of the field, she stops and tips her face to the sun, caught up in some sort of ultraviolet reverie, before she drops to the ground with her book. She looks so light and content, a world away from the stiff-backed girl of last night. Finn wishes she felt like that, instead of jagged and misplaced. The same way she's felt for weeks.

This is not her life. Finn's used to walking through her world like she's in a play that she wrote the lines for. One where she's worked hard to make sure she's always ready to deliver. Not anymore.

She wishes she could call Dan, so she could wallow in some familiarity for a minute. But mobile phones were handed over last night, and they're only allowed to use the public phones and the internet in designated communication times.

Even with all the tension, she'd settle for the comfort of home. Right now Dad will be waiting for the coffee machine to warm up, hunched over the paper at the end of the kitchen bench that catches the most morning light. He usually narrates every single thing he reads in the paper while Finn makes her lunch. Her teachers are always impressed by how well she is across current affairs. They don't know that she has no choice.

Behind her, voices start to call out into the morning, and her sunny world is slowly invaded. She watches the girl climb to her feet and walk towards her, as if she, too, has sensed the moment's over.

Curious, Finn waits for her to get closer before she climbs down from her perch. The girl frowns as she walks, like she's thinking hard. Her runners are pristine and her ponytail as perfect as last night. She gives Finn a fraction of a smile as she passes, a glance long enough for Finn to notice her eyes are a light amber, bright against the darkness of her skin.

Finn returns the smile a second too late, and she's gone.

CHAPTER 4

It must be Finn's lucky day. Her first partner for speed acquaintance making is the cocky guy who said he liked power. He slouches opposite her, his face in full smirk mode.

She makes an effort, though. "Hey, I'm Finn."

"Weird name." He stares around the room, like there are ten thousand things more interesting than her.

Nope. Proven douche. She no longer curbs the sass. "In my experience, in polite society names are usually *exchanged*. I mean, I'd hate to put you out or anything. It must be hard to converse while honing this effortlessly casual thing you've got going on."

His gaze slides back to her.

She smiles sweetly. "It's just I know you boys find multi-tasking a bit tricky."

The corner of his lips turn up as his eyes narrow, dancing a line between bitter and amused.

Before he can reply, Gus yells from his makeshift table podium. "Okay, first pairs, it's time!" He rings a bell above his head. "Get to your questions!"

The volume in the room triples as Finn scans the list. "Okay, favourite subject at school?"

"None."

"You must be good at something to get in here."

"I didn't say I'm not good at anything. I just said I don't *like* anything." His gaze roams the room again. "The modern education system is a waste of time."

"Right, of course." She rolls her eyes and scans the list. "If you could live anywhere in the world, where would you live?"

"A giant loft in New York."

"Favourite film genre?"

"Anything with zombies. I dig realism." The bell rings for them to swap. He leans forward and plucks the paper out of her hand. "Okay, my turn."

She braces herself for the worst. Or worse, for the obvious.

"So, got a boyfriend, Finn?"

And there it is. "Somehow I don't think that's on the list."

"Do share, though."

She just stares at him, wondering how to play him.

"Or is it a girlfriend?" He looks incredibly pleased with himself.

"I have neither, actually. Now ask me a question from the list."

"It makes sense, I guess." He reclines in his seat, considering her. "You do seem kinda uptight to be getting any."

She sets her face at pleasant-neutral and waits for the next question.

Finally, he gives up. "Do you believe in a higher power?" he reads in a dull voice.

"But I don't even know your name," she says, all innocence. "And I'm way too uptight to talk about something as deep as my beliefs without knowing someone's name."

"Why do you want to know my name so bad? So you can scratch it into a tree under yours?"

"I want it so I can warn the other girls about you." She leans forward and smiles sweetly again. "Or the boys, of course."

He opens his mouth, but the bell clangs loudly, stopping him.

She gives him a smile and a wave. "Bye, now."

He slouches off to his next victim.

Next is a girl from her team. It's probably the first time she's ever spoken to Zaki without Zaki's best friend Hana there too. In fact, she's never seen them apart. Around school they're known as this totally inseparable, comically opposing duo. Zaki is small and buzzy, with wide, brown eyes and the voice and body of a little girl. Hana is all curves and round cheeks, with this mumsy, middle-aged thing going on. She's one of those girls who's talked like an adult since she was ten and moves around like she's always on a mission to go tell someone something important. They look nothing alike, but they think and do everything together. They wear matching friendship bracelets, eye shadow, and hijabs every single day, and in the five minutes Zaki talks a mile a minute at her, Finn also learns that they volunteer at a cat shelter and worship Taylor Swift non-ironically together. A bff match made in heaven.

When the bell rings, Zaki smiles through her braces at her. "Hana and I both voted for you for school captain. You always seem like you're nice to everyone. I know it's not 'cool' to be nice, but..." She shrugs.

Finn just blinks at her for a moment. This girl is all kinds of sweet. "Thank you," she stutters.

She's still blushing when the girl leader sits down in front of her.

Her smile is tight. Guarded. "Hi. I'm Willa."

"Hey, I'm Finn." She smiles, but the moment feels loaded somehow. Then she remembers that they're opponents. Of course it's weird. They sit there, appraising each other as they wait. Finn's distance reading of her last night proves to be just as true up close: Willa's lovely but intense. Her mouth and eyes are languorously wide, but the thin press of her lips tells a different, sterner story.

The bell makes Finn jump. Flustered, she reads the first question off the list, an epically mundane one. "Which school do you go to?"

"Gandry Park."

Well that explains the crazy-good posture. Gandry girls probably take classes in it.

"You?" Willa asks.

"Brunswick Hill."

"I live near there."

"Really? Then your parents must have *really* wanted you to go to Gandry."

"What do you mean?"

"There are so many closer schools."

"I'm on a scholarship."

"Oh. Wow. So you're crazy smart too."

Willa shrugs, but her cheeks pink. "I don't know. I work hard." She looks down at her own list. "What's your proudest academic achievement?"

"Um, I won a state essay competition last year."

"What did you write about?"

"Why our politicians need to start believing in climate change, and fast."

Willa pauses, considering her. "So, do you think you're going to like this place?"

"Hey, that's not on the list."

She frowns and leans over the paper.

Wow, this girl is *so* serious. "I'm kidding," Finn says. "I really don't know what to expect yet. You?"

"Me either. I came so I could put it on uni applications. I *have* to do well."

"Well, I don't *have* to do well, but…" Finn tips her head in the direction of the idiot boy. By the expression on his latest partner's face, his conversation skills haven't improved. "I wouldn't mind doing better than him."

Willa follows her gaze. "Oh yes, him. I haven't had the pleasure of meeting the leader who *loves power*." She doesn't roll her eyes, but she's close.

"Oh, you're going to love him. I promise."

"I don't believe you for a second." Her eyes betray the smile she won't commit to. She opens her mouth to speak, but the bell stops her.

Finn flinches. "That guy is way too enthusiastic with that thing."

"He does seem to like it." Willa's smile is shy as she stands to leave. "It was nice to meet you."

"You too." Finn stares at her, surprised, as she strides away. Who knew that the girl who called out Gus for asking a stupid question in front of a roomful of people could do shy?

CHAPTER 5

Amy rubs her hands together. "Come on, Finn, get us something good."

Finn reaches in and pulls out a card from the hat Gus is holding out.

"Good luck," he says, sounding all solemn and ceremonious before moving down the line of leaders. When everyone has a card, he turns the hat upside down and spins it on his finger. "Okay, grab a map from the table, and go back to your groups. You've got five minutes to read over the cards before we explain the rules."

They sit in a tight huddle in the corner. Finn scrutinises the card, feeling her stomach sink.

Hana tugs on her sleeve. "What does it say?"

"Something tells me this is not good," Finn mutters.

"Oh God, what?" Amy leans in, trying to read over her shoulder.

"You are allotted no territory. You and your people are looking for a new place to settle. You have no land and thus no viable industry or income or—"

"What?" Jessie frowns. "I thought the point of this was we were all going to be given some territory?"

"Not us, apparently," Brian says.

Hana flaps a hand at him to shut him up. "Keep going, Finn."

"You must either seek refuge, find unclaimed land to live on, or find a way to gain land from other territories. You cannot camp in designated common areas. You cannot—"

"Camp?" Craig is wide-eyed. "Who said anything about camping?"

"I think it's just metaphorical. We have cabins." Zaki says nervously. "Right?"

"Well, if you'll let Finn finish, maybe we'll find out," Amy tells her.

"Your people are predominantly skilled migrants and intellectuals who have been forced from their homes because of political beliefs that are in conflict with the current regime. You have fled to avoid persecution or imprisonment. You must attempt to create your lives here. You function as a democracy."

Amy frowns. "So, basically, we're asylum seekers?"

"I guess?"

Jessie rolls his eyes. "Great, because we all know how well *they're* treated."

"Oh, goodie." Zaki rolls her eyes. "Being poor, overskilled, underpaid refugees. My parents already did this. Now I get a turn. Yay."

"What else does it say?" Brian asks.

Finn turns the cards over a couple of times. "Nothing."

Amy snatches the card out of Finn's hand and reads it again.

Jessie nudges Finn. "Don't worry. Maybe there'll be other groups even worse off than us?"

Maybe. Finn looks around at the other groups in the hall, trying to gauge the mood. One group looks positively miserable. But they're the same group that looked miserable last night, so it's hard to tell if it's specific misery. She looks around for the idiot boy, praying that his fate is worse than hers. He's in the corner, leaning back on his elbows, chatting away to his group. She can't tell if the look on his face is just his usual pleased-with-himself sneer or not. Willa and the Gandry girls are huddled together, composed and serious. But they always look like that.

Her fears are confirmed when Gus makes them all stand and read their cards. There's a definite murmur of sympathy as she reads.

Gus nods. "Ah, our wildcard group. You guys will have to be extra inventive."

"I thought getting a wildcard was supposed to be a good thing," Craig says. "You know, it gets you into Wimbledon. Or wins Uno."

When it's her turn, Willa stands and reads her card in a steady voice. "You own territory one. You have the largest territory and population." A few girls in her group give out little self-satisfied hoots. "Your workforce and economy are based on agriculture and cottage industry. You do not possess the industry to process the grain you grow. It is sold to Territory Three for processing and sold back to you. Your territory functions under a dictatorship."

Finn's eyes widen. This stuff is going to be complex. It's lucky that Craig's already scribbling notes in his exercise book next to her.

Next up is the idiot boy, Drew. "You possess Territory Three, a monarchy. You have the smallest territory, which is very densely populated. It has a rich populace, with a booming industrial sector. Due to your small geographical size, you rely on other territories for nearly all your food imports and water." He turns to Willa. "Thanks for that, darl."

Willa just looks at Drew, her face completely impassive, and then looks away.

As the others read their cards, Jessie turns to Finn. "What are we going to do?"

Finn shakes her head. Because the only thing she knows right now is that she has somehow managed to draw her group the worst possible card in that hat.

CHAPTER 6

All kinds of outdoorsy stuff are being flung from the deep, dark supplies cupboard onto the floor in front of them. Dusty tents and extra sleeping bags and tarpaulins and things Finn doesn't even recognise join the growing pile. She looks uneasily at her group.

Zaki's eyes are bug-wide. "I've never camped in my life."

"I'm just going to put this out there. I hate this place," Amy says.

Hana nods fervently. "It's definitely not my favourite thing that ever happened so far in my life."

"When the brochure said there might be some camping, I thought they were talking about an overnight hike or something." Craig shakes his head. "Not being subject to actual exile."

Gus slaps his hands free of dust and smiles broadly at them. "Chins up, guys. You can have a lot of fun with this if you try. Remember, the game is all about using your initiative and thinking laterally. This card really gives you a chance to do that."

"Oh, I feel so much better now that I know this will help me grow as a person," Amy mutters. Finn elbows her.

Gus pays no attention. He probably gets this every time. Finn wonders how many schoolkids have been tortured like this before.

"You can come back and get this stuff when you've figured out where you're going to set up camp," he tells them. "And let your teacher know, because he has to camp with you."

The Hulk bounces in his runners. "This is going to be great. Give you city kids some fresh air and some survival skills."

This is the most enthusiastic Finn's ever seen him about anything. Even Chemistry. And he teaches it.

"I *have* survival skills," Amy tells him. "I can get on any peak-hour tram or train, no matter how packed it is. *And* I can stay up for forty hours straight before exams and live to tell the tale."

He chuckles. "Not quite what I was talking about, Amy."

Amy just grunts.

"Suck it up, princess," Brian tells her.

"I am *not* a princess."

"You sound like one right now."

"Well, your face is about to become much, much better acquainted with my fist if you don't shut up."

"Come on guys, enough fighting," Finn tells them for what already feels like the millionth time. "Let's go."

CHAPTER 7

Amy stares at the house on the hill. "Look at it. It's huge. Maybe not a mansion, but it's at least *mansion-esque*."

It's the big brick house Finn saw yesterday morning.

"I *cannot* believe that place is part of the game territory." Amy shakes her head. "And I cannot believe that turd guy and his friends get to stay in it."

"While we freeze in tents." Hana throws her apple core into some shrubs. A bird flies out, squawking. "This sucks."

"I know, but maybe we should just focus on what we're going to do." Finn gazes at the map. The whole camp is divided up into sections, surrounded by differently coloured lines, outlining the territory each group owns. The game starts officially tomorrow, but tonight they have to move to their designated territories, an exercise designed to "enhance the experience of the game," says Gus.

"Designed to torture," says Amy.

Willa's group is sleeping in the same cabins as last night, while another group stays in a bunch of older ones that remained when the camp upgraded. Some people are staying in rough huts in the bush area behind the scrub on the other side of the oval, while Drew and his gang have the huge house. Only Finn's group is forced to camp.

"We need to worry about where we're going to sleep tonight."

"I say we kill turd boy and his friends and sleep in there." Amy points at the house.

"Agreed." Hana gives her a fist bump.

"I'm pretty sure murder's not in the game rules, Ames," Finn says.

Amy flops on her back and spreads her arms out across the grass. "I vote we do whatever is the fastest means of getting back into a building with plumbing."

"Hear, hear!" Hana cheers.

"There are a lot of rules, actually," Craig says, turning over the handout. "And a lot of homework for something called a *game*. We have to write every single thing up. Reports, analyses, proposals."

Brian spins his apple on his fingertip. "Why can't we just kick it old school and invade some territory. Colonise?"

"Yeah, let's take someone down." Amy rubs her hand together. "The idiot kid with the mansion."

"The idiot kid whose nation has a military and a huge population?" Finn pats Amy's leg. "Did you not listen this morning? We're supposed to be a small population of mostly educated intelligentsia kicked out of our lands for opposing political views. What do you plan to scare them into submission with? We going to stab them with our degrees?"

"Now, there's a point." Jessie holds out half a sandwich to Finn.

She stares at it blankly.

"Eat up, fearless leader. You haven't had any lunch."

"No thanks." Being responsible for all this is making her stomach churny. She looks around at the scattering of kids on the grass, peering at maps and reading handouts. No one looks as miserable as they do. Not even the misery kids.

"Besides, look how well that worked out," Jessie says to Brian. "Places like Australia, Canada, America. Colonisers basically destroyed entire populations of people who already lived there already, remember? Even if we had the means, would we really want to be *that guy*?"

"Yeah, that guy kind of sucks." A grin spreads across Craig's face. "Did you know that in Tonga, where my dad's from, they're super proud because they're the only Polynesian island nation that *wasn't* colonised? He says it's because warriors used to ride out in their boats and terrify explorers away before they could even get close to land."

"Sound methodology." Amy nods approvingly.

"And do you know what their tourist slogan is now?" He looks around at them, grinning.

"What?"

"The Friendly Islands."

Hana fires off a delighted laugh. "Perfect."

23

"I still say we try it," Brian says. "Mess with the mansion group and move in."

"I do not enjoy the fact that I agree with you," Amy tells him. "About the mansion part, anyway."

"Did you not just hear Finn?" Hana says. "We don't have the means to do that."

"We don't need resources. We just need brute strength," Brian retorts.

"Tell me, do you enjoy being a moron? Do you even understand this game? We don't actually go in and pummel them ourselves. How did you even get into this camp?"

He shrugs. "Basketball captain."

"Sport. Helpful."

"Yeah, shut it, ball boy," Amy adds. "Your jock status has no worth here."

"Well, if I'd known we'd be playing some Dungeons and Dragons crap, I wouldn't even be here."

"None of us would be, idiot." Hana screws up her sandwich wrapper and tosses it at his head.

"What's Dungeons and Dragons?" Zaki asks.

No one answers.

Finn sighs. "Sorry, Brian, I'm one of those boring, peace-loving types who doesn't like killing and pillaging. I think the only way we're going to get out of tents is by begging for asylum. Or we can suck it up, settle somewhere, and figure out a way to strengthen our resources and gain territory."

"All right. If we can't go for the mansion option, I'm for the first," Amy says. "We figure out what some group needs and fulfil it if they'll give us mattresses."

"I know what everyone wants." Brian grins. "We could become the prostitute nation."

Hana shakes her head. "It's official. You're a moron."

"But everyone wants sex, right?"

"I repeat, *moron.*"

"Prude."

CHAPTER 8

The sun beats down on Finn's neck and shoulders as she leans over the map. *Again.* She's been staring at it all day. But no matter how long she stares, nothing changes. The rest of the group is lying around, chatting about anything but the game.

She nudges Jessie. He's picking apart a dandelion and staring into the middle distance. "So, where's the east fence line?" she asks. "Is it the creek?"

He shakes his head, dragging himself back to Earth, and leans in. His finger slowly traces the creek. "Nope, it's a bit beyond. See?"

"Thanks."

"I never thought those years in Boy Scouts would pay off, but apparently I can still read a map."

"Scouts? I didn't think they even existed anymore."

"I don't know about in the city, but in the backwaters of this fine nation, the Scout movement is alive and well."

"You're a country kid?"

"Used to be." He tosses the shredded flower away. "Until two years ago."

"Why'd you leave?"

"Good old-fashioned divorce."

"Oh." She gives him a sympathetic smile. "I'm really sorry."

"It is what it is."

"I think my parents might be headed that way," she says quietly. "Divorce, I mean."

"Really?"

"They fight all the time."

"Yep. That's how it starts."

She nods, not telling him that they fight because of her, because of what she did. That makes the feelings close in.

"You have a lot to look forward to. Highly recommend it. Five-star experience."

"Oh goodie." She returns to the map. "Okay, we seriously need to start looking for a place to camp."

"And then we have to figure out how to get out. I mean, I'm okay with the whole tent thing, former Boy Scout and all, but a few of these guys are going to riot after a few nights of sleeping rough."

"I know." She sighs and runs her finger over the large section of territory that encompasses the cabins. "Hey, Craig?" she calls out.

He's flat on his back on the grass, using his notebook as a sun visor. "Huh?"

"Who has the big bit of land, again?"

He pulls the notebook from his head and scans it. "That serious chick."

"The *serious chick's* name is Willa," she tells him.

She looks over at Willa and her group. All the girls in her group are *so* Gandry Girls High. Impeccably dressed, even for camp. Even tans and on-trend everything, from shoes to hats to sunglasses. They're a magazine spread waiting to happen. Except for Willa. No sunglasses, no sunhat, no fuss. Still, she's the most likely to grace a magazine spread of them all. Finn wonders if it bothers the other girls. They're all trying so hard to look as good as Willa just naturally does.

"But she's *so* serious. I've never seen her smile." Craig shakes his head. "Not once."

"Maybe she just doesn't smile at *you*, Craigus," Jessie says. "And I don't think Finn's taking umbrage with the serious part."

"Yeah, don't call girls 'chicks'," Hana says sleepily from somewhere under the tangle of sunglasses and scarf that is she and Zaki hiding from the sun.

"Don't call us girls, either," Zaki adds. "We're women."

"Women?" Hana elbows her. "You brought a stuffed monkey here to sleep with."

"Shut up."

"Who's Territory Three, again?" Finn asks.

"Jeez, lady. Chill," Brian says. "We'll find someone to take us in. It can't be that hard."

Finn flops back on the grass, giving up the impossible task of getting them to stay on topic. She shuts her eyes against the sun and takes in a deep, slow breath.

"Allow me to take this short break to regale you with a tale of great humiliation from my scouting days." Jessie's voice is close to her ear. "It's a good one."

She smiles. She gets the feeling she's always going to be able to rely on Jessie to lighten the mood. "Go right ahead."

CHAPTER 9

"Are you people even supposed to be on my grass?"

It's Drew, the guy with the mouth, swaggering over from the big house. His group is from some rich, ancient, inner-east boys' school that Finn's mother talks about sometimes because she's vice-principal of a rival school. These guys are all expensive haircuts, T-shirt logos, and self-satisfied smiles.

One of the Gandry girls lifts her sunglasses, followed by an eyebrow. "It's not your grass."

"Um, I believe it is." He turns to Willa, his arms folded. "I'm thinking this territory is mine, Right, sweetheart?"

"Actually I'm thinking you don't know how to read a map," she says.

Finn catches Jessie's eye and smiles.

"Is that so?" Drew points at one of his clones, who's holding the map. "Well, my friend here says it's our territory."

"Then I stand corrected," she says calmly. "Your friend doesn't know how to read a map."

Amy sits up. "Ooh, I *am* enjoying Ms Legs' super-chill takedown method." She taps her finger against her chin. "I shall call her method *ice sass.*"

"Come on, you guys." Finn clambers to her feet. "We'd better go find some place to camp."

"You all better get going, actually," Drew says. "Unless you want to breach game rules." He turns to her. "Is that what you want, *Finn*?" He says it in this familiar voice, like they're old friends.

Finn pulls on her knapsack and sighs loudly. "Drew, buy a clue. Willa's right. Either you guys can't read a map, or you're colour blind." She holds the map up in front of him and traces her index finger over the purple line surrounding the small patch of land around the brick palace that he and his friends now call home. "See this part here? That's your territory, and…" she runs her finger around the black line containing the amenities and the football field and rec areas, including the lawn they are sitting on now, "*this* is common territory. Gus said no one can claim it or live on it."

"Got it, genius?" Amy jabs a finger in his direction as she stalks past. "You owe us a geography lesson."

Drew delivers a give-no-craps smile. "What do I care about a little patch of grass? You guys can have it. We've got *that*." He points at the house.

For a second, Finn thinks she's going to have to hold Amy back.

"Sucks for you homeless folk, doesn't it?" he says. "Finding somewhere to exist in your sad, cold tents."

"Oh, we'll be fine," Finn tells him much more confidently than she feels. "We'll find somewhere. We can read a map."

She catches Willa's eye. They trade small smiles. "Come on, guys. Let's do it."

CHAPTER 10

Brian kicks at a clump of dirt. "I say the spot near the barbecue place was better. Closer to the showers."

"This *is* kind of out of the way," Hana says.

"Yes, but do you guys want to have something to bargain with?" Finn reminds them. "A way to improve our situation?"

"If you mean not sleeping in tents, then yes." Amy nods fervently.

"Then we need to be here." Finn steps under the cool embrace of a willow tree and points at the busy rush of the creek. "This is where we settle."

"But isn't this part of the common territory?" Craig starts to unfold the map. "I thought we weren't allowed there?"

"We aren't. But we're allowed to settle over there." She points to the narrow stretch of grass on the opposite bank. "From the water to the fence line over there is no-man's-land."

"Awesome. We own no-man's-land." Brian tosses a stone into the water. "There's a reason it's called no-man's-land, you know."

"Well, it could be ours now," Finn says, playing confident despite the turbulence in her stomach. What if she's wrong?

"But why here?" Hana asks. "I don't get it. It's sort of pretty and all, but isn't it kind of small?"

"I know why," Craig says.

Amy squints at him. "Care to share with the rest of us?"

"Water."

"So? What do we need water for? We're allowed to use the shower blocks." Zaki turns to Finn, eyes wide. "Please tell me we are."

"Not water for us, Z," Finn says patiently. "For the game. We're the only ones with water as an asset."

Craig's grin is wide. "See? Genius."

"Sorry, call me dumb, but I still don't get it." Amy squats on a rock and dips her hand into the water. She yanks it out just as quickly. "Whoa, that's freezing! But everyone has access to the water. It's on the common territory."

"*This* side is on common territory. So no one can claim it for production or use." Finn points to the other side. "But that side is ours. And according to the game rules, we can do whatever we like with the assets on our land, right?"

"Yeah, I guess."

"So now we have a bargaining chip."

Jessie nods slowly. "Good one, Finn."

Finn smiles at him, more grateful she wants to let on. This leader thing is turning out to be harder than she thought. Harder than being intermediate school captain. Probably because she was actually given a school to be captain of. Not sent out to hunt one down.

Brian flings another rock. "I still say we camp near the showers. Who cares about the game?"

"I do," Hana says. "As in, I'd like not to go back to school a total loser."

"Me too," says Zaki.

"I *guess* here's okay. But remember," Amy points at Finn, "I will settle for nothing less than the mansion by the end of this. So you better be right."

Finn shakes her head. "No pressure or anything. Okay, let's vote. Hands up if you're happy to camp here?"

Jessie, Craig, and Finn raise their hands. Finn looks at Amy.

"Happy would be too strong a term, but alright." Amy raises her hand

Hana raises her hand. Then she nudges Zaki.

"Oh, yeah, right." Zaki raises her hand. Then she turns to Brian. "Sorry," she says, without an ounce of sincerity.

"Okay, I guess we go get our tents," Finn says, glad they've managed at least one decision.

"I still don't see why Drew gets to live in a mansion with his idiot boy band," Amy says as they trek across the oval.

"Because sometimes even losers win," Craig says cheerfully.

CHAPTER 11

Finn surfaces to the sound of tiny snores floating up from the bundle of sleeping bag next to her and lifts her arms out wide. Her back aches a little from sleeping on such unfamiliar flatness. It's been a long time since her parents used to take her camping. Last night wasn't so bad, though, once Amy stopped whining and went to sleep.

The birds are making a racket in the trees on the other side of the fence line. As she quietly unzips the tent, a cow lets out an indignant moo somewhere in the distance.

Jessie is already lounging on a rock down by the water. He looks totally at home in all this nature, his feet dangling in the water and his eyes half-closed to the sunshine. It's the total opposite of Hana, who squealed and jumped and asked a zillion questions about bugs and tent pegs and wildlife last night while the Hulk helped them to set up camp.

Finn sits in the entrance and gets used to the day.

Behind her, Amy becomes a flurry of rustles and groans as she wakes. She crawls over to sit next to Finn, still cocooned in her sleeping bag. "Well, I enjoyed that as much as I thought I would." She rubs a hand over her face. "Morning."

Finn smiles, but she doesn't feel like breaking the peace with words just yet.

Clearly, Amy does. She points at Jessie, still reclined on his rock. "So, you going to tap that?"

Finn pulls a deliberate *no comprendo* face.

"Oh, come on. Cute boy is cute. And he pays an unnecessary amount of attention to you."

"Thanks a lot."

"You know what I mean. So?"

"I don't know." Finn shrugs. "Cute boy *is* cute, I guess. If you like it so much, why don't you go there?"

"Because he doesn't look at *me* all the time. Besides, I don't date Chinese boys. It makes my parents too happy."

Finn grins. "Fair enough. Anyway, it's seven in the morning. This is no time to be making those kinds of decisions."

"Seven?" Amy crawls back into the tent. "This camping crap is bad enough without getting up at sparrow's fart for no reason. Shut the door on your way out."

Finn grabs her knapsack and zips her in. The Hulk's up now, too, chatting to Jessie. She gives them both a wave but keeps walking, skipping gingerly over rocks. She's going to find herself some whine-free sunshine before this day starts.

When she spots the figure lying in the middle of the oval, she knows immediately it's Willa, deep in her book.

"Hey. Morning," she says as she gets close to her.

Willa lifts her head, eyes wide, as if the last thing she was expecting was to see another human. Her ratty ponytail looks like it could be yesterday's. It's nice to know she can do ratty. "Oh, hi."

"Ready for a day of power tripping and deal making? Or if you're me, figuring out how to get my team out of this crap sandwich we're in."

Willa sits up with a frown. "Hey, you know I can't talk to you about any deals or anything."

"I wasn't going to. I wa—"

"Seriously." Willa puts her book down. "I can't talk to you about anything like that when there's no one around."

"I wasn't going to talk about any deal. I was just…" Finn shakes her head. "You know what? Never mind."

She stalks away. The heat fades slowly from her cheeks as she drops down on the grass at a safe distance from Willa. Why is everyone so damn cranky this morning? She was just trying to be friendly.

Finn yanks her sketchpad from her bag and digs around for a pencil. Armed, she begins to sketch a faint outline of the tree line down near the creek. She hasn't drawn for months. She's been too busy painting. At first, it's weird without music. She always paints with headphones jammed in her ears. But she gets used to it as her pencil roughly re-creates both the sweeping arcs of the willows and the graceless contortions of the gums behind them.

The soothing scratch of lead against paper does its thing, and she finds that place, that limbo between all the things in her life, where nothing can touch her. It's medicine. Finn always thinks it's funny that when her half-sister, Anna, turned up in their lives, that they discovered that they shared a love of art. Especially when the blood that tethers them is her father's, possibly the world's worst Pictionary partner.

And the bonus is, it's homework. Mr Kenworth told her she had to come back with a bunch of sketches. Kind of a Mickey Mouse assignment, because he knows she'll do some kind of art while she's there anyway. Because she can't *not*.

By the time the sun's right up above the trees and the morning siren sounds, she's finished, down to mapping out the tiny clouds peppering the blue sky. And with this hour tucked away, she feels like she can face the day.

As she walks slowly back to camp among the kids making sleepy trails between bed and shower blocks, she turns and looks for Willa. But she's already gone.

CHAPTER 12

Finn shuts her eyes, closing out everything but the feel of sun-baked rock and the streaming sounds of water careening over rocks. The peace lasts about ten seconds.

"So, we have a decision to make, right?"

"Yup." She exhales wearily and opens her eyes to Jessie making himself comfortable next to her, a mandarin in his hand. "Gus says we have to go through everything we learned yesterday and then put together our proposals."

Yesterday was intense. After a morning hike to a seriously underperforming waterfall, they spent the rest of it completing the day's assignment, trying to find real-world examples of places and times similar to the situations they've been given. Finn and her group researched different political refugees, from the rich Russian intelligentsia exiled in the twenties to the intellectuals forced to flee a revolution in Iran. Then they had to do the regular schoolwork they brought with them, under the Hulk's supervision.

"So what are our options?" Jessie asks.

"I guess it's a choice between asking one of the other territories to take us in with them or biding our time to see if we can find a way to make our settlement sustainable."

"If we do seek asylum, who will we try and join?"

"Someone who needs educated people. Brainpower."

"Yeah, I was thinking that last night. I reckon our best bet is Miss Ice Sass and her girls."

"If you keep calling her that, she won't be taking any of us in."

He grins lazily and digs his thumb into the mandarin, peeling away the bright pith. "I see your point. But trust me, it's only said in admiration. She's like this beautiful, scary ice queen."

"Okay, I get it. You have a thing for powerful women. Can we move on?"

"Why do you think I like you?"

She ignores him. "So why do *you* think we should ask them?" She agrees, but she wants to know why he's thinking it.

"Because of the education deficit in her territory. They have to outsource food production because they don't have the means do it themselves. But if they wanted to change that, to build industry, they'd need engineers and planners. And they'd need people to train them to be that. That's where our intellectual wealth would come in."

"That's what I thought too. But I'd rather hold out and see if we can find a way to stand on our own feet. I mean, it's possible, right?"

"I guess. But it could take a while."

"We have nearly a month." She tips her chin toward the cluster of tents. "But I get the feeling these guys won't like that."

"I hear you." He holds out a piece of mandarin to her.

She takes it, flinching at the first sharp, citric bite.

"Hey?" he says.

"Hey what?"

"If they took us in, would that mean that Willa girl would be our leader?"

She frowns. "Yeah, I guess."

"That'd be weird, having someone we barely know in charge."

"Probably." She doesn't want to admit it, but she's not that sure she wants to give up being in charge yet. Not before she's actually had a chance to see if she can make this lousy hand work in their favour. Because isn't that what they're supposed to be doing, trying to build nations? Not looking for the cosiest position possible? She *wants* to try. The doing, the planning, the making things happen—that's what makes her tick. Does she really want to just hand that role over to a stranger, a total control freak of a stranger, if this morning was anything to go by?

"So, how are we going to decide?" he asks.

"I guess we put it to a vote."

"Okay, but just so you know, I prefer you as our fearless leader."

She's still trying to figure out if he's serious or teasing when he says, "I do. You're good at it."

She smiles. At least someone's on her side. "Thanks."

CHAPTER 13

This time, Finn's sketching the opposite view from the oval. She's so deep into what she's doing that she nearly drops her pencil when someone crouches in front of her.

It's Willa, wrapped in a thick, red jumper, the sleeves pulled over her hands. She gives Finn an apprehensive smile. "Morning."

"Hi." Finn's arm slides over her drawing, knee-jerk protective, as she warily watches Willa settle cross-legged onto the grass.

"I'm really sorry about yesterday. I didn't mean to be so..." Willa presses her lips together, like she's not sure how to finish. She plays with the sleeves of her jumper. "You were just saying hi, weren't you?"

"Yep. Just saying hi."

"And I snapped at you." Willa blushes, and for a moment, she's a regular human-person, instead of the flinty leader-bot she's been so far. "I'm sorry. I take everything way too seriously. I was thinking really hard about the game when you came up, and I just assumed that's what you wanted to talk about."

"See, that's funny, because I was actually looking to talk about *anything* else."

"Again, sorry." Her lips press out into a contrite smile.

"That's okay. But now I've got to wonder if *you're* capable of talking about anything but the game."

"I can." Indignation sends her voice a note higher.

This is too easy. "I'm teasing. But the fact that I have to tell you kind of proves your point about taking things too seriously."

"Oh, don't worry. I prove it to myself all the time," Willa says.

"Okay, well, while we're being honest, the words 'loosen up' are not totally unfamiliar to me. And this game *is* kind of complicated. Which is why I was trying to escape it yesterday."

"I get it." Willa's expression turns thoughtful. "One of the girls said that you're captain of your school. You'd have to take things pretty seriously."

"Intermediate school captain. Years 9 and 10. Yeah, there's a lot of extra responsibility, I guess. And the whole setting an example thing."

"We don't have a captain. Instead we have three different student leaders at each level: academic, social, and sports. They divided it up years ago in some useless attempt to stop it being a popularity contest. But social leader is still a popularity contest. I'm academic leader. No one cares about that except the teachers. And me."

"I'd never be voted social leader. Not unless everyone's idea of a social life suddenly turned out to be study sessions, indie films, and occasional mild partying."

Willa lets out a small laugh. An actual laugh. It's a surprisingly girly, delighted sound. Then she leans forward. "Okay, I think we should make a rule."

"A rule, huh? Sounds like you might be doing the serious thing again."

Willa ignores her, intent on her point. "An oval rule."

"An oval rule?"

"We're kind of opponents, but we both hang out here. So since we both say we need to loosen up, let's make a rule that there can be no shop talk if we see each other."

"Only meaningless conversation?"

"Whatever, as long as it isn't about the game." Willa thrusts her hand out for Finn to shake. "Deal?"

A formal handshake over being more chilled seems kind of counterproductive, but Finn's willing to go with it. "Deal." They shake.

Willa takes in a deep breath, leans back on her hands, and sighs. "I love the mornings here. It smells good."

Finn gazes around her. "It doesn't look so bad either." The sky is picture-book blue this morning, flecked with equally picture-book white, fluffy clouds

"Have you been drawing?" Willa points at the sketch Finn's forgotten to keep covered.

"Yup. Art homework."

"Can I see?"

When Finn holds up the sketch, Willa's eyes widen. She takes the book right out of her hands. "Wow. You're really good." She stares in silence a moment and hands it back. "I can't imagine being able to draw properly. To make it look like what it's supposed to."

Finn never knows what to say to those comments, because she's always just known how to make things on the page look like life. Her paintings aren't like that, though. She doesn't want them to look like life. Dan says she paints the opposite to what she is, because they're all fanciful, twisted, and dreamy, when she's so down-to-earth and chilled. But she's never felt like she has any control over the paintings. They just come out like that.

"Hang on. It's not finished," she says. Tongue jammed between her teeth, Finn quickly sketches, totally showing off now. She tears the page out of the book and hands it back to Willa.

It takes Willa a moment to find it, but when she does, she smiles. There, in the middle of the oval, is a tiny figure lying on the grass, reading a book. "That's me, isn't it?"

"That's exactly how I saw you the first morning here. You looked so blissful."

"Reading my economics book. Total bliss."

"*That's* what you were reading? In my mind, you were devouring some fabulous work of literature."

"Nope. Only VCE-related books until holidays. I'm getting ready."

"That's impressive self-denial." Finn points at the tome Willa has abandoned to the grass. "Is that the culprit?"

"Nope. Done with economics. This is new." She holds it up. *The French Revolution in Context.*

"So, let me get this straight. In the time you've been here, you've polished off an economics textbook and just casually moved onto that? What do you read for fun? English grammar?"

Willa gives her a sliver of a smile. "I know I'm boring, but I want to do well. So if that's what I need to do..."

"Hey, you're not boring. Not so far, anyway. Though, honestly, I don't know if I'm the right person to judge."

"You don't seem boring either." Willa examines her. "You seem strong and smart and like people would want to listen to you."

Finn digs around in her backpack for a fresh pencil to hide her blush. "Well, that's alright, then. Okay, so we won't talk about the game, and we won't bore each other either. Can I ask you a question, though? It's kind of related to the game, but not."

"Maybe."

"Did you really put yourself forward as leader because no one would?"

"They say they were all holding out because they wanted me to volunteer, because it seems like "my thing". I don't know if that's good or bad."

"I'd take it as a compliment. At least your group let you decide. Mine forced me to do it."

"But that must mean they already think of you as a leader."

"Or they're just too lazy to do any work themselves. It turns out some of my school's future leaders are kind of slack."

Willa smiles but says nothing, and Finn wants to kick herself. That's not the kind of information you share with an opponent.

"Can I ask *you* a question?"

"Mm?"

"Can I keep this?" Willa points at the picture lying on the grass between them. Then she withdraws her hand, her cheeks pinking. "I mean, if it's not important or anything."

Finn picks it up and passes it to her. Even if it means one less piece for her homework folio. "Of course."

CHAPTER 14

They sit in a tight huddle around the fire the Hulk built. The payoff for this snug circle of heat was a lecture about fire safety, but it's totally worth it.

Finn glances around at them all, paper slips in hand. "Okay, so you guys understand what we're voting for?"

"Sort of." Zaki takes a handful of snake lollies from the jumbo bag and passes it on. "What are we going to offer in exchange for the Ice Queen taking us in, again?"

These guys have a million titles for Willa, and not one of them is her name. "They have large-scale agriculture, a huge population, and a lot of land, but they don't have the technical skills to build industry to process their agriculture for domestic food product. So they have to be processed in Drew's territory—"

"Um, I believe his official title is Idiot Boy," Amy reminds her.

"Then they have to buy it back from him at whatever price his territory fixes. But the theory is that if we were able to show them how to build the industrial resources to process their own food, they wouldn't be at his mercy on food prices."

Hana pops a yellow and an orange snake in her mouth at the same time and talks through them. "Do you think she'll even want to take us?"

"I don't see why not," Craig says. "It's a long game, but it's a sound economical choice for her."

"And we'd get to move back into the cabins with them?" Amy asks.

Finn nods. "That'd be the trade, yeah."

"I like it," Hana says with relish.

Jessie looks around at them. "Don't forget, guys, that it means we'd be under Miss Legs's rule, and her territory is a dictatorship. That means this is probably the last time you'd get a say in anything."

Hana stops chewing. "Wait, so their leader would decide *everything*?"

"Yup. But if we take option two and stay here and make a plan to settle, we'd have our autonomy and Finn would stay on as our leader."

Everyone falls silent.

"Okay, let's do this." Finn hands out the pieces of paper and pencils. She decided earlier that a private vote would be less awkward. "Everyone write down either a number one for joining the Gandry girls, or two for staying put."

She sits back on the log, scratches a two onto her paper, and folds it tightly. Everyone slowly hands their piece of paper down to the Hulk.

It's barely a minute before he gathers up the pieces of paper, counts them, and then throws them into the fire. "Okay, kids. It's option one."

It's as if Finn's blood thickens. And even though she saw it coming a mile off, it still stings. It's pretty easy to tell who else voted to join Willa's group, too, because they won't make eye contact with her.

"Remember," Jessie says, "this is just a vote to put in the proposal. She might not even go for it."

"But she might." Amy rubs her hands together. "And then I get to sleep in a bed." She turns to Finn. "Sorry, dude."

Finn forces a smile and stands. "Okay, so we'll see what happens tomorrow when we propose. I'm going to bed. Night, all."

She hears a muttered chorus of guilty goodnights behind her, followed by a short silence.

Then she hears Brian say, "Ice Queen better go for it. It's freezing out here."

Finn grabs her toiletries bag from the tent, wraps a scarf around her neck, and begins the long, slow trudge up to the shower block.

The ambitious, competitive part of her hopes that Willa says no. Either way, Finn knows she'll try her best to make her see the benefits of taking them in. Because that's what her group wants. And it's her job to help them, even if they turn into a bunch of disloyal idiots at the promise of a mattress and electric light.

Footsteps pound on the track behind her. "Hey, wait up." Jessie falls into step with her. "Don't take it personally, okay? I mean, they're a bunch of selfish, spoiled turds, but…"

"But what? But they're *our* selfish, spoiled turds?" She frowns into the darkness. "Is that supposed to make me feel better?"

"Something like that. But you know they weren't voting against you, right? They were just voting *for* something else."

"It's like they don't even want to try and actually play the game. The point is supposed to be learning this stuff, isn't it? It's not about finding the easiest option and coasting through."

"I know. It's annoying. Hey, who knows? Maybe if Miss Legs does take us in, she'll put them through their paces. Then they'll learn their lesson pretty quick."

Maybe. Finn doesn't care right now.

"As long as you know it wasn't about you."

She does. It just doesn't make it feel any better.

CHAPTER 15

Finn stares up at the sheer crag of reddish rock in front of her, the occasional tenacious shrub clinging to a crevice for dear life. It's as daunting from down here as it was from the top.

"I can't believe we just climbed down that." Amy kicks her boots into the dirt. "I'm feeling terribly outdoorsy right now."

Finn watches the last two climbers inch their way down, scrutinised by the burly, super-hyped husband-and-wife team who are enthusiastically bearing the responsibility of shaping them into well-rounded people this morning. Finn can't believe she just did that climb either. The worst part is right at the top, going over the cliff face, when you have to commit to the terrifying shift of the regular, upright embrace of gravity to walking backwards down a rock face, treating it like it's the ground. It was kind of exhilarating once she'd got past that.

When the last two climbers are done, the husband turns to them all. "Okay, people! Huddle!"

Finn raises an eyebrow as everyone obediently shuffles into a loose circle. Huddle? What kind of jock nightmare is this?

"Good job, guys," Wife says, jumping from side to side, like she's ready to take off at a sprint. "You really tested yourselves today."

"Sure did." Hubby crouches on the ground, picks up a stick, and draws a lopsided circle in the dirt. "That," he says, pointing at it, "that's your usual life. That's what we call your comfort zone." He draws another small circle a small distance from the big one. "But see that?" He digs the stick into the circle. "That was you today." He stares around at them, swiping a hand over his fauxhawk. "*Wayyy* outside your comfort zone."

"I'm not sure that was a complex enough idea to require a diagram," Craig whispers.

Finn stifles a giggle.

Wife claps her hands. "So, if you thought it was hard coming down the rock, it's a hell of a lot harder going up."

"She's right." Husband grins with that special kind of cruel glee Finn has only ever seen on personal trainers and in army movies. He checks his watch. "We've got a little time. So who's willing to have a go?"

There's a mass shuffle and a silence as all eyes return to the cliff face.

"Oh, come on," he crows. "Afraid of a challenge?"

"Yep." Hana sits down on a rock. "Terrified would be more like it."

There's another short silence. Finn's sure some sporty type or some dude trying to earn bragging rights will put their hand up, but they don't. No one speaks.

"I'm not giving out lunch until someone has a go," Gus tells them all, staring around at the group.

Wow, it's come to this. Bribery by stale, white bread sandwich.

"I'll do it," someone finally says. It's Willa. She steps out of the crowd. There's no swagger from her, though. She just folds her arms and contemplates the rock, as if she's just decided to get this over with so they can move on.

One of the Gandry girls lets out a small hoot. "Yes, Willa! Represent!"

"Good!" says Wife, thwacking Willa's arm in some form of commando congratulations. "Now we need someone for the other rig."

Again, silence.

"How about Drew?" Amy says quietly—but just loud enough for people to hear. Finn gives her a mental high five.

"Yeah, Drew should do it." Hana looks slyly at Amy.

And just like Amy wanted, the idea takes off. It's picked up by a Gandry girl and then one of Drew's friends, until eventually his whole team and a lot of other people are hooting and cheering for him to do it.

Finn sees the fleeting panic in his eyes as his gaze flicks up the cliff face and back down again. He quickly covers it with a slick grin, swipes his hair back from his face, and steps forward. A few people cheer.

"And we have our second." The wife claps loudly. "Let's do this, people!"

Finn sits next to Amy and watches, curious, as the husband and wife explain whatever needs to be explained. Drew stands slouched, hands in pockets, only half-listening as he looks back and forth between his teammates and the lecture. Willa stands straight backed and completely attentive, the same way she did that first night. Such a contrast to the girl hugging her knees and smiling on the oval this morning. Finn wonders which one of these girls she's more like when she's not at this camp.

After messing around with the ropes and more instructions, Willa and Drew start to climb. They take off quickly, easily finding handholds and footholds in the lower, less sheer parts of the cliff. Drew muscles himself from section to section with his natural upper body strength. Willa may be slender, but she's strong, easily keeping pace with him. Below them, Husband and Wife holler instructions, but they're nearly drowned out by cheering and heckling. It's not meant to be a race, but the crowd makes it one, picking sides and clapping and urging them on.

They get to the steeper, middle part, and while Willa slows to carefully pick out her path, Drew keeps racing. But Finn notices he sometimes has to retrace his steps when he's made a snap choice and finds himself at a dead end. The upper section is so sheer, Finn's glad she's not the one up there, hunting for places to put her feet and hands. The higher they climb, the louder people shout and cheer, and Finn realises her teeth are clamped down on her bottom lip as she mentally urges Willa to kick Drew's ass.

Hana chomps nervously on her gum next to her. "Ice Queen better beat Idiot Boy."

"Hell, yeah." Amy claps her hands. "Go Willa!"

"She's not even on your team yet, dude," Brian reminds her.

Amy holds up her hands. "*Look* at my choices. Come on, Willa!"

They're nearly two-thirds of the way up the rock when Drew suddenly loses his footing and slips. There's a gasp as he drops a couple of inches before the safety rope goes taut and catches him. He swings back and forth as he reaches wildly for the rock face.

"You're okay." Wife grasps his safety rope. "Just find your place and start again."

Meanwhile, Willa's steadily inching up the rock face, her long legs straddled impossibly between two holds, her fingers dug deep into a crevice. Finn can't resist letting out a loud "come on!" of her own.

As soon as he has regained a foothold, Drew starts to chase, closing the distance. It sets off another chorus of whistles and calls from below. But in his rush, he slips and is left dangling again. A few people laugh and boo.

"Try again!" Wife shouts.

Drew swears loudly and slaps the cliff face.

"Just calm down and find your centre," she soothes.

"Find his centre?" Amy cackles. "It's not his centre he needs to find right now."

By the time he's got a foothold again, it's too late. Willa's already scrambled up the last stretch of rock and, wrapping her hand around the trunk of a small tree, pulled herself onto the ledge. She gazes around at the view, as if she's forgotten everyone below.

Finn finds herself standing and cheering loudly with the rest of the kids.

"Great work," Husband hollers. "Come down whenever you're ready."

Willa nods and turns to climb down. Drew starts the descent too, but Wife shakes the rope. "No way, bucko! Finish what you started!"

"What for? It's over. She beat me."

"It wasn't a race, buddy. You turned it into one, which is exactly what slowed you down. It's about challenging *yourself*. Extending your own experience. Get to the top. You'll feel better for it in the end."

Finn seriously doubts it, but it's pretty great to watch him being forced to finish. His team starts calling out and whistling, but the tone has changed to something closer to mocking.

"Go on," Wife says when he doesn't move.

He punches the rock and curses but does as he is told.

Finn turns to Amy. "Happy? Now you've achieved public humiliation?"

Her grin is pure evil. "Oh, *so* happy."

Willa moves quickly down the rock, bounding down in a series of jumps the way they were shown earlier. When she reaches the bottom, Husband slaps her on the back. "Nice work. You're a natural. Have you done climbing before?"

Willa shakes her head as he unclips her.

"Well, you did good."

"Thanks." There's no hint of smugness or superiority as she goes back to her group. One of the Gandry girls clears a spot for her so she can sit on their rock, and another passes her a sandwich. And as the others relive the moment, Willa glances around the clearing, stopping when her eyes meet Finn's.

Finn gives her a small *I'm impressed* smile.

Willa gives her the smallest smile back and quickly looks away.

CHAPTER 16

Finn swaps her textbooks from one side to the other and stretches her free arm. There's a dull, satisfying ache in her shoulders from the abseiling trip this morning.

"Still feeling pleased with yourself?" she asks Amy as they toss their books back into the tent.

"Yup." Amy sighs happily. "And I hope that She Who Humiliated Drew decides to take us in. I like her now."

"I can't wait," Hana says. Then it'll only take a few seconds to get to the showers, instead of walking half a kilometre."

Jessie rolls his eyes. But Finn can't smile back, because it's still raw. She makes her excuses and leaves camp again. They have half an hour until dinner, and the last thing she wants to do is hear how much they'd rather that someone else be their leader.

She's not used to feeling like this. Powerless. But it's felt that way since her parents started fighting. Since Matt dumped her out of nowhere. Since she landed here, and the "natural leadership" her vice principal commended publicly is suddenly nowhere to be found.

Willa's on the oval. A shimmer of relief hits her.

"Hi," Finn says. "Do you mind if I…?" She bites down on her lip, suddenly wondering if she's assuming friendship that isn't actually there yet.

Willa pats the grass. "How are you?" She gives Finn a look as she sits, as if she's suspecting the question needs to be asked.

"Okay." That's all Finn can say. Because even if she wanted to be honest, she can't. Because that would be talking about the game.

She pulls the sharpest pencil she can find in the collection at the bottom her bag. "Hey, can I ask you a question?"

"I guess."

"The girls in your group, are you close?"

"Why do you want to know that?"

"I'm just curious."

Her brows furrow.

"Whoa, relax. This is *not* about the game. I'm not trying to gather intel or anything. *Seriously,* Willa."

At least she has the decency to look guilty. "I thought maybe…"

"Stop being so suspicious. I'm not that kind of person. I was just curious because they seem to really respect you."

"Sorry."

"That's okay." Finn smiles. "But you might want to add trust issues along with taking things too seriously onto your list of things that need work."

"You wouldn't be the first to tell me *that* either."

"Good to know."

She closes her book. "Well, to answer your question, the girls in my group are fine. They're nice. But we're not really friends."

"Right." Finn frowns. So Willa must just have that undefinable thing that some people possess. The one that makes people naturally do what you want. The thing Finn's starting to think *she* doesn't have. Or that she's lost.

"What about your group?"

"Same. I've known Amy for years, but we're not exactly close."

"And Jessie?"

"I didn't really know him before this camp. Why do you ask?"

Willa shrugs and traces her finger over the cover of her book. "Because you're always together."

"He's my deputy. We work on the game. It's not anything more, if that's what you're wondering." Finn can't help feeling a little like she's lying, though. Because she knows there's some sort of *something* between her and Jessie. She just doesn't know if she wants to do anything about it. "I kind of got dumped a while back, and I'm still getting over that humiliation," she says, leaving Willa to connect the dots if she wants. "What about you? Are you with anyone? Oh, wait. I guess if you're not allowed to read fiction during school time, you're probably not allowed to date, right?"

"Something like that."

"You should let yourself have a little fun sometimes. I mean, not necessarily a relationship. But maybe, I don't know, start small. Treat yourself to some chick lit between text books," Finn teases. "I'm sure it won't hurt your big uni ambitions, whatever they are."

"International relations."

"Should've known."

"What about you?"

"I don't know yet." Finn tucks her hair behind her ears, wishing it would hurry up and grow one more inch so she can tie it back. "My best subjects are Art and Biology, but I love English the most. What do you even do with that?"

"Something amazing, I'm sure." Willa's smile is shy.

"*You* were amazing today, by the way."

Willa brow furrows, and then she nods. "Oh, thanks."

"And, bonus, you made Drew look like an idiot."

"He made himself look like an idiot." Willa opens her book.

Finn picks up her pencil and sketchpad. She focuses on a dandelion shooting its starburst yellow out of the scrubby, pale grass, and wishes she had her paints here.

When they're packing up their things later, Willa suddenly says, "I was with someone. At the start of the year. But it's over."

"Oh." Finn blinks. "What happened?"

"She left." Willa traces a pattern on her jeans, frowning. But before Finn can think of anything to say, she goes on. "She knew she was moving away, but she didn't tell me. She let something happen, and then she left." She stands and brushes the grass from the back of her jeans. "So it's not just about focusing on my studies."

Finn nods. So Willa likes girls. And she's been hurt. Still, Finn's pretty sure you can't just close your heart for business like that. She never could. She shoves her sketchpad in her bag and clambers to her feet. "Well, I don't think something that brutal could happen to a person twice. I hope not, anyway. Maybe just make sure they're not leaving the country or anything before you make a move next time?"

"Probably a good idea." Willa stares down at the grass, hugging her book. "You know, I have no idea why I just told you about that."

"Because we're becoming friends. That's why. So you're going to have to learn to trust me now, aren't you?"

The corners of Willa's mouth inch upward. "I guess so."

"And you shouldn't let one bad experience stop you from being open to something else, you know. Otherwise no one would do it."

"And maybe you should take your own advice." Her smile is part teasing, part earnest. "I better go. See you later."

As Finn watches her walk away, and wonders which is worse, the quick dump or the slow fade. Because she was left, too, in the slower, excruciating way. She liked Matt. Really liked him. Enough to think it was real. Enough to sleep with him—her first time. Then things changed. He went suddenly distant and stayed like that. Then he came back from the school ski weekend, which she didn't go to, and broke up with her. Said he wasn't feeling it. Now they avoid each other.

And when the initial sting was gone, there was a worse one in its place. Aside from the fact she could have judged something so badly. It felt so shocking to have gotten something so, so wrong. How was she supposed she trust herself after a mistake that epic?

Even though she told Willa that one bad experience with the wrong person shouldn't stop you, there's been no one since him. Unless you count that night on the trampoline with ditzy, cute Ruby Shipman and the kissing. But that was different. That was the product of a party (rare), a beer (extremely rare), and a little flirting (rare lately). They both knew that Ruby preferred guys and Finn preferred brains. But the impossibility of it was exactly what made it possible. And fun.

She's shoved out of her thoughts by the sound of her name. It's Jessie, loping towards her. "Don't look so innocent. I saw you conspiring with the enemy."

"What?"

"Miss Legs. I saw you mingling. Talking her up before we beg her to take pity on us?"

"No." Finn sighs. In the distance, the crowds of kids drag their feet to the rec hall for dinner. It's hard to muster enthusiasm when the biggest your dining dream can go is edible. "We weren't talking about the game."

"I'll choose to trust you on that." He pulls his sunglasses up. "Are you ready for tomorrow, Finn? It's the big one."

"As I'll ever be," she mutters.

CHAPTER 17

Tomato and lettuce sandwiches again. A perplexing cocktail of stale and soggy. She's contemplating the second half when Zaki skips up and hands her an envelope. "You've got mail," she says with cheesy glee. Then she drops a package in Craig's lap. "And it's your lucky day, Craigus."

Finn turns the envelope over. Her mother's writing. Inside is a small card with a beautiful, hand-painted bird on it. Her mum never could just write a note. It's not her style.

Hey hon, your dad and I have decided to drop down on Saturday and see you on visitors' day. We miss you! Let us know if you need us to bring you anything. See you after lunch.

The thought of seeing them gives Finn a little prick of homesickness. Bring on Saturday.

Craig scrabbles at his parcel. "Yes!" he cries as chocolates spill into his lap like coins pouring from a lottery machine. "Make it rain! Hey, Finn, look sharp!" A mini Snickers flies onto the table in front of her.

"Ooh, thanks." There's been a distinct lack of chocolate at this camp. What if she hits a spoke in her menstrual cycle, and there's none to be had? She reminds herself to get her mum onto it before Saturday.

Jessie nudges her. "Eat up, because we're going in soon."

A pinch of dread overtakes her. They're about to present their offer to Willa.

"So, how are you going to play Miss Ice Queen Serious Sass Legs?" He wrinkles his brow. "Did I forget anything?"

Finn swallows her last mouthful of peanut-chocolate goodness and shakes her head. "Well, for one, I'm going to ask you not to speak. At all. Maybe ever."

He chuckles. "Fair play. I'll be on my best behaviour. No name-calling, I swear."

"Good," she says dryly. "I don't even know if I want her to say yes; but I don't want to look like an idiot either."

"Finn," he says, catching a flying Kit Kat, "you don't even know how to look like an idiot."

CHAPTER 18

They sit in a formal face-off across the table. Around them, other groups meet under the fluorescent lights, discussing proposals in surprisingly serious indoor voices. Where once raucous jokes about the lack of internet and broken board games prevailed, there is a sombre, board-meeting kind of mood. People have really gotten into this game.

Willa, of course, is the most serious of them of all. She sits straight-backed and straight-faced as she listens. Finn can't read her expression at all. It's unnerving. She wishes she were talking to the girl on the oval instead of this poker-faced statue. As she winds up her spiel, she shifts slightly in her seat. "So, basically, if you were to accept this offer, my group thinks it could be of benefit to your group."

Finn didn't even think it was possible, but Willa sits up even straighter. She raises an eyebrow. "Your group?"

"Yes." Finn stares at her. "My group."

Her gaze is unflinching. "But what do *you* want? You're the leader, aren't you?"

Finn folds her arms over her chest. "I would like th-the same," she finally says, knowing she left it too long. Her cheeks turn hot as she rues that small stammer.

She sees her uncertainty being absorbed.

Damn. Finn straightens in her seat. She will not be cowed. "This is what we, as a group, have decided on as the most beneficial option," she says. "Beneficial for us and for you." She tries to look like she doesn't really care. "It's up to you if you think the same."

Willa's eyes narrow a little, but Finn doesn't blink. She's not letting go of any more power in this meeting.

Finally, Willa nods. "We'll consider it among our options." She turns to the blonde next to her, who is scribbling on a notepad. "Have you taken it all down?"

The girl nods. "Uh-huh."

As she turns back to Finn and Jessie, Willa squares her shoulders. "We'll be considering all proposals over the weekend. Thank you for speaking with us."

Finn gives her a businesslike nod and pushes her chair back. "Okay, thanks."

Standing hurriedly, Jessie glances back and forth between them. He hasn't said a word so far, as instructed. "Uh, yeah. See you later," he mumbles, following Finn.

Finn strides back to the group. They're all sitting under a leafy sprawl of trees. She shakes her head, frustrated. That microsecond of uncertainty made her look stupid and weak. It's almost as if Willa knows that Finn doesn't want their groups to join up. But how could she know that? And even though they're supposed to be keeping the game and their friendship separate, she can't help feeling betrayed by Willa's polar caps-level ice act.

Amy squints up at them from her Chem text. "So, how did it go?"

"That was…" Jessie sinks onto the grass, shaking his head. "It was like the Ice Queen Play-offs. Total power play."

"Yeah, but what did she say?"

"We'll know after the weekend." Finn kicks at the grass and frowns.

"So we still camp 'til Monday?"

"Yes."

Amy lets out a long, loud moan.

"Seriously, Amy," Finn says. "Would you please stop whining about it? We did the best we could to get you what you want, and now it's out of our hands."

"Yeah, leave Finn alone," Jessie says. "She's basically giving up being leader to do this, and she still went in and asked for what you guys wanted."

Finn turns on him. "I can defend myself, thanks."

"Sorry." He holds up his hands.

She feels instantly guilty, but can't bring herself to apologise yet. She's too annoyed at herself. At everything.

"I'm sorry, dude." Amy hooks her arm through Finn's. "Thanks for trying. I'm being a brat."

"You really are."

"I'll stop complaining, I promise. Hey, did you hear Idiot Boy has invited everyone to the mansion on Saturday night?"

"Even us?"

"Yep. Rumour has it they're laying on some booze someone smuggled in."

"But why did he invite us? He hates us."

"Wants to show off his pad, I guess. Make sure we really know what we're missing out on."

Finn rolls her eyes. "That'd be right."

CHAPTER 19

Finn drops onto the grass, panting at the stars. There's too much exercise at this camp. Even the rec activities are just thinly disguised sports.

Jessie saunters over, holding out a can of home-brand lemonade and an ice-cream. She gazes lovingly at them. "There should be a halo of light over this ice-cream."

"I know, right?"

These chocolate-coated ice confections are the most decadent treat they get here, and they're only doled out every now and then, usually after being forced to do something highly physical.

Jessie devours half of it in one bite. Not Finn. She's making this last.

"Who knew an ice-cream would be the top thrill of a Friday night?" he says.

"You used to be a country boy, didn't you? How many thrills could you have had?"

"Oh, believe me, country kids know how to make their own fun." He seems to have forgotten she snapped at him earlier. Either that, or he doesn't do grudges. "We are nothing if not resourceful."

They've been playing torch flag tag on the oval, their mandatory Friday night fun. Finn was mixed in with one of Drew's boys, a Gandry girl, and a pair from the wood-hut team as they fought to win as many points as possible. It's a still, balmy night, and it secretly felt kind of awesome to run around, yelling in the moonlight. Dumb, but fun. Jessie's team won. He was put with Brian and Willa and a bunch of other kids she doesn't know so well.

"Turns out Brian's good for something," Jessie tells her. "He earned about half of our points."

"Now we just have to figure out how to get him to channel that into being useful for us."

"And Miss Legs knows how to use hers. She's *fierce*. But I guess we're not surprised."

"No, we are not."

"Hey, your parents are coming tomorrow, right?"

"Yup. They better bring coffee. And good snacks. What about you? Anybody coming?"

"Not sure."

There's a loud clanging sound. Gus and his bell. "Alright, everyone, off to bed! It's late!" he shouts into the night.

Jessie sighs. "It's Friday. Cut us a little slack."

"It's nine thirty. He probably thinks he is." They start the trudge back to the creek. "They've given us until eleven tomorrow night," she tells him. "Did you hear about Drew's party? We're actually invited."

"Yeah, I think I'll give that a miss."

"Me too."

It's such a beautiful night. It makes her want to swing her arms, cutting them through the air. So she does. She feels loose and almost happy for the first time today.

The rest are up ahead, gathered around The Hulk, who's gesticulating wildly as he talks.

"What precious nuggets of knowledge do you think we're missing out on right now?" Jessie asks. "How to most effectively roll one's sleeping bag for space optimisation? Geological structures and how they affect tent pegs? The lost art of bush tucker?"

"Possibly all of the above." They stop when they get to the ridge where the track to the creek starts. She loves this spot. You can see the epic sprawl of the night sky over the paddocks.

He turns to her, can held aloft. "I think we should take this moment and use this sugary beverage to toast your efforts this morning."

She raises an eyebrow instead of the can. "Really?"

"Seriously. You totally held your own. Even though you didn't want to do it."

"No, I didn't. I messed up when she questioned me about it being my choice or my team's choice."

"I didn't notice."

But Willa did.

"Seriously, Finn. I think you did good."

"Thanks." They touch cans and drink in silence.

She stares up at the thick scatter of stars between the trees. "Thanks for sticking up for me today. With the group. I was pissy about it in the moment, but I'm actually grateful."

"Well, that's not confusing." She looks at him. He smiles, his eyes almost blackish in the darkness. "Anyway, of course I stuck up for you."

"Why?"

"Why?" he says, like she already ought to know. Then, before she sees it coming, he steps in and kisses her lightly on the lips. "That's why."

She's surprised, even though she knows she shouldn't be. This has been coming for a while now. She scrambles to keep it light. "Um, do you really think we should be mixing work and pleasure?"

"Who said anything about pleasure? That was all work." He grins, but she can see he's nervous. "You're still our leader for now. I need to keep you on our side."

"Oh, right. That's what that was."

Before she knows it, he's leaning in and kissing her again. It's a little slower this time. A little more lingering.

"That one, though," he says as he pulls away. "That one was pleasure. Night."

The next thing she knows, he's taking off down the trail in short, leaping steps, disappearing into the darkness.

At least he has the decency to kiss and run. To give her a moment alone with this possibility. Now she just needs to figure out what she wants to do with it.

CHAPTER 20

She wakes early, even though it's the weekend. On some kind of sleepwalking automatic, she heads for the oval, but then halts on the track. Does she really want to see Willa after that meeting? Can Finn trust herself to keep her bruised ego under wraps? She doesn't usually do rattled. Not out loud, anyway. But this camp's got her all kinds of messy. She steels herself to play normal and heads for their spot.

Willa isn't even there. Finn stares at the scrubby, green space where she'd normally be sitting, somehow still graceful as she slouches over a book. She wouldn't have picked Willa for the sleeping-in type.

Irritated by the flecks of disappointment spoiling her resentment, Finn sits on her lonesome and sketches. And when she's done feeling betrayed all over again, last night invades. Every time she thinks of Jessie's kiss, there's this low thrum in her stomach. But she doesn't know how to read the feeling. She likes Jessie. As a human being. In general. And she might be vaguely attracted to him, in some kind of benign, cute, funny-boy, sure-it's-possible kind of way. But she also knows he doesn't give her *that* feeling. That exquisite, painful sensation that you can never really describe. Shouldn't she be chasing that? But then maybe she needs something easy and comforting while everything else is so damn hard, to help her remember that she does know how to make unstupid choices.

When she's trudging back to camp, she sees Willa and her group carrying towels and water like they've been exercising. Willa gives her a quick smile as she saunters past, all long brown limbs. Finn returns it, kicking off her campaign of being unruffled Finn, even though her stomach says otherwise.

Down at the creek, everyone's easing into the day. Jessie gives her a wave but doesn't come over. She's grateful and maybe even a little impressed.

Ignoring the girls' calls to come hear Hana's latest carefully-harvested camp gossip, she goes to her tent and pulls out her books, determined to get on with her other project. She spreads out her map, lays out her notes, and starts to work on a contingency plan. Just in case things don't work out with Willa's group. They may never use it, but at least she can prove to herself she *could* come up with something if she actually gets the chance to try.

CHAPTER 21

Her parents are being weird. Great, but weird.

Armed with coffee and pastries, they sit opposite her, a united front of indulgent, smiling parenthood.

"So, are you having a good time?" her mum asks brightly. Too brightly. Not that Finn's mother is not a positive person. She is. But she's also kind of serious. Comes with the territory of being a vice principal. "What are they making you do?"

"It's fine." Finn brushes the flakes of pastry and cinnamon from her hands and fills them in on the game. They love the idea, of course. Right up their geek alleys. With these two as her parents, how could Finn not have ended up here?

They tell her about everything back home. How the dogs have taken to howling in unison in the morning to be let out. How her uncle crashed his motorbike on holiday in Vietnam and got twenty-six stitches on his leg. How her gran sent her dad a birthday card meant for his sister.

At first, Finn can only sense the weirdness. Then, all of a sudden, it's crystal clear. It's not a united front at all. They're talking to *her*, but they're not talking to *each other*. Haven't even made eye contact.

"What's wrong?" Finn asks right in the middle of her dad's story about the neighbours.

"What do you mean?" Her mum busies herself, tidying up the rubbish.

"Something's wrong. You two won't even look at each other. I'm not an idiot."

"I trust you'll field this?" her mum says without looking at her dad.

He nods slowly and turns to Finn, running his hands through his thinning hair. "Listen, we didn't want to worry you with it while you're on camp, hon, but I was forced to resign from the paper."

It happened. It actually happened.

"And, well, you know why, don't you?"

Finn nods. Her throat tightens.

"So, as you can imagine, I'm looking elsewhere for work." He presses a hand over hers.

This time, she just blinks, wondering what it will mean. Why the hell does she feel like crying? He did something brave and amazing. But it's not that. It's the tension between them. Still there. Still thick. Will they fight even more now?

Her mother grabs her other hand and squeezes it. "Don't worry. We're okay for money."

She pulls her hands away. It's too much to have them both touching her while not looking at each other. "I wasn't worried about that."

"Then what is it, Finn?"

Finn shakes her head. Why go there? "Nothing. I'm really sorry you lost your job."

He gives her a wry smile. "Worse things have happened to better people, haven't they?"

He always says that. "You're a good person, Dad. Otherwise you wouldn't have done it."

"Thanks, kiddo. I'm glad you think so."

CHAPTER 22

Finn wanders back from the car park, her hands jammed in her pockets, her stomach an acidy mess of anxiety and baked goods. What's going to happen to her parents now? Will they keep battling this out in angry whispers behind closed doors? Or will they find a way past it? She hopes so. It's the first time in her life she's been relieved to see them leave her. Right now she'd rather be in the wilderness than in that car with all that unspoken tension.

"Yo, Finn." Hana's sitting on the fence at the edge of the oval, filing her nails and dreaming.

"Hey." Finn leans next to her, watching the steady stream of bickering or bored families, the joy of reunion clearly dissolving fast, as they traipse back and forth across the sun-yellowed grass. "Your parents visit?"

"Nah. Next week. The whole lot of them. Mum and Dad, all six brothers, the grandparents, probably a second cousin or two. And my mum will bring everything in the fridge." She rolls her eyes. "You got brothers and sisters?"

"Just an older half-sister." Finn climbs up next to her.

"How old?"

"Twenty-eight. She's a gynaecologist. Lucky me. Free pap smears for the rest of my life."

Hana lets out an extravagant laugh. "Yeah, lucky you."

"We never lived together, though, so I was kind of an only child."

"I don't know whether to feel sorry for you, or jealous."

"Probably sorry. Six brothers, though. That's a lot of testosterone in one house."

Hana shudders. "Tell me about it. So much boy stank. I love them, though. Most of the time."

Finn's about to ask more when she spots Jessie walking across the oval with a girl she's never seen. She's short and curvy with long brown hair and walks with this slow saunter, like she believes the world will be willing to wait for her. She says something and laughs, bumping Jessie's shoulder. Finn stares, suddenly uneasy.

"Well, I guess the break's over, then."

"What?"

"See that girl with Jessie?"

"Yeah," Finn says, carefully casual.

"That's Mel Somes. She's on our soccer team. She was with him all last year. Was. Is. I don't know, actually. She told me last week they're on some kind of trial break. Whatever that means."

"Right." Finn's jaw tightens. Part of her doesn't want to hear another word of this, while the other part wants to ask Hana to hand over every single nugget of information she possesses.

She doesn't need to, though, because Hana keeps gossiping. "She was telling me all about it after netball. Apparently, they've set a date after camp when they're going to *re-assess*. They weren't supposed to talk to each other or see each other for the month. Like a trial separation. I say if it comes to that, just break up already. We're sixteen, for crap's sakes. Why drag this stuff out? It's not like they have a mortgage."

Finn nods, but she's only half listening. She's too busy wondering why the hell Jessie kissed her if he's got something—something *year-long serious*—going with this girl. She wouldn't have picked him for the wandering type. But then, Finn's not so sure she's good at picking types anymore.

That acid feeling slinks back. It's not fair. She wasn't even one hundred per cent sure she wanted to go there with him, but he forced her to consider it by kissing her.

Feeling the familiar ugly flicker of betrayal, Finn jumps off the fence. "I have to go."

"Uh, okay. See you."

CHAPTER 23

When things get messy, Finn's the kind of girl who likes to face it and get it out of the way. But it doesn't mean she actually likes doing it. After dinner, she goes back to camp, feeling an icky combination of relieved and queasy when she finds him lying on his rock, reading.

He smiles as she approaches, but she can feel his wariness too, like he's wondering if she knows. This camp is like a gossip lightning rod. Even if Hana hadn't been with her, Finn would bet money she'd know about Jessie's visitor by now.

"So." She digs her hands into her pocket. "Mel?"

He nods, like now it's confirmed, and puts his book down. "I didn't think she'd come here."

"I don't really care what you thought about that. I *do* wonder why you kissed me last night when you're with someone else."

"We're not really together. We're on a trial break."

"I know."

"How do you know that?"

"Hana."

"Oh." He chews his lip and sits up. "Listen, Finn, I wasn't cheating, and I wasn't breaking any rules. I don't do that crap."

"Sure," she says evenly. "But how about the fact it's breaking *my* rules?"

So what if she's making them up on the spot? He doesn't need to know that. "Do I get a say in whether I want to be a part of whatever messy thing you've got going on?"

He lowers his head. "You're right. I'm sorry. But I want you to know we're not together."

"But you're not *not* together."

"I guess. But I like you." He looks up at her, his eyes wide, like he's pleading with her to believe. "It's all been so confusing, but meeting you has been what's helped me see that this thing with Mel is done, you know?"

"So you broke up with her?" Not that it matters.

He hesitates. "Not exactly."

"So happy to be of assistance, then. Listen," she says calmly, even though a part of her would love to let fly at him right now, "I'm sorry you're all mixed up about whatever you've got going on with her, but I don't want to be a part of it. And I should have been given that choice."

He nods but won't look at her.

"Some advice, too, for your future dating plans: being on a trial break with someone else? It's kinda one of those need-to-know things, okay?"

"I'm sorry, Finn. I really am. And I really do like you."

She shrugs. "We can be friends."

"Right. Got it." He frowns. "Why are you so mature about this stuff? Mel would be screaming."

It's like he *wants* her to be upset. Expects it. That's her cue. "I'll see you around, Jessie."

She marches up the track, putting as much distance between them as she can.

Mature? What does that mean, anyway? She doesn't even know what it means to be mature about something like this. She's just reacting to a moment the only way she knows how. Maybe he's right, though. Finn's mum always says that Finn put her out of a job by raising herself. She doesn't *feel* that grown-up. It's probably not that grown-up to shove him in the creek, but she really wanted to just then.

No way is she going to waste any time feeling upset about this. She's got no room to spare for feeling anything more than a little ego-bruised and glum. There are too many other things needing her misery right now. Like the state of her parents' marriage. Like her pathetic efforts at leading her group. Like rejection from a guy she actually liked.

Jessie will have to get in line if he wants her anger.

68

CHAPTER 24

Finn does what she always does when she feels like this. She talks to her best friend. Trades the last of her weekly technology minutes for the comfort and sanity of Dan.

He picks up in half a ring. "What? I'm busy," he says when he hears her voice.

"No you're not."

"No, I'm not. How's Dictator Camp? Learning anything?"

"Not much. That I miss you."

"I miss you, too, stupid."

Finn smiles. She can see him right now, curled up in his giant checked spread, some obscure sci-fi thing paused on his laptop, an array of junk beside him. And Finn pines to be where she belongs, stretched out next to him, begging to be able to watch something—anything—else, and then talking through whatever they choose anyway.

"Speak, Finn."

Finn does as she's told. And as she fills him in on the Jessie situation, she spies Willa on the phone on the other side of the hall. She dials a number and smiles widely when it picks up. Finn fleetingly wonders who it is that makes her look like that.

When she's done telling Dan her sorry little tale, he crunches loudly on something at the other end of the phone. "Wow, that sucks."

"And I hate that I have to feel embarrassed about this. That's the worst part—to be humiliated by someone you're not even a hundred per cent sure you liked." She sighs.

"Again, shitty. And kind of insulting."

Exactly." Finn stares at the chipped noticeboard next to the phone, picking at the graveyard of old pins and staples. "Anyway, it doesn't matter. It's not like I was invested or anything."

"Well, I've been saving this nugget up for you: Tamika dumped Matt. Your Matt."

"Very much not my Matt."

"Said he came on strong and then went all emotionally distant. Sound familiar?"

"Yep. Totally, horribly, familiar." Does Dan really think she'll feel better knowing she was just one of many victims of an emotionally stunted behaviour pattern? Boys are so stupid sometimes. "Can we please not talk about it?"

"Sure. Just thought it might feel better to know it isn't just you. Anyway, in good news, I was going to see if I could catch a ride with your parentals next week and see this breeding ground of greatness."

"Yes, please." Finn's smile spins into a frown. "It might be weird, though."

"Why?"

"Dad lost his job, and now they seem to have moved from forced pleasant to non-engagement."

"Ouch. That's bad. You know you're like one calamity short of a shitstorm right now? How did you manage that?"

"I don't know," she says softly. A sneak attack of tears threatens. She swallows hard.

His tone mellows. "Hey, you'll be okay. Just focus on winning that dumb game you're all playing."

"I will, if my team will let me." She can't talk about any more bad things, so she changes the subject. "What about you? How are things?"

"Oh, good. You know how it is, being an internet sensation."

"Yeah, yeah." Lucky for him he only speaks like that to her.

"And how're things with Rosie?" Finn prays this girl sticks around. She seems cute and funny and, unlike the last one, doesn't see Finn as some kind of threat just because she's a girl.

"Good. She's coming over in a bit."

"And how's the fam?"

"Exactly, precisely, happily the same. Life is blissfully dull."

"Good." Boring is the desired option for him after his mum's sickness last year. "Listen, I better go. My time's up. I'll talk to you soon?"

"Yup. I love you. Keep passing the open windows, okay?"

"Ha-ha. You too."

She hangs up and looks around the hall. Willa's gone. Everyone's gone. They're probably at the party. Even the girls decided to go earlier. Hana said it beats the hell out of another fireside survival lecture from the Hulk. Finn's not so sure.

She stands on the top step of the rec hall verandah and weighs her options. If she goes back to camp, Jessie will be there. And if she goes to the party, Drew will be there. It's a lose-lose. But at least everyone *else* will be at the party to dilute Drew.

She's about to turn up the path to the mansion when she sees a glowing light moving near the back of the rec hall. As she moves in closer, she immediately recognises Craig from the hulking shape on the back steps. He's hunched over a phone, playing some game, his fingers careening over the keypad.

She tiptoes up to him. "Boo," she says quietly.

He jumps a mile, whipping the phone behind his back. When he realises it's her, he grins guiltily. "Hey."

"Packing some contraband there?"

"Got to. If I don't get at least half an hour of mindless gaming a day, I'll lose my mind here."

"I feel you. Not the gaming so much, but definitely the need to escape."

"Yeah, I didn't realise until I got here how much I love my downtime."

"You know what I miss?"

"What?"

"Music. I miss just shoving my headphones in my ears and blocking everything and everyone out."

"I'd lend you this." He points at the phone. "But it's my brother's old one. And unless you like obscure Polish death metal, I'm not sure you're going to find your jam."

"Obscure Polish death metal? Is that a tautology?"

"My brother's one of those guys who's just got to be different."

"Hey, so I'm going up to the party. Interested?"

"I'd rather stab myself in the eye with a plastic fork."

"Fair enough. I'll see you later." She starts to leave but then turns back. "Oh, and Craig?"

"Yeah?" He's deep in his game already.

"I could see you from a mile off. Might want to work on your stealth."

"Copy that."

71

CHAPTER 25

Party sounds spill down the hill as she approaches. There are people sprinkled over the wide brick stairs out front, and in the cavernous front room, there's a loose circle of kids sitting, a bottle of something being passed around. Tinny music shrieks from a contraband phone. The mood in here is already at fever pitch, everyone shouting each other down for punch lines and attention.

Drew's in the middle of it all, back to being pleased with himself now that he's party meister. Amy and Hana and Zaki wave and call out to her, but she just waves back and goes outside. She's not ready for that scene. Might never be.

She follows the wraparound balcony, stopping to chat with the scatter of splinter groups she finds every now and then, searching for a vibe she already knows she won't find. She's nearly all the way back round to the front door when two Gandry girls round the corner. They give her polite smiles but don't stop talking, so she turns again and stops at an empty section looking out towards the dining hall where the staff gathers at night to drink cups of tea and play cards between routine checks for miscreants.

She inhales deeply, taking in the fresh, lemon-scented air. It's another beautiful night. Still, there's not a single shred of party in her—a fact made pretty obvious by the fact that she's found the one spot at the whole party where there are no other humans.

"Hey," a low voice says behind her.

Scratch that, because Willa's curled up on a wide stone bench behind her, busy being another human. "I was going to leave you to it, because you looked like you wanted to be alone," she says. "But then it just got awkward, me silently sitting here behind you."

A weirdness steals in. The sticky residue of resentment from yesterday. Finn clings to a casual smile. "Yeah, you *are* kind of creepy."

"Are you okay? You looked—"

"I'm okay," Finn says. It's hard to reconcile this concern with the girl who was so willing to pick at her confidence yesterday. How does Willa slip between these two versions of herself? How do they even coexist?

"You sure?"

"I guess I've had better twenty-four hours in my life."

Willa nods, not letting up with the stare.

"I'm fine. Life's just kinda complicated right now." Finn quickly and deliberately changes the subject. "I'm surprised to see you here. Given how much you love Drew."

"I guess you could say I'm checking out the enemy."

"No you're not. You're hiding in a corner."

"Also true. But so are you."

"I came here to avoiding thinking. It's not really working, though."

"It never really does, does it?" A breeze rushes across the porch, blowing Willa's hair over her face. It's one of the first times Finn's ever seen it all out. It softens her edges.

Finn jerks her thumb at the house. "I guess they're forgetting how to think in there too. Not your thing?"

"Definitely not my thing."

"And aren't they worried the teachers will catch them? I mean, they know we're here. They couldn't exactly miss this."

"A couple of them came up before and said they'd be checking in every thirty minutes. So now the kids are just keeping time and hiding the booze on the clock. There are only two bottles, anyway. I think there might be just as much fake drunk in there as there is actual drunk."

"Probably. And the teachers?" Finn shakes her head. "I can't tell if that's plain dumb or lazy."

"Both."

Finn stares out at the skeleton-white outline of the gums on the horizon. It's so much darker out here than in the city. The world seems vaster too. It gives her this unanchored feeling, like if she doesn't stick close to people and buildings, she might disappear into the nothingness.

"Was that your parents I saw with you today?" Willa asks, waving at a moth that's diving for the light beaming through the window behind them.

"Yep."

"Was it good to see them?"

She can tell Willa's fishing, still trying to locate the source of her mood. "Good and bad. Good to see them, but…" She bites down on her lip and then decides to say it. "My dad lost his job."

"Oh, I'm sorry."

"We kind of knew it was coming. He's a journalist. And he found out this senior opinion writer was bullying some of the younger writers. He was so angry that instead of reporting him, he wrote this amazing op-ed about the shitty workplace culture at newspapers and published it in another paper. He didn't name names, but it didn't matter. People knew."

"I'm guessing they didn't like it."

"Not even a little bit."

"Your dad sounds cool. I'm sorry he lost his job."

Finn shrugs. "Like I said, we knew it was coming. But now my parents fight all the time because Mum didn't want him to do it."

That's not the whole reason for all the fighting, but Finn's not ready to talk about the rest. "And they're being weird and tense. They have been for ages. I hate it."

Willa doesn't say anything. But she gives her this look like she gets it.

"What about you?" Finn asks, changing the subject to avoid the resurgence of that enemy ache in her throat. "Your parents come?"

"Nope."

"Next week?"

"No."

"Oh, okay."

Willa's lips thin, like she's deciding something. Then she curls her arms around a knee and pulls it to her chest, hugging it. "I don't live with my parents."

"Oh. Do you board? I didn't know Gandry had dorms."

"No. With my grandmother."

"Am I allowed to ask why? I mean, it's none of my…" She stumbles and stops.

"It's okay, Finn. You can ask."

"Okay, then…why?"

"My mum died when I was seven. A car crash." Willa says it quickly, like she wants to move past it before she even starts.

But Finn can't. "Wow, I'm so sorry. Do you remember her?"

Willa stares straight ahead. "A bit."

"And your dad?"

"He tried doing the dad thing for a while, but he was pretty terrible at it." She plays with the thin, threaded cord around her wrist. "He was only nineteen when I was born. Wasn't ready. Never really got ready either."

"My dad and his first girlfriend had a baby when he was eighteen. They gave her up for adoption because they weren't ready."

"So you've got a half-sister you've never met?"

"No, I've met her. She found Dad when I was twelve."

"Was it weird?"

"At first. I knew she existed, but I never thought I'd *know* her. But now it's like we're friends. You can get used to most things, my mum says."

"That's true," Willa says.

But Willa's had to get used to a lot more than her. And a lot worse stuff too. Finn wishes she knew how to acknowledge that without it looking like pity. So she simply leans her shoulder against Willa's for a moment.

Finn almost can't believe she had Willa so wrong. She'd had her pegged in a regular, uptight suburban existence, with maybe some demanding parents to explain the intensity and the aggressive high-achieving. Wrong.

"So when did you go live with your grandmother?"

Willa rests her chin on her knee. "We moved there a year after Mum died. Then Dad left again. He'd been working out on fishing boats for years in Queensland. Couldn't get used to being in town. Or around people again. So he went back."

"Do you like living with her?"

"Yeah, Nan's great. She taught in a boarding school for years, so she's used to kids. She's not that strong these days, so I have to help a lot, though. And I don't know what will happen if anything happens to her."

"Would your dad come back?"

"I don't know. I suppose. He sends money every month, and birthday cards, but he hardly ever visits. Maybe once a year."

"What about your mum's family? Are they around?"

She shakes her head. "When Dad met her, she wouldn't talk about her family at all. All I know is she was born in India but grew up here. So there's no one on that side that we know. And on Dad's there's just Nan."

"Oh, wow." Finn is pricked by shame over whining about her family situation. Because, you know, she *has* family.

Willa nudges her. "Stop it."

"Stop what?"

"Looking like that. It's not one of those things you need to feel sorry for me about. It just *is*."

Finn obediently changes the subject. "And so you won a scholarship to Gandry?

"One of my Year Nine teachers at my old school convinced me to sit the exam. I never even thought about it. I mean, we're not poor or anything, but there was no way I was going to a private school. He said I should give it a try. And Gandry gave me one. Now I want to get one for university too. That way, when I start working, I won't have to pay off debt later."

Finn shakes her head. Who thinks about all these things at their age? She remembers their first conversation, Willa biting her lip and saying she *had* to do well. "And that's why you came on this camp, right? For uni applications?"

"Exactly."

"Which is why you play the game so hard."

Willa's brow furrows. "I don't play it that hard."

"Trust me, you do. I mean, you did just admit you only came to check out the enemy." She elbows her lightly, grinning. "Do you do anything that's not work?"

"I talk to you."

"Well, remember what I said," Finn says hurriedly to cover the awkward combined assault of flattered and embarrassed. "Try to have some fun some time."

"I'll try." Willa's smile is bashful. Finn feels a thread of something intangible but good being stitched between them.

Still, she doesn't expect Willa to kiss her. But that's exactly what happens. One moment, they're smiling at each other, and the next, Willa's lips are on hers. It's just a brief, delicate press, but it's enough to shock the hell out of Finn.

Willa pulls back a little, breathing softly. And when Finn doesn't respond, she moves in again. This time, Finn kisses her back, cajoled by the honey-thick feeling that drifts through her. And it keeps her in the kiss until the touch of Willa's fingers on her arm bursts a bubble of panic in her chest, yanking her back to reality.

"Whoa." Finn's face is burning. She pulls away. "I'm sorry." She shakes her head, too stunned to make words. "I'm…just… It's just…"

Willa presses her lips into a thin line and stares downward. "Jessie?"

Finn nods. "But not… not like you think. There's just a lot right now." What was Dan saying about her being one crisis off a shitstorm? Maybe she just got there.

Before Finn can try and explain, Willa says, "I'm sorry." She stares at her lap as she says it, her palms pressed against her thighs.

"Don't be sorry." Finn nudges her. "I don't want you to be sorry. It's me, not you." She cringes at the triteness of that statement. But what else can she say? She has no idea how to make sense of the mess of thoughts stampeding her brain right now, let alone how to explain them to Willa.

Willa gives her a small, pink-cheeked smile and stands. "I better go."

"Hey." Finn grabs her wrist. She doesn't want to leave it like this. Not after Willa trusted her enough to tell her things tonight. Willa's the kind of person where you get the sense it's special when she tells you stuff. Finn holds her gaze. "I'm sorry. I just can't right now."

She doesn't know if she ever could, either. Doesn't think she's even got the room in her brain to inspect the feelings that came with that kiss. Or all the reasons why the two of them would be a bad idea. Worse than a Jessie-and-Finn bad idea.

Willa nods again, but before Finn can say anything, shouting erupts inside. And it's different from the earlier shrieks and hoots. Tense.

It gets louder. Finn stands. "We should check that, right? The teachers will be all over it if it gets any louder."

Willa nods again, and they stride around the porch together.

CHAPTER 26

It's Amy. She's standing there, facing off an inch from Drew, arms folded, face bright red. Beside them, Hana's fussing around Zaki like a mother hen, pinning her scarf more securely into place. All eyes are on the four of them.

"You're a pig!" Amy yells.

Drew puts his hand in front of Amy's face. "Jesus, just chill out, woman. He didn't mean it. Be cool."

Finn strides over to them as Amy slaps his hand away. "You know what's worse than a guy excusing male piggery? It's a guy telling a woman to chill for being pissed about it!"

The guy standing next to Drew puts an arm between them and wavers on his feet a little. "Guys, stop it." He turns to Zaki. "I'm really sorry." His voice is slurred.

Zaki nods but steps back a little.

Finn grabs Amy's arm. "What the hell is going on?"

"Oh great. Another one." Drew rolls his eyes.

"Another what?" Amy snarls. "Another woman who might have an opinion about what a dickhead you are? You *and* your friends?"

"Hey, guys, calm down. Or the teachers will come." Finn stands between them. "What's happening?"

"If you don't like it here, just go." Drew waves at Amy over Finn's shoulder. "Bye-bye."

"Oh, don't worry. We're gone—pig!" Amy drags Zaki to the door with her.

Drew shakes his head. "*So* uptight." He looks at his friend for support, but his friend just walks away.

A silence hangs in the air before the room gradually fills with the sound of breathless recapping. Finn looks around for Willa, but she's nowhere to be seen. None of the Gandry girls are. It figures. They're totally the kind of girls to know the right moment to cut and leave.

Finn hurries out the door, passing a handful of frowning teachers coming up the hill. She catches up with the girls on the moonlit oval. "What happened?"

"That dickhead happened," Amy snarls. "God, I hate him."

Finn turns to Hana and Zaki, hoping one of them can use some actual verbs.

"Zaki was talking to one of Drew's mates. He was really drunk and tried to kiss her. Out of the blue. And when I had a go at him, Drew started giving Zaki crap for being uptight. Gross macho bullshit." Hana throws her arm around Zaki's shoulder and pulls her against her. "Z isn't allowed near any dudes."

"Are you okay?" Finn rubs Zaki's arm. She always seems so young, compared to the rest of them. Almost like a little sister.

"I'm fine. As long as my parents never, *ever* find out that happened." She shakes her head. "I don't get why he thought he should kiss me. We were just talking. About *dogs*."

"Drunk." Hana rolls her eyes. "Some guys think the word *hello* is a come-on when they've had a few. That's why I don't let my man touch booze. Makes him act like an ass."

"At least Cameron was sorry," Zaki says. "He was really embarrassed. It was Drew who was being mean."

"Drew's a dick," Hana mumbles, pulling her best friend closer.

Watching them, Finn has another pang of missing Dan. Because now she's even more desperate to burrow down with her best friend and solve all the problems of the universe together.

Amy's still glaring into the darkness next to her.

"You okay?" Finn asks. "Not going to murder him in his sleep tonight?"

"Not gonna lie. I do have murder on my mind. But you know what they say about revenge, right?"

"Yeah, I know what they say, Ames. But don't start a war, alright?"

Amy's grin isn't promising. This could get ugly.

Finn grabs her toiletries bag from her tent and begins the trudge to the showers. It's quieter at night, she's learned. Less shrieking and oversharing, and more hot water.

The shower block stinks of wet brick and cheap girl deodorant, but it's blissfully empty. She dumps her things on the bench, stares at the fogged-up mirror and sighs. What the hell is going on?

First there's her parents. Now things are going to be worse with Drew. And let's not forget her sudden clusterfuck of a love life. But how can she be in this mess without actually having *done* anything? And why does everyone suddenly want to kiss her out of the blue? Has she been magically teleported into one of those movies where the geek girl wakes up as the hot one? Maybe somewhere out there, there's a girl on a cheerleading camp who's turned into an earnest geek with a penchant for painting.

Finn's never had two people like her at the same time. She's just not that kind of girl. And unless being in the middle of nowhere has some magical transformative powers, why would that change now? She's pretty sure she's the same old Finn. Regular, short, snub-nosed, blonde-but-not-in-the-*blonde*-way Finn. It's weird.

And now, after that aborted kiss with Willa, the awkward levels on this camp have doubled. With Jessie, she kind of saw it coming. But Willa? That came out of nowhere. Willa's so confusing. Sometimes she's this sweet, sensitive thing. Other times she's like a flaming arrow that you hope isn't coming for you.

It felt good to kiss her. There's no way Finn can deny that. Willa is underline it, bold it, put it in all caps gorgeous. But she's also a hot mess of conflicting elements that Finn can barely fathom in a friend, let alone anything more.

She sighs loudly into the steam. She liked it better when her biggest problem on this camp was being leader of an unruly pack of lazy overachievers. Sure, it's been like herding cats, but it turns out it's simple in comparison to this. So that's what she'll do, she decides. She'll ignore these out-of-nowhere subplots and put it all into the game. If that's even possible.

CHAPTER 27

Finn focuses on the basics of putting one foot in front of the other until they reach the top of the slippery gravel ascent. The air is thick with panting breaths and a chorus of whining from people who've still got air left to complain. And even though she'd love them to shut up, Finn can't blame them. It's Sunday. Whatever happened to that hallowed day of rest? Apparently that only applies to the rest of the world.

For future leaders, it means a hike.

Maybe that's the difference. Maybe the great leaders never slept in on Sundays. Maybe they got up while the rest of the world was snoozing and then got things done. Someone needs to do the research. But if this early Sundays thing turns out to be part of the deal, Finn's feeling pretty lukewarm about this leadership deal.

"Look at those guys," Craig mutters as he huffs next to her.

About ten kids walk in a tight pack, dragging their collective feet. She recognises them from the thick of last night's party gang. And if their complexions this morning had to be mixed on a palette, hangover plus hike would blend to a puke-y, pallid white. "They look like they just love being alive right now," Finn says.

At the top of the trail, a gut-churning steep cliff drops away from them. Everyone but the Hulk keeps a ginger distance as they gaze dully out at the view. The world before them is all grey-green paddocks specked with sheep. Thrill city. No one says a word. What did the powers that be expect? Full, rabid commitment to an early-morning walk uphill? Excitement at seeing yet another view of distant livestock and grass? It's lucky they didn't choose abseiling for today's activity. The total lack of enthusiasm could have gotten ugly.

Gus hands out snacks. Trying not to sigh, Finn takes a muesli bar. Now her life is complete. She perches next to Craig and unwraps it. Don't look a gift horse in the mouth, right? Even if the gift is more chew than taste. She screws up the wrapper, tucks it into her pocket, and slouches against a tree. Sleep avoided her last night. Too much to think about. Annoying, because the list of things she'd like *not* to think about is getting longer by the minute.

She hears Craig settle in next to her, making the most of the weak sunshine prison-breaking from a thick belt of cloud. He's the perfect hike partner. Doesn't feel the need to fill up every moment with mindless chatter, but good to talk to when he does.

She turns to him. "How do you think they chose us for this camp?"

"At school?"

She nods.

He tears his wrapper into strips. "I've thought about this a bit, actually. I reckon they just got lazy and chose the top people in a bunch of subjects. I mean, think about it. Everyone here's really good at something, but we're not exactly leadership material. Okay, well, you are. But me? What the hell am I doing here? I couldn't lead a monkey to a banana parade. I'm just awesome at maths."

"I don't know if I could lead a monkey these days either."

He cocks an eyebrow at her. "Okay, right. Whatever you say. Anyway, my theory has to be right. How else do we explain Brian? I mean, basketball's all he's good for. Sure, he'll probably be sports captain one day, but I definitely wouldn't trust *him* with the monkey. Or any sentient being."

Finn laughs, feeling instantly better. Craig gives her a comradely grin. "That's my theory, and I'm sticking to it."

She nods. It makes perfect sense, too. A wind whips over the top of the hill and slices through the sun's warmth. She zips her jacket to the neck and pulls her beanie down around her ears. She's probably topping some glam charts this morning, but she does not care. It's that kind of day.

The Hulk is working the groups, eagerly hike-chatting and backslapping with whoever will listen. Apparently, this little nature ramble was his plan. She shoots him a dirty look. Betrayed by one of her own.

She's about to let her eyes drift closed when she spies Willa leaned against a tree at the edge of the clearing. She's bundled up in a thick coat, her arms folded across her chest. In profile, she's all cheekbone and frown.

They haven't spoken to each other today. Finn thought about going to find her first thing and say hi, to clear the air, but there wasn't a moment when Willa wasn't surrounded by Gandry girls. Now would be it. She's gathering her courage when she sees Drew break from the small cluster of kids who are now sitting right near the edge of the cliff face. He saunters over to Willa and says something. She simply nods as the wind whips her ponytail across her face. When she swipes it away, her eyes are narrowed at him.

What does Drew want with Willa? Whatever it is, he's doing most of the talking. Willa simply stares at him as he speaks, like identity software experiencing a total lack of facial recognition. Finn always enjoys Willa's non-engagement tactics. Especially when it's with Drew.

"Okay, kids!" The Hulk suddenly yells, waving them over to the side of the clearing. "We're going to stroll back a different way so I can show you how the flora and fauna changes on the other side of the hill."

Stroll? If only he meant it.

"Please keep an eye out for snakes if you wander off the track," he shouts. "This is the one time where we encourage you to make as much noise as possible. But don't worry. They're more scared of you than you are of them."

"You sure about that?" Hana says. "I'm pretty terrified."

When Finn turns back to look, Drew's walking away from Willa, a small smile on his face. Something stirs in Finn as she watches Willa frown across the valley. Another unnameable something weaving itself into the tangle of today's strangeness. But before she can decide whether to go and talk to her, the crowd starts moving downhill again.

CHAPTER 28

Finn sidles up to the newspaper at Gus's elbow, acting like a seagull after a chip. She points at it. "Hey, are you done with that?"

The camp leader sits back, eyebrows raised. "Of course. Knock yourself out."

"Thanks." She tucks it under her arm.

"Hang on. You're going to read it, aren't you? Not set fire to something?"

"Of course I'm going to read it. I mean, I might burn it after, of course. But only to keep my tent warm." She gives him a grin and scuttles away, hoping his smart-ass tolerance is at a high today.

She carries her precious cargo across the oval, skirting a rec-time soccer match in progress. The sun's come out, and it actually looks like it means it this time. She finds a quiet spot near the barbecue area, where she can see the curves of the dusky hills melting into the horizon. She's been meaning to try and capture them all week.

But they'll have to wait. First she unfolds the paper and smooths it over her lap. Then she takes a delicious, anticipatory breath. She may be out-geeking herself right now, but she can't help it.

News. Actual information about what is going on in the world. The best she's gotten on this front is a quick update from her parents between tense smiles and chitchat on visitors' day.

She sips her tepid coffee in its foam cup, leans over the cheap print, and devours. And she doesn't move until she's scanned it from the headlines to the classifieds. Of course, there's not much good news to be had. Politicians are still fighting about how to make marriage equality happen and still busily ignoring the climate crisis. People are still fleeing terrible situations and ending up in only marginally better ones. There are still kids in detention centres. There are still senseless accidents. And it all gives her that same melancholic, fed-up feeling she always gets when she reads the paper.

This summer, she's going to help somehow. Maybe volunteer with the Greens, or write another essay. Like her dad says, feeling bad about it isn't enough.

"Don't be one of those people who gets all depressed about the state of the world and just sits there," he's always told her. "Be one of those people who does something. Even something small." This summer she'll find that something. Because she doesn't want to be that person.

Only when she's sated does she open her sketchbook and let her pencil slink over the page, capturing the hills. The calm pours in. She wonders if this is what mediation feels like. Empty but full at the same time. This is where Sunday should always be found, she thinks. Not on a cold hilltop.

Just when the sunshine's finally lulled her pencil into trailing off and her eyes are fixed sleepily into the middle distance, she spots Willa emerging from a track in the scrub. Willa usually has a head-up, straight-backed stalk of a walk. Slow, but with intent, like she's using the time it takes to get somewhere to figure out exactly what she'll do when she does arrive. Not today. Today's she's head down, hugging her book like it's a long-awaited parcel, and frowning in that thinky way she does. Maybe she's been hunting out the quiet too.

Before Finn can decide whether or not to call out to her, she sees Willa spot her. Willa's hesitation is a fleeting thing, but it lasts long enough for Finn to see her hang, suspended between uncertainty and her usual determination.

And that flash of vulnerability does something to Finn. Makes her decision for her: she will not abandon this hard-won friendship over last night. She marshals a casual smile. "Hey."

Determination clearly triumphs, and Willa moves in closer. "Hi." She stops on the grass in front of Finn, and a silence threatens to drop again.

Finn rushes to fill the gap. "What have you been up to?"

"Reading. But it's so windy on the hill."

"It's nice here." Finn pats the table next to her.

There's that thing she always does, where she presses her lips into a taut little line, deciding.

"*Sit.*" Finn pats the table again and smiles hopefully at her. "We're better than being weird with each other, aren't we?"

Willa's smile is even slower to come than usual, but there's relief in it when it does. "Yeah, we are better." She settles on the weather-beaten wood next to Finn and opens her book.

It's not easy, though. Not like it usually is. Whenever Finn says something, Willa just responds briefly but takes it no further. Finn can't tell if she's upset about last night or tired or something else, but that small, chafing tension between them is impossible to erase. It surprises her how much it bothers her. Like she hasn't realised how much her Willa time has become a Camp Nowhere sacred space.

And she really doesn't want Willa to feel bad or awkward about last night. Because she didn't do anything wrong. It just wasn't exactly...*right*. But in the brand new light of today, Finn's still completely deficient in ways to articulate that.

When it's time for dinner, Finn slowly closes her sketchbook. "Hey, are we okay?"

Willa turns to her, amber eyes narrowed against the bright sun, her voice soft. "I hope so."

And then she's gone.

CHAPTER 29

Gus claps so loudly it echoes around the hall. "Red herring! Today you need to make decisions based on last week's proposals and plans, but first you need to know this. The summer was unseasonably hot due to climate change, resulting in some crop damage, water shortages, and industrial issues across all territories. And things may get worse. Please read the brief I'll be handing out, and calculate the effects into your decisions. You'll be awarded team points on how you negotiate these issues and the reports you write about the adjustments to your plans."

Finn's group is instantly bored and fidgety. They have no deals to consider or crops to ruin. Who knew climate change would be a bonus? Craig's pen dashes across the notebook he always seems to have stored on him.

"Some of this might turn out to be good for us, if Gandry rejects us," he mumbles as he scribbles.

"Because we've got water, right?"

"Exactly." He leans over the notebook. "On the downside, sourcing food might be more of an issue because other groups will be low on supplies. But agriculture is an easy starter if you have irrigation and manpower."

"Good."

When the time is up and the leaders are meeting, Finn tries not to fidget as Willa talks to Drew and then to the leader of the group who has the bush area. Finally, she approaches, clutching a folder in her arms. Finn's fully expecting cold, businesslike Willa, so she doesn't even blink at the remote expression. Instead, she crosses one leg over the other and leans back against the seat.

Willa doesn't sit down. Just says quietly, "I'm sorry, but we won't be able to make the deal."

Coldness grips Finn, but she's careful not to blink. She didn't realise until now that she honestly believed Willa would accept it. She simply nods. "Thanks for letting us know," she says in her calmest voice.

Everyone's under the tree, quiet for once. Finn stares at the ground, her arms folded across her chest. She braces herself for the whine fest.

Amy yanks impatiently at the cuff of Finn's jeans. "So?"

"They're not taking us."

"What?" Her mouth drops open.

Finn shrugs. "That's what she said."

"Did she say why?" Hana asks.

"Nope."

Cue instant, noisy outrage.

Finn sighs. She can't do this. This will not be a part of her day. Not if she wants her sanity intact by the end of it. She spins around and strides off. And she doesn't stop until she's right in the middle of the stretch of sun-scorched grass in the middle of the oval. She drops to the ground and thumps it with her fist.

There's a highly uncomfortable pattern forming around these last few days. It's called being forced to feel bad for being rejected for something she didn't even want in the first place. Finn doesn't get it. When did she stop being in charge? Of things she's never had trouble being in charge of before? In Year 7, Ms Fawkner told her mum that Finn was one of the most self-directed thirteen-year-olds she'd ever met. When did that stop? When did she stop being the protagonist of her own existence? And how does she get it back?

"Hey, are you okay?" It's Jessie, come to the rescue. Of course.

She plucks viciously at the grass. It's so dry, it dissolves to dust in her fingers. "I just can't listen to them whinge about it all day."

"I feel you." He crouches next to her. "They're talking about who else's team we can join now."

"I don't want to join another team. I just want to play the game. You know, we could do this if they weren't so freaking lazy."

"Tell them that."

"What's the point? Amy and Hana will just whine about sleeping in tents. Zaki will do whatever Hana says. Brian will just say 'duh', and then we'll be outvoted again."

"You just need to find a way to convince them. You know, Finn, there was a reason why we picked you to be leader."

"And I feel like I have no idea what it was anymore." She stares at the grass so she doesn't have to meet his eye.

"Well, I do. I never even met you before this camp, but I remember when you guilt-tripped the entire school administration into proving the school was recycling properly. *And* when you convinced all of Year 9 to raise money for that school in the Northern Territory." He nudges her. "Now *you're* going to have to remember."

CHAPTER 30

Someone shouts her name. She lets out a weary breath. For half an hour, she'd actually been able to lie on this sunny rock and forget everything.

It's Jessie and Brian jogging down the path towards her.

"What?"

"Got something for you." Jessie's all sweat patches and stink, his hair hanging limp around his ears.

When he crouches besides her, boy stank takes over from the sweet smell of grass and sunshine. She wrinkles her nose and leans away from him.

"Sorry." He plucks at his T-shirt. "I've been playing hoops. But guess what we just heard?"

"What?"

"Drew told Willa that if she took us in, he'd up all prices on their food trade," Brian says.

"*What?*" Finn sits up. Somewhere amidst the shock, she registers that her half of the conversation so far has consisted of one single word.

"Yup. Apparently he's got a real bug up his butt about something between him and Amy on Saturday night. She didn't go there with him, did she?" Jessie looks horrified.

"God, no. She just handed him his ass in front of everyone."

"Well, I think it's kinda hurt his cred with the ladies."

Finn's nose wrinkles. "He *had* cred with the ladies?"

"I don't know. But the boy is bitter." Brian shakes his head.

Finn thinks of that tense conversation between Willa and Drew on the cliff's edge. Drew is such a pig. Amy was right about that. She frowns. "But how did he even know about our deal with Willa?"

"Maybe Willa told him?" Jessie suggests.

"No way." Even if Willa did respond to his threat, Finn is certain she would never have told him anything. "It had to be someone else."

"I don't know. I just thought you'd want to know." He stands. "I gotta go shower."

"Thanks, guys." As they jog up the track, she frowns. So maybe Willa's weird mood yesterday might not just have been about their kiss. It could just as easily have been something resembling guilt. What's Finn supposed to do with that kind of betrayal?

CHAPTER 31

Finn scratches the pencil idly over the paper, making abstract swirls and shadings. She's not in the mood for actual form this morning. Form requires concentration. Requires her to find that quiet place. And she's too busy scratching the itch of her irritation to find it.

Everything feels worse today. And it should feel better, shouldn't it? But no. Waking to a grumpy Amy was annoying. Facing another day of the game without a plan is depressing. And Willa's betrayal *definitely* feels even crappier.

"Hi."

And, bam, there's Willa, standing in front of her. Hands at her sides, chin up, like she's thinking maybe this encounter is going to require the formal game version of Willa.

"Hey." Finn looks down at her page. Doesn't this girl know when she's being avoided? Finn chose the picnic area precisely because she's not sure if she can keep her end of their no-game-talk-on-the-oval embargo.

"You're upset, aren't you? About us not taking you."

Finn smiles blithely at her. "Us? I thought you were the leader, Willa? Wasn't it *your* decision?"

Willa's lips purse slightly as she registers her words being thrown back in her face.

"Don't worry, I'm fine." Finn tells her.

"You're mad. I know you."

"I thought we didn't talk about the game." The flicker of anger in Finn's chest becomes a flame. "And you *don't* know me."

"And I thought we weren't letting the game affect our friendship." Willa sits on the table next to her as if to announce that she's not going to let this go.

"It's not like you're keeping that rule either. You weren't weird with me yesterday because you kissed me. You were weird because you knew you were about to betray me."

Finn turns to face her, on a rage roll now. "I saw you with Drew yesterday. I wondered what you were talking about. I guess I know now."

Willa's silent for a moment, staring at her lap. Then she turns to her with pure Willa calm. "Finn, I didn't *want* to take that deal. I had to. After Gus threw the crop thing at us yesterday morning, I had no choice. I can't fight back with damaged crops."

"But we could have helped you with that. We could have helped you produce more food."

"I know, but it would have taken time. We needed a quick fix. We can revisit your plan later." The way she says it, like a mother trying to put off a cajoling child, just annoys Finn more. The rational part of her brain knows Willa doesn't mean it like that, but trapped in the hot caul of her anger, she only cares how it feels. And again, she's arrested with that same bitterness: when did she become the reactor? Not the actor?

That's it.

She snaps her sketchbook shut. "Don't bother. We won't be needing that deal any more. I wouldn't team up with someone who'd sell out to a shit like Drew just for the sake of a win."

Willa doesn't even blink. "You know, you shouldn't let this affect you so much. It's just a game. It's not personal."

Finn scoffs. "Just a game? Rich coming from the girl who turns from a normal, nice human being into an ice-cold dictator every time she starts playing it."

Willa just keeps staring, but Finn can see the flicker in her gaze. She's hurt. Still, Finn can't stop with the bitter. "Do you know why Drew blackmailed you?"

"What do you mean?"

"It wasn't about you or your team. He's angry with Amy about what happened on Saturday night. This is his revenge on us. He just didn't want you to take us in."

Willa blinks. She didn't know.

She recovers quickly, though. "It doesn't matter. I didn't do it for personal reasons. I did it because we needed to. I'm sorry, Finn."

"Don't be sorry." Finn stuffs things into her knapsack. "I didn't even want this deal anyway."

"Then why did you ask for it?"

"Because the others voted for it."

"Then it's your own fault."

Finn stops, sketchbook in hand, and stares at her. "I beg your pardon?"

"You're their leader. Why are you letting them decide what happens?"

"Because we're democratic."

"So? They voted you as leader, didn't they? Which means they granted you the power to make decisions on their behalf. As far as I understand, that's how most democracies work."

Finn jams her sketchbook book into the bag. "Thank you, Willa. I'm aware of this. I, too, go to school."

"Then it's not their fault if you weren't strong enough to make decisions. It's no good having ideals if you're not tough enough to fight for them."

She doesn't say it in a bitchy or snide way. Just as a statement of fact. And Finn's blood boils at the sneaking suspicion that she's right.

"Not tough enough? Tough like you, I suppose?" Finn folds her arms over her chest. "Well, thanks a lot for trying me and deeming me unfit to lead. We can't all be as good as you."

"Yes you can. You're just not doing it."

Finn stares at her. She has no idea what to do with *that*.

Willa shrugs. "You wanted to talk about the game." She jumps down from the table. "And I *do* know you, Finn."

Seething, Finn stares after her. She was supposed to be the one to walk away. She grabs up her bag and marches back to camp. At the top of the track, she stares down at their raggedy little encampment. She's so sick of this. She's going to get her old self back. She *has* to. Maybe her way isn't Willa's way, but she's got her own thing.

Below her, people are trickling out of tents, sitting around in the sun, groaning and yawning their way into the day. She storms down the hill and claps her hands loudly, Gus-style. It ricochets through camp.

"Meeting in ten minutes. Be there!"

At the sound of her shout, Zaki and Hana jump and turn.

Hana salutes cheerfully. "Aye, aye captain."

Finn just stalks past her without a word or a look, channelling her rage into harnessing that old, confident Finn. The Finn who makes speeches at assembly at the drop of a hat. Who argues with the principal on behalf of the students and doesn't let up until she is heard. The girl who spoke to a TV journalist about their school after Examgate last year without a flicker of nerves. The girl who was voted in because she believes in things. And in herself. The girl who doesn't let someone like Willa tell her how it needs to be. Because she already knows. No more hiding out. This is the girl she will be again.

CHAPTER 32

Zaki slaps her hands over her mouth, eyes bugged wide. "I am *so* sorry, Finn. We were just chatting about the game. I didn't think."

That solves the Drew mystery. "Don't worry about it now," Finn says. "But from now on, *no one* talks to any other camper about any of our plans, okay?"

They all nod. They're gathered around the fire pit, a sad circle of spent ashes. Amy's still half-asleep, her sleeping bag wrapped around her shoulders, her hair a spectacular mess. Brian's yawning into his hand, and Jessie's got his eyes shut as he leans against a rock.

Finn takes a deep breath, preparing herself for the inevitable. "Okay, so we're not going to try to seek asylum with any other groups."

Amy's awake now. "What? Why not?"

"Because I decided." Finn holds up a hand before Amy can utter a word. "You know what? You guys wanted me to be a leader because you were all too lazy to do it yourselves. And then you whine and moan about everything and make me choose things I don't want to do." She crosses her arms over her chest. "No more. You chose me, and I'm choosing for us. We're staying here, and we're trying my plan. And if you don't like it, you know the rules. You can vote me out on a no-confidence."

Finn looks around at them as if to say *bring it on*. But they don't. In fact, no one brings anything. Not even Amy. When Finn meets Jessie's eye, he gives her an encouraging smile. But she doesn't need it. She's on a roll.

"You say you want to win." She turns to Amy. "*You* say you want to kick Drew's ass. But you say this while we're wasting the precious time we could use to focus on doing that, on taking the easiest route to get back into a cabin." She shrugs. "What for?

That's not playing the game. We all got picked because we're really good at something. So, I don't know. Let's actually *try* to be good at it?"

Craig breaks into a slow clap. Finn gives him a withering look, but he just grins. "For what it's worth," he says, "I think you've been right all along."

"Thanks," she says calmly, even though she feels like running over and hugging him.

"Me too," Jessie says. "Let's actually have a go at this thing."

Finn allows the small spring of hope in her chest. At least she hasn't *lost* any supporters with her little diatribe.

"Okay," Amy sighs. "If you promise me that we'll beat Drew, I vote yes."

Finn's just about to remind them they won't be voting on this one when Zaki puts her hand up.

She can't help laughing. "It's not school, Z."

Zaki drops her hand. "So, what do we do now, then?"

"Now we have to find out who needs our resources most." She looks at Craig.

He smiles, clutching his notebook. "I've got some ideas about that."

"Me too." She looks around at everyone. "We can talk about it after breakfast."

And as she strides up the path toward the dining hall, she feels like her heart is going to burst out of her chest. It's *that* kind of victory.

CHAPTER 33

Leon, the leader of the group from one of the bush allotments, sits back in his seat, leg crossed over knee. He's the picture of chill, Willa's antithesis. "So, how would it work?"

"We propose that our people design the pipeline, and your people build it," Finn says. "And then, in return for a ten-year lease on free access to our water, you give us a trade deal for food."

He nods slowly. "I like it. But we need to work out what we can actually spare after the summer. Let me think about it."

"Of course." She knows he's going to go for it, though. She knows because it turns out Brian's good for something: playing the mole. And people really like to chat on the basketball courts. Even though Finn's put the gag on her group, some of the others haven't been smart enough to. "If you could let us know by tomorrow, it'd be appreciated."

There's a flicker of unease in his eyes, but he nods. "Sure. We should manage that."

"Great. See you later."

"What's all that about needing to know by tomorrow?" Jessie asks as they saunter back to their table. "We have time."

"He needs to think we have other offers on the cards. Otherwise he'll take his time, and someone else might get wind of it. Willa's smart, and so are Drew's minions, even if the jury's out on him." She sits down and rests her elbows on the table. "They might figure out how we're going to use our assets."

Jessie rubs his hand together. "Sneaky. Girl's got game."

A streak of pride shoots through her. Not because *he* says it, but because she knows he's right. And it feels good.

When they leave the morning session, they pass Willa's group talking on the porch. Finn doesn't even look at her. They haven't spoken since their argument the other day. It's easier this way, she's decided. Because to be game-changing Finn, she needs a clear line between friend and foe. This is how it's going to have to be.

CHAPTER 34

When Finn finishes her highlights reel, Dan sighs loudly into the phone.

"What?" Finn asks, worried.

"Nothing. I'm just relieved."

"Why?"

"Because you'd kinda lost your Finn mojo for a while there."

"I did not," she retorts, even though she knows she kind of did.

"You kinda did."

She laughs at his thought-echo. He always does that.

"But hey, even Superwoman gets to have a crap couple of months, you know," he says gently.

"I'm fine."

"Yeah, but according to you, you're always fine. I, of the superior insight, beg to differ."

Finn smiles as she folds the corner of an ancient notice reminding them not to feed the magpies. Dan never lets her get away with a moment of denial. It's brutal but loving.

"Anyway, it's not like you didn't have good reason to feel less than your glitteringly stubborn, wonderful self. The thing with Matt, the thing with your parents—which you continue to stupidly blame yourself for. And this camp thing? You and I know that the Finn from a few months ago would have had that raggedy bunch of whiners whipped into shape and all over this game from day one. I'm just glad something has pissed you off enough to get you back on the horse."

"You know, you really do paint a delightful picture of me. I'm truly grateful."

"Oh lighten up. I've told you a million times you get away with it because you're kind and smart and you're a total believer without hitting annoying levels of earnest.

No one gets bitter when you always take the lead, because you're actually good at running things—including my love life, upon request."

Finn smiles. She can't deny that. Talking Dan out of bad romantic decisions has been a significant duty of their best friendship. Dan calls her out, Finn rescues Dan from terrible relationships. This is the story of them so far.

"I do feel better," she admits. "I don't know why, but I do."

"Because you're kicking ass again. So just go with it, babe. Because I love all my Finns—even the mopey one. But I do miss my lightning-bolt girl. She gets it done."

"You suck," she tells him fondly.

"Yeah, I do."

Finn leaves the rec hall, feeling light and happy and the tiniest, sweetest bit homesick. Outside, a group of guys are hooting and catcalling their way down the path, doing that satisfied, macho parade they do when they're high on being testosterone in pack form. As they get closer, she realises they're all eating ice creams. Wow. They must have made Gus seriously happy somehow. And they're attracting campers like flies, all out for a share. Drew leads them like some deranged boy Pied Piper as he hands the ice creams out from a box.

"Hey, Finn, want an ice cream?" a guy called Michael calls out.

She shakes her head. "What'd you do to deserve those?"

"We didn't." Drew grins, shaking the box. "We, uh, liberated them from the kitchen."

"You mean you stole them?"

"It's not really stealing if our parents paid for them, is it?" He holds one out to her.

She shakes her head. "Whatever you say."

"Priss," he mutters as they walk away. But she just lets it wash over her. Because nothing is going to shake the loose, confident feeling that today has brought on. Because today she remembers what being Finn feels like.

CHAPTER 35

Gus looks serious. Dead serious. Not-angry-but-disappointed serious.

He stands out the front of the hall, his arms crossed, his shaggy brows hunched over his eyes. "Is someone going to tell me who did it?"

There's a silence, chock-full of every single camper and his dog knowing who did it but not wanting to be the one to say.

"It might seem like a harmless game, but what you are actually doing is stealing. Stealing from the camp, and from the other campers."

Some of Drew's guys start to shift nervously as Gus puts their stupid kitchen looting in a new, guilt-making light. Not Drew, though. He smirks and nudges the guy sitting next to him, the straw-haired one who tried to kiss Zaki. The kid doesn't react, though. Just folds his arms tighter over his chest. Finn thinks of the party night, when that boy walked away from him, and she wonders what he really thinks of his leader.

"Anyone care to shed some light on this?" Gus taps his feet against the worn linoleum and waits.

But the silence is tenacious. As if the longer it goes on, the less anyone is willing to step forward.

"Okay, then," he finally says. "If that's how we're going to play it, I can only assume you're all responsible. Which means you're all on punishment. Everyone's tech time is cut off until after the weekend."

There's a ripple of silent outrage, but still no one speaks. Until someone from Leon's group calls out. He sounds pissed. "I don't know who did it, but I'm lactose intolerant, so it sure as hell wasn't me."

"Dude, TMI," Amy mutters. "Seriously, buddy." Craig guffaws loudly but stifles it when Hana elbows him.

"And I don't eat crap," some hippie girl adds. "Sugar's evil. Why punish us all for this?"

Gus shrugs. "Because some of you know who did this. And it's just as irresponsible not to report it as it is to be the one who did it. This punishment might give you some encouragement towards honesty."

Finn shakes her head. Does this guy know nothing about sneak code? No one is about to turn anyone else in. Not even an idiot. Unless revenge is in the cards, of course. She turns to Amy, curious. "Aren't you even a little bit tempted?"

"A little," Amy says out the side of her mouth. "But not enough to snitch."

"Okay, well, that's that, then," Gus says wearily. "Everyone's tech time is removed for the two days. No internet, no phone, no Facebook or Snapchat or whatever it is you people do. If anyone would like to talk in private, they're welcome to come and see me in the office. I'm disappointed in you all. Dinner's in an hour."

"Great," Finn mutters to Jessie as they trudge down the steps of the hall. "Now we're completely cut off." She was going to call her parents tonight.

But Jessie's too busy staring to listen. He points to the lawn. "What's going on?"

Finn follows his finger. Willa's standing in front of Drew, her arms folded tightly across her chest. Even from here Finn can see she is a tight coil of anger. She says something to Drew. He replies with a shrug, making Willa coil even tighter.

Finn and Jessie move in closer as more and more kids stop to watch.

Willa steps forward, right into Drew's space, her back and neck rigid. "You're an idiot," she snarls. "Everyone knows it was you."

"Whoa," Jessie mutters.

Finn nods. It's definitely something, seeing stiff, remote Willa suddenly turned spitfire. She doesn't know whether to be impressed or worried.

"Everyone knows," Drew retorts. "Yet no one told. Not even you."

"I don't rat. But I *would* have the guts to admit it was me. Not let everyone else take the blame for my show-pony thieving." She shakes her head. "Winning friends with ice cream. Pathetic. No one's impressed."

"Yeah, not impressed," a guy calls out from the crowd.

Drew just shrugs again, but Finn can see how his stance has turned into a taut nonchalance.

She goes over to the Gandry girls, who are standing in a concerned huddle off to the side "What's up with Willa?"

The blonde one, Willa's deputy answers. "I think it's about the punishment."

"I got that part. But why's she so angry about it?"

"I have no idea."

"How did you get to be leader, anyway?" Willa suddenly asks, loud enough for everyone to hear. And there's plenty of people to hear. Finn's pretty sure the whole camp is watching by now. Luckily, all the teachers seem to be gone. Teatime, probably.

"Oh, that's right. You chose yourself." Willa looks him up and down slowly. "Well, thanks for ruining everything for the rest of us."

"Oh, don't be such a drama queen. Sad you'll miss talking to your mummy?"

Finn flinches, but Willa just fires him a particularly potent death stare.

"Whoa, I have *never* seen Willa pissed," a Gandry girl mutters. "It's kind of amazing."

"And kind of terrifying," another adds.

Finn pulls a face. Willa's not terrifying. Not to Finn, anyway. But she *is* pissed.

And Willa doesn't seem the type to lose it just because some idiot did something predictably idiotic. She usually minds her own business, sticking to her group and her game. She doesn't do ruffled either. She does full, public composure. The fact that she didn't react to the "mummy" comment proves that. Finn wonders if Willa's team know about her mum. Maybe not. They didn't even react to Drew's comment.

Willa turns to Drew's group, who are all standing in a loose cluster behind him. She haughtily examines them, turning on her queenly Willa. Finn has to admit, it's pretty impressive.

"Some of you wanted to own up to it," she says. "I know you did. So why didn't you?"

No one answers, but there's a collective shuffle as hands dive into pockets and eyes look the other way.

"So every single one of you is too gutless to face up to him?" Willa points at Drew. "*Him?*"

Again, no one says anything.

"You're worse than he is, then." She turns on her heel and marches straight through the crowd of people. It's as if they aren't even there. As she storms past Finn, her face is tight with anger. She disappears into the day.

"Are you going to go after her?" she asks the Gandry girls.

The blonde one cringes slightly. "Uh, I think we'll give her some time to, you know, chill."

"Yeah, she's not exactly the huggy, feelings type," another girl says. "I think we should leave her alone."

CHAPTER 36

But Finn doesn't know how to leave things alone.

She finally hunts Willa down on a table at the edge of the barbecue area, partly hidden by branches of a willow. She's all hunched over herself, elbows on knees, chin in hands, staring down at the grass.

Finn hesitates. Because now she's here, she doesn't quite know what to do with the fact she's here. She'd just been following an instinct. But now, confronted by the full strength of Willa's mood, she has no idea why she's chasing down this girl she hasn't talked to in two days. The girl whose friendship she thought she might so easily leave behind.

But she's here now, so she sits down on the table in that same insistent way Willa did the other day and asks gently, "Hey, what's wrong?"

"Nothing. It doesn't matter."

"Clearly."

Willa doesn't register her sarcasm. Not that Finn was expecting her to. "I could kill him."

"I noticed."

This time, Willa concedes a flicker of a reaction.

"And as much as I enjoyed your verbal assault, I have to wonder why? You don't lose it over stolen ice creams."

Finn recognises Willa's lip-thinned reaction. She's deciding whether to tell her something.

"I just really needed to call someone. Tonight."

"Okay."

"And now I can't. And I promised." She drops her chin into her hands. "I knew I shouldn't have come here."

Finn has no idea why Willa says that and no idea if it's okay to ask, so she gives her the one comfort she knows she can give and sits beside her, just *being* there.

They sit in silence until Willa swipes surreptitiously at her cheek. And it's that rogue tear that does it. Whatever it is that could make someone like Willa cry—even tears of rage—must be important. More than important.

"Sit tight. I'll be back." Finn marches through the buttery late-afternoon sun to camp.

And when she returns, Willa's still sitting there, hunched, her chin cupped in her palms.

Finn beckons to her. "Come on."

Willa looks up at her, bewildered, like she got so caught up in her feelings again that she forgot Finn was ever there. Finn tries to ignore the small rake of hurt. "Hurry. We don't have much time before dinner."

They trudge up the steep track. And when they get up to the first clearing, Finn slips Craig's phone from her pocket. Two reception bars. It should be enough. She thrusts it at Willa. "Here. Make your call."

Her eyes widen. "Where did you get this?"

"Never mind my sources. But there's a robust technology trade if you know where to look." Finn grins. "Be quick."

Willa's still staring at the phone like she found another Christmas present she forgot to unwrap.

Giving her some privacy, Finn wanders away to sit on a rock. From here she can see the camp going about its business. Life trickling on below them. There's the never-ending basketball game in action, full of sweaty, sporty types battling it out. She spots Brian in the thick of it. On the other side, the Gandry girls sit on the steps of their cabin porches, trading chitchat. She picks out Hana and Zaki from their matching maroon headscarves as they leave the rec hall, arms linked. It's weird how quickly this place has become her world. She hardly thinks about home—and not just because of the tension. Besides the occasional yearnings for her own bed or for real coffee or some time alone, it's become a distant other to this weird little camp universe.

As she watches everything go on without them, there's a strange sense of calm. A satisfaction. And she knows it's from being able to help Willa, to find a way to soothe whatever sting she's feeling. There's relief in the mix too. Because Finn didn't know that during these last days, maybe she's missed Willa. That underneath all the doing, she was still feeling her feelings.

When Willa joins her, she's smiling like something has loosened in her. She returns the phone. "Thank you."

"No problem." It takes everything Finn has not to give in to her curiosity and ask Willa who she called. Who or what it is that can push her to a threshold like that. But she doesn't.

A wind rushes through the clearing. The cockatoos screech and erupt from the trees in clouds of boisterous white, only to dive down again and continue the fight for roosts.

Willa shivers and pulls her jacket around her. "I had to call my sister."

"You have a sister?" Finn stares at her. This girl is like a human plot twist, sometimes.

"And a brother. They're ten and eleven."

"Do they live with your nan too?"

She nods.

"But if your nan's sick, how does she look after you all?"

"I look after them too."

"So let me get this straight. You look after your brother and sister, take care of your nanna, earn scholarships, and get chosen to be a future leader?"

Willa tears a slender leaf into strips. "I do."

"And you also have a full-time job as a big-time business exec. Am I right?"

"No. Just a crappy part-time job."

"I was joking, but of course you have a job. So, is your sister okay?"

"She is now. I was worried because I got a letter from her this morning, begging me to call her. And Riley's usually really chilled. And she *definitely* doesn't write letters." She lets out a tiny laugh. "But she got her first period and freaked."

"Oh. And she needed her big sister. Cute."

"She wanted to ask me things. None of her friends have it yet."

"I know the feeling. I was only ten when I got mine. Total shock. I mean, I knew about periods, but I didn't think it was going to come for ages. I sobbed in the nurse's room until they got my mother on the phone." Finn smiles, remembering the excruciating wait on a cold plastic seat, tears falling, a hot water bottle pressed on this new, humiliating ache, as the nurse tried to get in touch with her mum.

"I was thirteen, and I was sleeping at my best friend's house. On white sheets. I had to tell her mum the next morning." Willa lets out a breath of a laugh. "So embarrassing."

"My sister said she got hers on school sports day. I wonder if there's a girl in the whole world who got her period in the comfort of her own home with someone around she could talk to."

"Maybe it's like preparing us for life," Willa says. "For the fact that nothing *ever* goes to plan."

"Maybe. Anyway, I can't believe you have a brother and sister. *Or* that you didn't think it was worth mentioning?"

"When was I supposed to tell you that? You've been avoiding me for days." Willa's face is stern, but her eyes gleam. "And you know, you've been super busy playing the game," she says pointedly.

"Maybe." Finn shrugs. There's no way she's discussing that with Willa now. That's what got them into this mess in the first place.

"Oh, so we're back to not talking about it? Good." Finn shoots her a look, but Willa just says, "I like it better when we're friends."

"Me too," Finn admits. Because it's hard to deny that, despite everything, she likes being around Willa more than anyone else here. She somehow manages to be utterly familiar and a total surprise at the same time.

When the dinner siren rings, Willa takes a deep breath, looking the calmest Finn has seen her all night. Her smile is slow and sweet. "Thanks, Finn."

Suddenly awkward, Finn says, "It was nothing. Come on. We better go."

CHAPTER 37

Leon leans over the table and holds out his hand. "Okay, let's do this thing."

A thrill whisks through her, but Finn's careful not to betray it. They're going to make this work. She just knows it. She takes his hand. "Deal."

He sits back. "Okay, so we'll talk later? I think we have to draw up some sort of plan or agreement thing for Gussy."

She chuckles at the nickname. Gus would adore it. "For sure. Later."

Her team is watching her as she saunters toward them. She keeps a perfectly straight face until she sits down, with her back to Leon. Then she gives them a quick grin. "Be cool, guys."

"Really?" Hana wriggles in her seat. "We have a deal?"

"Sh," Finn warns her.

"We have our *first* deal." Craig twirls his pen between his fingers. "And now we can start planning more."

"What will we be trading for?" Zaki asks. "We have food now."

"We have to pay for it somehow," Finn says. "And it's not just about surviving, it's about developing too. There's lot of stuff we could do."

"This is going to be fun." Zaki rubs her hands together.

"Let's not get ahead of ourselves." Finn reminds them. "We've got a whole bunch of stuff to write up first."

"True," Amy sighs, looking at the assignment sheet.

Of course they don't win the game just by theoretically making plans and deals. Nope, they have to provide plans and analyses and historical precedents for everything they do. Then they're awarded points based on their work and the decisions they make for their metaphorical territories. But now that everyone's finally scraped up some enthusiasm, it's kind of fun working together. Between them, they've got all the brain parts covered.

And everyone's in the zone today. They huddle around, tapping away at the camp laptops, scribbling into notebooks and mainlining caffeine. They're a testament to outrageous geekery. Finn stares around at them like a proud mother.

"By the way, Finn," Zaki suddenly says, "killer idea."

"Thanks. It was Craig's, too."

"Crap. I just helped you develop it." He points at her. "Take the credit, Finn. It's yours."

She likes Craig more and more every day. She likes all of them, actually. She can imagine them at school after camp, greeting each other like long lost war buddies in the halls.

"Well, you're both evil masterminds," Hana says.

"Hardly evil," Craig replies "We're supplying water to drought-stricken nations. But we'll take your compliment."

"When do the others find out," Amy asks, "and be totally impressed?"

"Don't know." Finn sips her stone-cold coffee and leans back over her work. In her universe, homework equals copious coffee. How else is the brain supposed to function at the speed she needs it to? Luckily, the rec hall's been supplied with a giant tin of caterer's blend instant crap, long-life milk, and an urn. It's awful, but it does the job.

Jessie nudges her. "Hey, I had a thought."

"Congratulations. Make the most of it." She smiles at him and instantly wonders when she can stop being so conscious of trying to keep things light between them.

He flicks an eyebrow at her. "Oh, you're hilarious. I was reading about this tiny town in the Balkans the other day where a river just erupts out of nowhere. Divers go there every summer, trying to find the source."

"And this is important because?"

"Well, Finn, because it's *interesting*. This sleepy little town boomed in the fifteenth century. Before that, it was kind of remote, and the area was primarily agricultural and kinda dozy. But they built all kinds of mills on the water source that people in the agricultural areas needed to make goods, and then a market for trade, and it became this economic hub for a few hundred years. Could we do something like that?"

"But we have no agriculture to process in mills. Not yet."

"Yes, but there are lots of other territories that need to process stuff. And groups that need lumber mills and wool mills. And they're all relying on Drew."

"But he has a fully modernised industry. How can we compete with him?"

"We don't. Not yet. We just start small. Survivalist style. Take business from the bordering areas. That way we just look like we're making enough to survive. Then we expand."

Finn taps her pen against her page. "It's a thought. I like the market idea too. I was thinking about something among those lines yesterday. Like we'd be part of a trade route, or something."

"Like the Silk Road, but a waterway." Craig's been listening.

"Exactly."

Zaki leans in. "And we could try to undercut whatever costs Drew's group put in place."

"Then they'd come to us for sure, even just to avoid him," Hana adds.

They're all listening. Yep, this group has definitely changed their game. She nods. "Exactly."

"We should start researching as soon as we're done with this." Craig's brow is hunched over his eyes, already deep in thought.

Finn gives him a knowing look. "You love this, don't you?"

A smile splits his face. "Yup. Love it."

She can't blame him. She's kind of loving it too.

CHAPTER 38

It might just be the perfect morning.

Finn opened her tent to a shockingly balmy day. The first threat of proper spring. Usually when she gets up, the sun hasn't even come close to shredding the last, bracing traces of cold. But not today. Today smells thick and sweet and gentle. And it reminds her that when she gets back to school, she'll only have three weeks left until September holidays. That's a thought to wake up to.

Even the oval is looking springtime pretty, nightly rainfalls giving it a reality TV-level makeover from withered yellow to a pale, promise-of-lush green. Every night this week, Finn has woken up to a busy patter on the canvas of her tent, only to burrow deeper into the depths of her sleeping bag, enjoying that delicious feeling of being toasty while it's raining outside. And when she emerges in the morning, the sky is blue again, and there's that fresh smell in the air. Greenness itself.

She and Willa are back to their morning meet-ups on the oval. Even now, with the whining slowed to a near stop (face it, Amy's never going to embrace camping), Finn still loves this quiet time. In the hushed mornings, there's no need for either of them to lead. No need to make decisions. No need to be an example. They can just quietly *be*. And even though Willa joked yesterday that leading her Gandry team is much less torturous than dealing with her little sister back at home, Finn knows she likes these stolen hours too. Some mornings they talk, trading life stories. Other mornings they just coexist in the sunshine. Either way, it's become Finn's favourite time of day.

This morning, Willa's reading, a picture of engrossed. When Finn joins her, she's cross-legged, back straight, her hair falling over her face. But it isn't long until she's stretched out, lulled by the sun, and her legs are lean, brown stretches sprawled out of her denim cut-offs to her bare feet. Her chin rests in her hand as her eyes roam the page. Only Willa could look that peaceful while reading a textbook. She could be a model for the camp brochure.

Finn flips open her pad, an idea forming. "Hey, can I draw you?"

Willa's eyes go wide. "Me?"

"See anyone else around?"

"I guess you can." She frowns. "But why?"

"I need the practice. And why not?"

"I don't know. I always think you have to be someone interesting to have your portrait done."

"It's just a sketch, not a commissioned work of art," Finn teases. "And, Willa, you are definitely interesting."

Willa pulls a face at her. Then she shrugs. "Sure. You can draw me, I suppose. What do I do? Just sit here?"

"Just keep doing what you're doing. I don't want you to pose or anything."

"Good." She settles back on the grass and returns to her book. Her expression is self-conscious at first, like she can't shake the awareness of being watched. It's always like that when Finn draws people. She just waits patiently until she sees Willa forgetting, and then she properly begins.

Finn works more slowly than usual. She's not great at portraits, but she wants to translate Willa just right, to render that wide mouth and those knowing eyes just as she sees them. To find the precise balance of light and shade that will create her jawline. It takes the whole hour to produce something she's halfway happy with.

As the morning siren sounds and kids begin to appear, snail-pacing between bed and bathrooms, Willa sits up. "Finished?"

Finn frantically shades in a section around her mouth. It's hard to work with Willa sitting there watching her, expectant. When she's as done as she's going to be, she reluctantly hands the sketchpad over.

Willa's tongue is caught between her teeth as she stares at it. When she finally looks up, her eyes are glowing. "You made me look good."

Finn flaps a dismissive hand. "You already looked good. You must know how pretty you are. Like, it's a bit ridiculous."

Willa's still staring at the picture. "It's hard to know what you look like, don't you think?"

"I guess." Finn tries not to think too much about what she looks like. Dan says she's definitely cute, but Finn has no idea. When she looks in the mirror, she just sees shortness and that small snub nose that her sister Anna says is adorable but Finn thinks make her look like a kid.

"The girls at school say I am. And a lot of random guys ask me out."

"I bet they do." Finn looks at her, curious. "Do you ever say yes? I mean, do you—"

Willa screws up her nose and shakes her head.

"Do the girls in your group know?"

"I don't like people knowing things about me."

"Fair enough."

Willa stares at the picture again, her teeth scraping gently at her bottom lip as she catches an escaping smile. Her reticent pleasure sends a warmth through Finn. She gets the feeling Willa doesn't think about herself much.

Then Finn's suddenly wondering what would have happened if Willa had tried to kiss her in another time or place. Like, if she and Finn met as strangers at a party, without all the complications that come with them being at this camp. Would her reaction have been different?

She's forced to abandon the thought as the breakfast siren cuts through the morning calm. She plucks the sketchbook out of Willa's fingers with a grin. "You can't have this one. It's mine."

CHAPTER 39

"Hey Finn!" It's Hana at the door of the rec hall, chomping on a carrot. "What's up?"

"Your dad's looking for you."

Finn just stares at her for a second. "My *dad*?"

"Says he is. I mean, he could be an imposter serial killer, but if he is, he's done a killer match on the eye and hair colour and you should at least meet him to congratulate him."

"But he didn't say he was coming."

Hana throws her hands up. "Dude, I am but the emissary. I know nothing except that a mini-van full of my blood are going to be here soon and I need to go tidy my tent. So I'm going to need you to stop gaping like a dummy and try to fully comprehend my words, okay, honey?"

All Finn can manage is to nod slowly and close her maths book.

"Good, I'm out."

Finn blinks at the space where Hana was. Why the hell is Dad here? Not that she doesn't want to see him. But a surprise drop-in doesn't scream promises of happy news.

Outside, she spots him immediately and hurries over. He's leaning against the edge of a picnic table in the sunshine. "Hey. What are you doing here?"

"Finno." He folds her into a hug. "Want to go get some coffee? They said I could take you out."

She nods into his shoulder. He's all Dad smell—aftershave and wool. She lets herself breathe in its comfort for a second and then pulls away. He's smiling, but she can see new lines have set in around his eyes. "Okay."

"Great." He shakes his keys and turns for the car.

For a moment, she just stands there and watches him stride ahead, an icy feeling forming in her chest.

He small-talks their way to the nearest town. And she cautiously goes along with it until they're in a tiny café, drinking weak white coffee out of lurid yellow mugs.

She stabs her teaspoon through the stiff foam at the top of her drink as he chitchats with the owner. As soon as the woman and her hot-pink apron disappear behind the counter, she looks him straight in the eye. "Dad, why are you here?"

His cup stops halfway to his mouth. And then he nods, like he should have known Finn would call him out for procrastinating, for trying to soften a blow with this caffeine escape.

"I'm going away for a while."

"What?" She leans back and folds her arms. "Where are you going?"

"Not sure yet. Tasmania, maybe."

She doesn't say anything. Just clenches her jaw and waits for the reason.

He turns his mug slowly around in circles on the table. "There's been some media attention with what happened, and lots of calls. And, weirdly, job offers from a few places. I need a minute, though." He pushes the plate over to her of halved blueberry muffin, coated with thick yellow margarine. "I need to decide what's next."

She ignores the proffered treat. "What does Mum think about it?"

"She thinks it's a good idea."

The iciness spreads, colonising the upper reaches of her stomach as she translates his words. "So you're still fighting?"

"We just see things a bit differently on this one. You can never know these things about a person—how they're going to react or feel—until you're there."

She rolls her eyes. What worldly, painfully obvious wisdom. She's sixteen, and she knows that already. Knows why honesty is always the better choice too. "Are you going away because you're splitting up?"

He sips his coffee instead of answering.

"Just tell me."

"You know we've been having a bit of a rough time lately, right?"

She nods. How can she not?

"Well, we both decided some time apart to figure out our priorities might not be a bad idea."

"What does that even mean?"

He finally meets her eye. "It means we're going to see how things are when I get back."

She stares past him, suddenly aware of the cheesy country music in the background and of the owner chatting loudly behind the counter. "So you *might* split up?"

"I don't know, Finn. I just don't know. I just know the next step is something we can't figure out in the same house."

Finn wants to ask *what about me?* But she also knows she doesn't deserve to. If it weren't for her, it might not have come to this.

"You okay?" he asks.

She shifts her gaze back to him, and something hot and molten suddenly begins to melt the ice caps. "I want to go back."

"Home?"

"To camp." She pushes her mug away. "Take me back."

She stalks out to the car. She doesn't really want to go back. She just doesn't want to be with him and his news. Doesn't want to suffer through him trying to smooth the edges of this for her. Why bother? It still comes out the other end sucking.

He leaves her to her silence until they're on the dirt road leading to the gates. Then he turns to her. "You can call me whenever you want. You can even come visit."

"Great," she mutters.

The visitors' area is teeming with kids and their families saying their goodbyes. He pulls gently at her ear, like he used to when she was a kid. She flinches.

"I don't blame you, honey," he says. "And you shouldn't blame yourself, either."

Then why acknowledge it? And if he knows she feels like this, why is he leaving her? Leaving her with more uncertainty than she can carry? She envisions her house now. With her mother always working late and her dad gone, it will be an unbearable silence to fill.

"Well, I blame you." She unclips her belt, climbs out of the car, and stalks away before he can say anything else.

The thing is, she doesn't blame him. Not really. Okay, maybe a little. But really, she just wanted him to hurt. Hurt enough to maybe change his mind about leaving them. But the fact that he doesn't even try to call out to her tells her she hasn't changed a thing.

CHAPTER 40

Over the achingly long afternoon, the anger turns into something else. A numbness. No, not a numbness, exactly, because it still hurts too much. Whatever it is, it's dragging and thick. It's like a force field between her and the rest of the world. Nothing penetrates.

At dinner, she sits at the edge of the mealtime complaints and stupidity, saying little and getting away with it because Amy and Craig have created some weird eating version of a drinking game, and everyone is completely caught up in it.

During the after-dinner talk from a visiting pair of hippies who own a self-sustaining farm nearby, she sits with her back against the wall and stares past them. When question time finishes and everyone is eating their loose, grazing supper of fruit and biscuits with tea, she takes a blanket from the camping supplies cupboard and slips out to the porch. She drapes it around her shoulders and moves away from the kids clustered on the porch, throwing shade and trading food.

She sits there, lost in her deliberate non-thoughts as the dusk begins to dissolve the edges of the day. And she doesn't move until someone lowers themselves onto the step next to her.

Willa. And there's this flooding relief. Like Finn's been waiting for her but didn't know it.

"You okay?"

Finn can't bring herself to agree or disagree. Or speak at all. So she shrugs.

And Willa just sits there, matching her quiet. And when the Saturday night mood escalates around them and Finn still hasn't spoken, she stands again. For a second Finn thinks she's giving up on her, a betrayal enough to scratch at her numbness. But instead she beckons. "Come on. Let's go somewhere."

Obedient, Finn follows her across the oval, along the path, and up the steep hill track. When they reach the clearing, Finn spreads her blanket out on the grass, wishing she could claw her way out of this mood and *speak*.

"You looked like you needed out," Willa says as she sits gingerly next to her.

Finn nods, feeling an unfamiliar clench in her throat. How does Willa notice that? How does she see what no one else does?

The ache grows.

Finn can't remember the last time she cried. And if she did, they've always been tears of anger or frustration. And now she knows why. For a few minutes she quietly gives in to a few choked, hot, and deeply unsatisfying ones. And she doesn't feel any better.

When she's done, Willa, who's been staring out at the darkened sky and leaving her alone, turns to her. She doesn't say anything, though.

"My parents might be splitting up."

Willa's voice is soft. "I'm so sorry."

"And it's partly my fault." And before she can even decide if she wants to share, she's doing it.

Finn tells her how she heard it all one Saturday afternoon when she was trying to finish an assignment in her father's study. Pete, a shaggy salt-and-pepper journalist, was visiting. One of her dad's best friends, a connection built on ten years of working on competing papers but on the same beats. They sat in the kitchen over beers, chatting.

She wouldn't have tuned into their conversation at all had it not been for the tension in the room. Their conversations usually lost her. She used to try and keep up when she was younger, because it made her feel grown-up to sit with the adults, but their talk was always so specific and insider and impenetrable that she stopped bothering years ago.

In fact, she was so deep in her schoolwork it took her a while to notice the shift in tone. Hushed, incensed whispers began to drift in from the deck where they'd moved at some point. And when she finally registered the atmosphere out there, it shocked her into listening. Her dad and Pete never argued. Didn't even raise their voices, even when they talked out their very different political ideas.

"It's not worth it," she heard Pete say.

Her father's voice was steady. "I think it is."

"Nope. Bad idea. I'm serious."

Finn sat there, her fingers at rest on the keyboard, her ear cocked toward the window. "Not sure I care."

"You will when you lose your job and nothing actually changes once you spill. Because that's exactly what'll happen."

There was a silence. Finally, her dad answered. "Don't know if I believe that."

They argued around this same circle for a while. And by the time Pete left, the two of them at an impasse, Finn had a vague sense of what they were talking about. It worried her so much she asked her dad outright a few nights later when her mother was at work.

Reluctant but cornered, he explained the situation he'd discovered at his job and talked about the story he was thinking of writing about it. She also found out that he hadn't told her mother about it. And he urged Finn not to say anything to her until he was ready to make a decision about the article.

The secrecy made her even more uncertain. It was unnerving to know that her parents, who were borderline ridiculous-happy as far as she knew, had this secret between them. She waited two weeks in her promised silence, but the time never came. Her mum never said a word, and he didn't either. Then one morning, she snatched his empty coffee cup from the bench and interrupted his morning news diatribe. "When are you going to tell Mum?"

She'd put the dripping, clean mug in the dish rack and turned back to him before he answered.

"I told you. Not until I've made a decision. Only if I need to tell her."

She'd nodded but had known in her gut that he'd already made his decision. He was just putting off admitting it to himself and to her.

And she became so caught up in all the worries that she couldn't think of anything else. Even the breakup with Matt, a month old by then, faded into triviality in the face of this. All she could do was ask herself the same questions: What would her mum say? Would she want him to do it? Would he work again if he did? The questions had run an endless parade through her mind, taunting her with their unanswerability.

She tells Willa how it all got too big, this burden. How before this moment Finn never had a problem she didn't know how to fix or feel better about. And then how one day in the car, she let something slip to her mother by accident. How she's sure it wasn't really an accident.

She'd stupidly expected her mother to solve this problem from her usual place of pragmatism, and not from the place where she felt betrayal and anger at not being privy to a secret even her daughter knew. Finn had watched her mother's lips thin out as she drove, noted how she braked more heavily than usual at an intersection. And a doomy sensation had filled her stomach.

That night, the first in a long line of fights erupted in hushed, harsh undertones from behind the study door. From that day onward, tension slunk into the house and stayed there, a pervasive, unwelcome guest. And this has been her life until she left for camp.

"I'm sorry. My problems seem so small compared to what you've had to deal with."

"It doesn't work like that, Finn. Your problems are your problems, and they hurt right now."

"I guess." She lies back on the blanket. Above her, a great big sky is turning an inky blue, on its way to black. Like always, she feels like a useless speck under its massiveness. Problem is, it doesn't make her problems feel any smaller.

"You didn't do anything wrong, Finn. Not really. Your dad was always going to do what he did, and your mum was always going to find out." Willa lies next to her. "And she was probably always going to feel betrayed because he kept it a secret. Nothing changed because of what you said. It all just happened maybe a little quicker."

In her head, Finn knows Willa is right. But it doesn't stem the misery. Because the simple fact remains that this is happening. Her parents are at some sort of marital crossroads, her father is jobless, and he is leaving them.

A loud cheer invades the night. Rec time. All slapstick and stupidity around the hall, probably. She's glad to be on this blanket on a hill with Willa, away from it all. "Thank you for rescuing me."

Willa takes a loose hold of Finn's hand on the blanket between them, her eyes fixed on the stars. "I'll always rescue you." She says it so simply that it makes Finn draw in a breath. Willa squeezes Finn's fingers and releases them. "Not that you'll ever need it much."

Finn suddenly has to fight the urge to nudge her forehead into the nook of Willa's neck and shoulder. Has to remind herself that she's got no right to seek comfort like that. Not after she rejected her. But just the fact Finn wants to begs the simplest of questions: why resist?

There are so many reasons not to cross this line, probably. Always have been. At first, it was the mess of Jessie, which was still stinging and strange that night Willa kissed her. Now there are other things in its place. Like the game. The fact that she and Willa could be enemies tomorrow. There's also the simple fact that they are both headstrong and stubborn, with an inborn tendency to lead not follow. It hardly sounds like compatibility.

Finn knows all this already. But in this moment, she's not sure she cares. For the first time in a long time, she can't be bothered logic-ing her way out of something. So she rolls on her side to face Willa and allows herself to examine this new recklessness.

Pulled by her stare, maybe, Willa mirrors her. She looks peaceful and content, like she'd be nowhere else. And that's what gives Finn all the brave she needs to take Willa's hand from where it rests on the blanket between them. As she lets her fingers graze over Willa's palm, Finn lurches between terrified and excited before being yanked back to her favourite land of overthinking. Is she doing something dumb and impetuous here? Probably. But she can't seem to make it matter, because right now Willa's a beam of light flooding through a crack in a curtain, and Finn can't look away.

So instead, Finn just surrenders to the moment she's making, stroking stray strands of hair from Willa's face to clear room for her stare. Willa's expression hovers between intrigued and wary, and when she finally meets Finn's eye, she frowns slightly. Bold now, Finn leans in closer and presses her mouth against that small, confused purse of Willa's lips, doing her best to dissolve it.

The kiss sends a buzz over Finn's skin, a telegraph passed down all the wires, sending good news for once. Even the touch of Willa's knee to Finn's leg as she shifts closer sends her insides scattering. It's a sensation both shocking and unsurprising at the same time, and Finn realises she could live in this kiss for a very long time. Survive on it. Eat and drink and take succour from it. If her mornings hanging out side-by-side with Willa were momentary sanctuaries, this kiss is desert-island-for-a-year fodder.

And just as she's about to retreat, Willa's fingers slide into her hair. She draws Finn deeper into the kiss, as if she, too, finally starts to believe in this moment.

Part Two: Willa

CHAPTER 41

She must have dozed, because when she wakes, Finn's not with her.

The last thing she remembers is the feeling of Finn's head resting against her cheek and the curl of her hand in hers. Now there's just her.

Willa is suddenly awash with dread. Not again. The last time she fell asleep next to a girl, this, too, was how it went. But then the fear cures itself at the sight of her standing at the edge of the clearing by the rocks, looking down at camp. Finn's back is to her, but Willa's so used to reading her from afar that she can tell Finn's thick with thought.

Willa doesn't go to her. Instead she watches Finn contemplating whatever it is she's contemplating, her hands thrust in her pockets. And Willa hopes she has not just become an added complication in Finn's life. Because she understands how easily it could become like that. Finn's life right now is difficult. They, too, could be difficult. They have been so far.

When Finn finally turns, Willa freezes as she sees Finn recalled to her existence, sees her remember. And she sees the other part, too, that fleeting moment of hesitance, a kaleidoscope of microfeelings running over her face in a matter of seconds. It's like watching a lottery machine spin while you pray it falls on the prize you want. And her stomach churns until she sees it land on a small smile. Just this once, she wins.

Finn doesn't come to her, though. Instead, she sits down on the rock—the same rock they sat on nights ago, when Willa thanked her for helping her to call Riley. For helping Willa, even though she didn't know why exactly why Willa needed help. For this is the kindness of Finn.

As an excuse—an offering—Willa picks up the blanket and brings it with her. She hands it to her and sits.

"Thanks," Finn says softly as she drapes it over both their laps. Then she rests her chin in her hand and leaves Willa again, chasing down her thoughts. Finn's not thinking about her. Willa knows this. She's thinking about her parents. Or maybe about what her life will look like when they leave this place. Or maybe she's not thinking much but is just letting the hurt and the sad wash through without attaching it to anything. Sometimes that's easier. And Willa doesn't disturb her. Because she knows what it's like to have your problems take up all the room inside you. How sometimes, just when you think you've pushed them back to manageable size—showed them their fair share of space—they burst out again, filling you up.

Below, the camp is alive with noise. Saturday night in full flight. It must be close to curfew. Willa's stomach clenches at the thought of leaving things here unsaid. She wants to take her hand, but now that Finn's all quiet and not touching her, Willa doesn't know if she's allowed to, or if Finn wants it, or if what happened on the blanket back there was a moment in time. A sad, heartsick, looking-for-distraction kind of thing. Willa wants to ask, but she doesn't want to burden her. Tonight's hurting and hard enough for Finn already, and Willa doesn't want to be a part of that. She wants to be her escape.

They sit in this claustrophobic silence as the Milky Way spins out its dusky track. They sit there until the siren sounds below, the end of the day in Camp Nowhere. Which is precisely where Willa is—nowhere. Half an hour ago, they were a supernova of lips and breath and hands through hair. Now they are silence.

"I guess we should go," she finally whispers.

Finn nods. When she gets up, she pulls the blanket from them, holding it tight in a bundle against her chest. Then she meets Willa's gaze, because it's not like Finn to not look you in the eye, but immediately glances away.

As they walk, the silence becomes so big that Willa doesn't dare try to fill it. In fact, she's so paralysed by it that when they get to the bottom of the path and Finn turns to her and gives her a half-smile, Willa simply stares at her for a few seconds before she remembers to smile back.

"Night," Finn says and walks away.

"Night," Willa says after her and swallows hard.

CHAPTER 42

Eva glances over the edge of her book as Willa steps inside the harsh fluorescent light of the cabin. "And where have you been, Missy?"

"Stopout," Amira teases. She's already got her hair a mess of bun and hairspray for the night, her preferred method of attaining next-day beach hair in the wilderness. Willa knows all about this now. These are the things you learn at camp. She also knows Ling has nicknames for everyone, that Maria gets her period every two and a half weeks, and that Holly fights with her boyfriend in her sleep. Willa doesn't think they've learned much about her, but that's the way she likes it.

It takes everything she has to haul herself into the moment and answer/not answer Eva. "Around."

And that's all she needs to say for Eva to nod and return to her book. Because her curiosity was never real. Besides, Willa has them trained in when to leave her alone. Without even meaning to, she has somehow made a world where she lives both among these girls and apart from them, depending on the needs and time of the day. And everyone is happy with that arrangement. Because it's just a microversion of what they have at school.

Her friend Kelly says she's lucky they're nice to her. But Kelly says that because the only private school girls she has ever known are the plaid-skirted mean girls of film and TV. Gandry girls aren't really like that. Well, they can be sometimes, but not with Willa. Mostly because she doesn't count, compete, or care socially. She doesn't want a place in their playground pecking order. At the same time, her brains impress them, so at school she straddles some fine, unseen line of acceptability, located somewhere between unthreatening socially and vital scholastically. She wins their debates. She tops their state lists. She gets handed the framed certificates. Her hungry mind earns their respect, as do her looks. Being intimidating has its pluses, Kelly says.

And here on camp, she has somehow become their cute little anomaly. Both leading and lost. In the cabin it's all "oh, Willa doesn't care about those things" when someone tries to drag her into one of their girl-world, mascara, thigh-fat, boyfriend conversations. And when they do try, Willa feels like this weird, puritan thing, a girl who's been stuck in a basement or a cult for years and emerges into a world that functions beyond her grasp. All the references fly over her head: the social media stuff, the pop culture, the dropped celebrity names. They are only vaguely recognisable echoes to her. At home, her eleven-year-old sister absorbs them into her being, while Willa remains clueless. And even if she wanted to join the endless chatter, she'd never catch up. Not if she studies for the rest of her life.

So she doesn't participate. She plays neither Truth nor Dare, nor does she divulge secrets or make-up tips or advice about relationships. And the only two hairstyles she knows are a ponytail and not a ponytail.

Adorably clueless genius is the role they have decided for her. Because in their version of the world, someone who looks like they say Willa does would only be this no-frills because they don't know any better. Thus, when she isn't their leader, she's relegated to being their quaint, slightly odd, but highly useful little sister. A palatable version of different. Other girls at school aren't so lucky.

But in the world of the game, the patronising affection disappears, and she is the one they look towards to speak first, to act first, to make their decisions. Because although no one else at this camp would know it, every single girl in her group wants to win this game. Because winning is what they do.

Gandry girls are competitive. It took Willa a while to figure this out when she first arrived in Year 9. On the outside, they are airbrushed, high-resolution versions of jaded, worldly girlhood. And they make it appear like school is just a place they go while they are being that. It all comes together in a perfectly rendered illusion of carefree.

But she quickly noticed that to gain status in this world, you have to give a crap while perfecting the art of looking like it hasn't occurred to you whether or not you should give a crap. Study hard, but don't look like it's an effort. Don't come too close to the top. Just below the top is best. Win at sport, but don't show how badly you want the point. Always punch your weight or better in the dating game, and act like it's expected. Be a testament to effortlessness. There are so many unspoken rules. And luckily, she doesn't have to follow them.

She climbs onto her bunk and stares at the ceiling. Below is a delicate patter of girls chatting an endless nothing. They ran out of substance to talk about at the end of week one. How could they not? They are together so much. In the corner, Emma sings softly, their own personal radio. And no one tells her to shut up, because she has a beautiful voice and she's never loud or a show-off about it. She simply cannot not sing. So they let her, bathing in her husky, mellow tone.

Willa's eyes close, and her thoughts inevitably slide back to Finn.

She kissed me. She kissed me. She kissed me.

She grips the pillow as the memory makes her insides want to fold in on themselves. And Willa kissed her back, because if there's a moment in time where Finn decides she wants to kiss her, Willa's going to go there, even if she knows the odds are against it working out the way she wants it to. She knows maybe Finn's reasons weren't her reasons. Maybe Finn needed to feel something else for a minute. Maybe she just needed to *feel*. And maybe Willa was just there.

Willa wants to not let it mean so much. But how can she when she has nourished herself on two facts: first, that for a moment, on that night on the porch, Finn kissed her back. Second, that she said she couldn't *right now*. Not a simple, finite *couldn't*. Not couldn't *ever*. She couldn't *now*.

Willa likes *now*. *Now* has the potential to change. To become *someday* or *next week* or maybe even *soon*. That *now* has the semantic potential she needs to dwell in and hope on and revisit that kiss again and again. Ever since that night, she has driven herself crazy in the wilderness of variables of that *now*. Her stupid, hopeful heart has clung to it. And the fact that Finn walked away again this time means Willa might have to cling to it some more.

"Hey Will." A block of chocolate is waved in her face.

"No, thank you." Her voice cracks a little. She rolls over and pushes her face into the pillow, because she doesn't know if she can hide this mood. She breathes out slowly into the dusty-smelling pillow. This is exactly what she was supposed to *not* do—let herself fall for a girl who might not know her own feelings. *Again*. Because it's too hard and too hurtful to wait for them to catch up. If they ever do. Willa already knows that this is the one time in life where it doesn't pay to be an advanced learner.

Willa's so far inside her misery that she barely registers the tap on the door.

"What the?" Eva slaps her magazine down and scuffs across the concrete. She pulls the door slightly ajar. "Hi?" Her voice sounds doubtful.

"Hey."

Willa's heart seems to stop beating for a second. It's that familiar, crystal tone. She'd know it anywhere.

"Well, you're a brave one, aren't you?" Eva drawls. She's right too. It's the hardest and fastest rule of this camp: No leaving sleeping quarters after curfew. It's a sent-home kind of transgression.

"Uh, yeah. Is Willa there?"

"I'm coming," Willa says calmly through a seasick surge of fear.

Eva turns, giving Willa a vaguely questioning look before dropping back onto her bed and picking up her magazine.

Willa shuts the door firmly behind her before she makes eye contact. Because she'd like her roommates' complete lack of curiosity to stay that way.

Finn's wrapped in a jacket now, a dark green scarf looped around her neck. It tugs at the tiger-y flecks in her eyes. "Hey."

"Hi." The choke of nerves makes it come out sullen. Willa flinches. Why does she get this stuff so wrong?

"Do you have a second?"

She nods, tongue-tied, and follows as Finn trots lightly down the steps, looking around for rogue teachers. Willa's stomach is a queasy mess. Why is Finn here? Is she going to make the cut now? It would be like Finn to do that. To come and finish the job she didn't do at the bottom of the hill. Make things right before bed.

When they get to the picnic area, Finn stops. "Hey, listen," she says slowly. "I forgot something."

Willa shivers and crosses her arms over her ribs. It's too cold to be out here without a jumper. But she's too tangled with fear and curiosity to care. "What?"

Then Finn smiles. That wry Finn smile. The one that usually chases her, saying something dry and funny, because it's her way of dealing with life's little stupidities.

132

But this time it's not. This time it's a prelude. A prelude to her rising onto her toes and kissing her. It's just one swift, soft touch to her lips, but it's more important and more magical than all those other kisses back in the clearing. Because this one makes all of those ones *real*. And suddenly Willa can breathe again. She takes hold of Finn's jacket pockets, holding her in close.

"I'm sorry," Finn whispers into the air between them. "Do you ever just scare yourself for a minute?"

"All the time."

"I'm sorry," she says again.

"You didn't have to come back," Willa lies.

"Yes I did."

Of course she did. Because she's Finn, and she doesn't leave things badly. Finn steps in closer, pressing her forehead to her shoulder. Willa combs her fingers through her mess of short blonde hair, still stuck on the fact that this incredible, summer storm of a girl is letting her be this close to her.

Finally, Finn sighs. "I better go. Don't want to get caught. Besides," she rolls her eyes. "I'm not setting a very good example."

Willa dares a teasing grin. "I think you are."

Finn lets out a little breath of a laugh, but then her smile fades into something sad, and Willa knows she's back to remembering.

"Hey, you'll be okay."

"I know."

Willa's not sure if she believes it, though.

"Goodnight." Finn kisses her again and strides away into the darkness.

"Working on the weekend, are we?" Amira says as Willa comes into the cabin. "The things you do for us."

Willa feigns a complicit smile. But she doesn't answer, because she doesn't like to lie. And they don't expect her to answer anyway. Being the silent, stoic leader has its upsides. Like right now, when all she wants to do is lie on her top bunk and wallow in that kiss and that smile and that reckless rule breaking Finn did just for her.

CHAPTER 43

Sunday is strange.

It's strange because it's both melancholy and lovely.

It's lovely because Willa gets to carry the fact that Finn kissed her—*twice*—around all day. And she holds it like something precious she doesn't want to drop. It's lucky she owns the memory, too, because Sunday is jammed with team-building exercises and group hikes and camp chores, and they are rarely in the same place.

Even from the distance she's forced to keep, Willa sees how Finn bears traces of last night's sadness. Of course she does. During meals, Finn is turned inward until one of her team yanks her out of it with a joke or comment. And Willa wants to go to her and take her hand and promise her it will feel less bad soon. She doesn't, of course. But when their eyes finally meet in the line to return dirty breakfast dishes and Finn smiles at her, it feels like a sunburst radiating through her chest.

Then there's the melancholy. It's a nebulous, unfamiliar sadness that drifts in while they're cleaning the cabin. Willa doesn't recognise it at first. Finally, it takes identifiable shape: she's homesick.

She runs the mop over the concrete floor, and as the hot pine stink of disinfectant cloys the air, she suddenly aches to have woken in her own room. Willa loves Sunday mornings. Sundays start slow and stay slow. She doesn't have to wake earlier than everyone and cram in the last of her homework before the day starts. She doesn't have to drag dozy, grumpy Riley from her bed and force her to get ready for school while Willa helps make breakfasts and lunches and checks that Nan has what she needs for the day. She doesn't have to rush them to school and jump on the last bus that will get her to Gandry on time, already weary.

Not Sundays. On Sundays they make piles of Nutella toast, and her brother and sister are allowed to ease into the day via television. Willa will sit outside in Nan's tiny, verdant jungle and wait for Maida and Kelly to surface. When they do, Kelly will sit on the high brick wall between their houses while Maida spreads her long skirt out on the grass, and they'll tell her about what they did last night. And while she listens to their tales, Willa will remember there's a world beyond this house and school, even if she can't always be persuaded to go there. Nan will come out to check what happened to her garden overnight and tell Kelly in her schoolteacher's voice to get off the fence and act like a lady. Kelly will just laugh and tease, and within minutes, Nan will be laughing, too, because she loves Kelly as much as she disapproves of her.

Willa's realises she's homesick because it's her best friends she wants to be around while she begins learning how to live with this thing that is her and Finn. She might not tell them about it straight away, though, because Willa loves that covetous feeling when you're holding onto something before you share it. When it's all deliciously, untouchably yours. But she'd tell them eventually, because they are Kelly and Maida, and they are the only repository of her secrets. They are the only people outside of her family who know her whole story. And now there is Finn.

She also wants to just sit and listen while Kelly and Maida argue about anything and everything. And even though they fight so close to a knife's edge, they will never truly hurt each other, because at heart, they are sisters. Willa won't even mind that bitter little bite of envy when the argument ends and they throw their arms around each other, laughing, and she remembers that she is third wheel to a friendship older than her time on this street. They love Willa, but they love each other more because they are bound by history.

Willa's always wondered what it's like to have a someone. She is someone's someone. Two people's. For she is Riley and Jack's. But she doesn't have *her* person. She wonders what it's like to have someone who likes you more than they like the rest of the world. Who'd choose you first. Who'd get impatient wanting to be near you when they couldn't be. Someone you could call or message at any time of the day and night, and they'd always be happy that you did. It must be a good feeling.

CHAPTER 44

During free time, Willa wants to go and find Finn, but she can't. She can't because she has to work on the game.

Willa must work on the game because she has a secret: she doesn't know what to do.

This is totally unknown territory. Willa knows she's clever. Very. She knows this because she has never not understood anything a teacher has told her. While others around her have been lost, she's never known what that's like. Not when it comes to the things harboured between the pages of textbooks, anyway.

But now, suddenly, she's the one that's lost. They had a plan. They would tighten everything up. They would strengthen their resources, and then they would reroute trade. The end goal was total independence. For their territory to no longer be at the mercy of that childish boy and his dumb power games. It was a long game, but a good game. Then everything fell apart with one forced hand.

The thing is, Finn will never know now that Willa was always going to take her people in. That she and her team were going to be a part of this new scheme. But Drew and his petty need for revenge happened, and now Gandry is more at his mercy than ever.

Willa is sure that Finn's found a way for her team to play the game on their own terms. Can tell from the shift in Finn's behaviour in the days before her world crumbled a little. Willa's team has not. *She* has not.

Tonight, she and Eva, her deputy, work through their notes in homework time, thinking and talking contingencies, discussing other ways to free themselves from Drew's economic grasp. But without Finn's people, they cannot industrialise, and without anywhere else to process their food, they cannot feed themselves adequately yet.

The irritating thing is that their territory can easily survive like this, stuck in the status quo they began the game with. They could even thrive, as long as they continue to manage everything well and not get in Drew's way. But that's not how these girls play. They win. And Willa is supposed to be the one to make it happen. And for the first time in her life, she's not sure how.

Eva's confident, though, in that automated Gandry way. "You'll think of something," she assures Willa as they pack up their things. "You always do."

But what if there's a first time she can't?

CHAPTER 45

Finn's not there in the morning. Instead there's just Willa, an unopened book, and a sleepy sun hefting its way over the horizon. And as it works its way higher, the butterflies she woke with flutter and die and form a dead weight in her gut. And when she hears the morning siren from her spot on the grass, her last shreds of hope evaporate.

Willa doesn't look for her during breakfast. Because she's too scared to know why Finn didn't come. Instead, cereal swirls around her spoon as she absorbs the snatches of chatter that flit around her.

"I'd just tell him you've already made up your mind."

"My mother swears by honey and shea butter for that."

"But if I do it in postgrad, won't it take a year longer?"

Gandry is on clean-up duty after breakfast, and she loses herself to the soothing clamour and rhythm of stacks of dirty dishes. Over and over in the hot fug of the kitchen, she loads them into the industrial washer and pulls them out clean.

Don't let this be like it was with Freya, she prays as steam billows in her face. With Freya, she had to learn to live with the constant push and tug of uncertainty, because Freya liked it like that. But Freya was as different from Finn as could be. She was fragile and needy. She insinuated herself into Willa's world by treating Willa like her saviour. She made Willa think that her survival depended on Willa's complete and utter attention.

Finn would never do that. Finn's solid. Not in body, but in being. She's gravity and kindness and all those good things that anchor. Safe but never boring. Finn doesn't demand or inveigle. She doesn't need to.

Willa stacks piles of plates roughly. She is suddenly both smitten and annoyed—smitten because it's Finn, annoyed because she is smitten. Because Willa has broken all her own rules.

She wasn't supposed to do this again. At first she tried to fool herself, to pretend it was something else. She told herself this attention to Finn was curiosity, because she was the only other girl to lead a group. Because she was smart and kind and *present*. Because she led so differently to Willa and didn't act intimidated when they met. Because that night when they all had to pick out a leadership quote that they liked from a list, Finn stood and read in her bell-like voice that a leader was a dealer in hope. Only Finn could pluck beauty from pages of corporate speak.

Willa told herself it was because Finn is so radiant when she talks about something she believes in and *not* because Willa always found herself looking for her in crowds. Not because one early morning, catching a glimpse of pale collarbone and black bra strap when Finn's shirt shifted as she drew, an instant, exquisite flicker jolted Willa recklessly into waking.

Still, she tried to tell herself that she was simply intrigued by this small, dirty-blonde dealer in hope. It didn't last long, though. Because that's the trouble with being smart. You can only fool yourself for so long. So when she saw Finn walking toward her on the oval each morning, she soon recognised that responding thump in her chest for exactly the rude, beautiful thing it was.

CHAPTER 46

Protected by the low sling of a tree, Willa draws the postcard from her pocket: There's a photo of a tram, covered by a gleeful entreaty to *Fall in Love with Melbourne!* The back holds a commemorative stamp and a cocktail of deliciously familiar scrawls.

Hey there. We brought the midgets to High St for a hot chocolate. Your gran says they're behaving and to tell you not to eat too much rubbish. Haven't you learned to rule the world by now? Come home!!!! Kel.

I miss my friend Willa. Come back and drink tea under the tree with me. Love you. Maida.

Nan says I can get my ears pierced, but that you have to take me. Maida says my birthstone is sapphire, which is blue, so I'm going to get blue studs. Hurry up and come back so we can go! Love Riley

Dear Willa come home soon love Jack.

It's that clumsy little *love Jack* that does it. Makes her throat ache with the silent hum of home. Of things known. Of things loved. Of things unchanged.

She shoves the card into her pencil case, pulls out her Legal Studies notes, and tries to smother the excess feels with homework.

"Hey."

But she can't, because now Finn's standing in front of her, the sleeves of her pale-blue shirt rolled up in that cute, businesslike way she wears them, her short hair tucked behind her ears. Willa blinks up at her. How can she manage to sneak up on her like this when all Willa has done is think about her?

"I'm sorry I didn't meet you this morning. We had a little ant infestation problem." Finn rolls her eyes. "Someone's been hording snacks."

Willa smiles, and notes the way Finn's hands are clenched a little by her sides. Could she be nervous? Willa could never have imagined it—or being the thing that made Finn so.

"Are you doing anything in free time this afternoon?" Finn asks, digging the toe of her boot into the grass.

Willa shakes her head. She'd planned on reading and dreaming and thinking about Finn, probably.

"Want to go for a walk?" She looks hopeful. And Willa's heart hums. Does Finn think she would ever say no?

She taps her pencil against her book and nods. "Sure."

"Meet me at the picnic tables?"

"Sure," she says again.

And she's gone.

CHAPTER 47

Finn jumps from the table the minute she sees Willa coming. "Hey. I want to show you a place. Up the creek." She lets out a little laugh, stupidly, cutely delighted at her accidental joke. "Not that kind of creek."

Willa laughs and follows her between the sweeping green curtains of willow. They walk along the banks without talking for a couple of hundred metres, the scrub becoming a dense green press at their sides. It thickens so much that eventually, there's no way to get through it.

Finn turns and gives her a conspiratorial smile. "This is where it gets fun."

In one quick leap, she bounds from the banks to a rock that sits high and dry in the rushing water. And from there, she leaps to another. Then she turns to Willa, cheeks pink with cold and with what Willa thinks might be happiness. "Come on."

And she's so glowing and alive, how could Willa not follow her? She obediently steps onto a rock, gathers her balance, and steps again.

And this is how they go for a while, leaping from rock to rock, making their slow way up the creek. Around them, spidery-lush ferns huddle on the banks, while trees battle for space in the sky above. Willa lingers a moment so she can take it in. She thinks of her grandmother, who never wanted to go anywhere. Never wanted to travel. Never really left the state. Willa thinks of all the things she hasn't gotten to know because of it. All the places she's never seen. Beautiful, secret places like this. Places that give Willa a soft ache. Willa wants to discover each and every one of them.

This creek reminds Willa of a national park her dad took her to once when she was little. They camped for the night by a river, all piled in one tent. She loves rivers. They're so furtive. They don't announce themselves, noisy and vast, like the ocean.

Sometimes they just flow, quietly wearing their groove. You could live a hundred metres from a river and never know if you didn't look.

Finn stops and turns and, maybe thinking Willa's stuck, holds out her hand. And even though she's not, Willa lets her take it and pull her across.

She tries not to feel bereft as Finn releases her. "How did you find this?"

"Jessie showed me yesterday. There's a track to where we're going on the other side, but it takes a lot longer than coming straight up the creek. Some of the kids run it in the mornings, even though they're not supposed to."

Willa nods and tries not to think of Finn and the hot boy together. The thought of them walking together makes her chest constrict. She's a jealous creature, she's finding out.

A little further, Finn points to an old post covered in frayed chicken wire. It lists towards the water. "That's the fence line for the camp." She turns and grins. "I thought I should let you know, because for about a hundred metres more, we'll be officially breaking rules."

Willa shrugs. There's no way she's going back. Not now that they are alone and now that Finn's smiling more than she has seen for days. "We'll just tell them you were looking to expand your new empire," Willa says.

Finn's smile is dubious. "I somehow don't think that will fly."

They round a bend in the creek, and soon after that, it shallows out into a wide, calmer stretch of water, specked with large, flat rocks. The trees part ways above them, letting the sunlight in, dotting the water with flecks of light. It is a tiny, hushed paradise.

Finn finds a rock bathed in the little patch of sunshine that slides through the trees. She sits. And Willa has a feeling—or maybe a hope—that this will be their rock now. She drops down next to her.

They fall into a silence. Willa is suddenly not sure what to say or do, and she gets the feeling that Finn isn't either. It's funny how just adding the fact that you want to touch each other to a relationship is not a mere addition but a whole reconfiguration. And maybe they don't know how to reconfigure yet.

It's Finn who starts it. Willa's still busy in the happiness of sitting next to her. And also maybe she still needs Finn to call the shots. To let her know exactly what this is. So Willa's watching a leaf be dragged into a tiny whirlpool circling between two rocks when it happens. It's sucked in and spat out again in the time it takes Finn to draw Willa's arm over to her own knee.

Finn's fingers drift along her wrist to her elbow and back again. Willa's eyes fall closed at the intoxicating sweep. Nobody's ever touched her in such a simple, intimate way before. She and Freya did so much more, but they jumped from zero to infinity in one night. They moved so fast they skipped these parts, these tiny but epic acts of touch. Willa wants them all now.

When she opens her eyes, Finn is smiling at her like she knows how good it feels. And Willa's stuck again with the problem that she wants to kiss her, but she's not sure of the rules.

Before she can muster her courage, Finn leans in and kisses *her*. Then she gives her another one of those small, playful Finn smiles. Willa didn't know it was possible to be more smitten. She wishes she possessed words to say it.

Finn suddenly shuffles closer, takes her hand, and leans against her side, right where Willa has imagined her before. "Tell me about your brother and sister. About Riley and…Jack?"

"Mhm." Finn's hair smells of something sharp and fragrant. Lime, maybe.

"Tell me about them. What's Jack like?"

"He's sweet and smart, but sometimes you have to make him talk to you. He's better than he used to be, though." She smiles, thinking of the little boy she has to bully-love sometimes, because it's the only way you can get *in*. "The people who moved in across the road this year have a kid his age, and they've gotten tight. He'd hang out there all the time if he could. They game and play soccer together. He has a best friend for the first time in his life. He's still quiet, but I think he's happier now."

"That's great."

"It is." Willa doesn't know how to tell her about the other part, though. The part where she's selfish because she feels flickers of bitterness that this family can give him the kind of comfort Willa can't. She could never make him feel safe enough to stop hiding and take a look at the world and even find he likes it a little, like he does now. She knows she should only be purely, beautifully happy for him, but it stings sometimes.

She can't sit with these feelings, and she can't share them, so she changes the subject to her bull-headed charmer of a sister. "Riley could raise herself. She tough and smart and popular. She likes boy bands and charm bracelets and intrigue, and her teachers say she's got savvy."

Willa's almost shocked by the rush of words leaving her mouth, but she never gets to talk about her brother and sister. "I think they might mean she's got a smart mouth. Which is true."

"She doesn't sound like you."

"She isn't. I know it's dumb, but it never occurred to me that she could turn out so completely unlike me or anyone else we know. She's like her own autonomous, incredibly bossy little person. She even tells me what to do."

"Someone tells *you* what to do? I don't believe you."

"Believe me. She's unhappy with my social life, she's informed me."

"What's wrong with it?"

"It doesn't really exist."

Finn laughs and stretches out her legs. "I have one of those social lives, too. So you look after them a lot?"

"Nan does everything she can, but she gets tired, and she has problems with her back. I have to do a lot around the house. One of her old students came to stay so I could come here."

"Where do you work?"

"For a catering company on Saturday mornings. I'm saving as much as I can. Then later, if Riley and Jack want to go to university, they'll be able to live with me and not have to worry."

Finn's fingers curls around hers. "You're incredible, you know."

"So are you," Willa tells her.

Finn's nose wrinkles.

"No, really. It's true."

Willa knows Finn won't hear it, though. Doesn't know that just because her story isn't air quotes "special" like Willa's doesn't mean that she's not special. Because she is. Finn *earths*. She's kindness and strength in one person. And one day, she will use this power for more than good. Willa knows it. She'll use it for something *amazing*.

Finn's cheek is a downy glide under Willa's fingertips. "How are *you* feeling today?"

"Like I don't want to think about it," Finn says.

"Okay."

Finn sits up and shimmies, as if shaking herself free of that thought. Then she presses the tip of her nose to Willa's for a moment before pushing a swift kiss on her. And when she pulls back, Willa follows her, because she wasn't nearly ready for it to end.

They kiss, slow and sweet, in a mellow drift of lips meeting over and over. Willa smooths her hand over the sun-baked cotton at the back of Finn's T-shirt. And when Finn's tongue finds hers and her hands move into her hair, Willa doesn't know if she'll ever be able to leave this rock again. They are so electric and so soft at the same time, she can hardly stand it.

When they finally part, Willa hears a little intake of breath, like maybe she has some kind of effect on Finn. She doesn't know why that surprises her, but it does. Because Willa's still learning to believe. Her feelings for Finn have been an aching familiarity ever since that night of the party, but Finn's attraction to her is still a shocking, new fact.

Finn checks her watch and frowns. "Hey, we should go."

When they are standing, Finn's arms wind tightly around Willa's waist. Her head almost fits under Willa's chin. Finn's so strong and so lively that Willa forgets how small she really is. "You're such a shorty," she teases.

"I am aware," Finn says drily. "Some might say you're too tall."

Willa's about to step to the next rock when Finn grabs her hand.

"Wait a sec. Come here." She grabs Willa and positions her at the front of the rock, facing upstream.

"What?" Willa asks, wary.

"I want to show you something cool. Look down." Her hand is a tiny electric charge on the small of Willa's back. "Look right down at the water. Let the periphery disappear and try to only see water flowing around the rock. Just stare."

Willa frowns, but does as she's told. Finn's hand disappears, leaving her alone on the edge of the rock. Willa ignores everything but the scurrying water and the edge of their small granite island. It takes a moment to narrow her focus, but when she does she's taken over by this uncanny, queasy sensation that they're the ones moving, not the creek. And it makes her lose her balance, falling backward slightly.

Finn grabs her by the waist, her bellbird laugh chiming in Willa's ears. "See?"

CHAPTER 48

Willa grinds to a stop, her lungs trying to haul air faster than it can get in. She jams her hands on her hips, bends at the waist, and peers over Holly's arm at the map. "Are we close?" she manages to gasp.

Behind her, the other girls huff and pant up the steep stretch to the clearing.

Holly glances between the compass and the piece of paper and nods. "About another three hundred metres, I think."

"Good." Willa bends over again, and surrenders for a minute to the fight for oxygen. Around her, the girls do the same.

They have been driven to a patch of thick bushland for the purposes of completing what is apparently the next step in becoming future leaders. Each team has a trail they must complete, their routes marked out in different, winding coloured lines on the map. All that they have to guide them is the map, a compass, a list of coordinates, and the distance between markers. They're supposed to complete the trail and return to the meeting spot with the correct list of numbers they will find etched onto the markers. It's impossible to get lost, Gus tells them. The park is fenced, and there will always be a trail and due north to find. Willa's glad to hear it, because everything here looks the same, an endless terrain of gangly trees, embedded rocks, and the occasional meeting with a creek.

Gus calls this game The Great Hunt. Holly says it's really just glorified orienteering, some outdoorsy thing kids do with compasses on school camps or in Scouts. Willa never did any of those things. Luckily, Holly did.

The Great Hunt is a race. Of course it's a race. Everything is a competition at this camp. And because it's a competition, they all want to win. Well, Willa *needs* them to. Because she needs the prize. Today's dangling carrot is not the cleanest cabin title, or earning a great camp report to take back to their school. This winner, Gus told them, receives an advantage of their choice—within reason—in the future leader game. He hasn't said what is within reason, exactly, but they need whatever they can get.

With the gift of Holly's experience, they were able to hit the trail first while other groups were still noisily comprehending compasses and maps. Only Drew and his group were ready at the same time. As the two groups took off along the tracks at a sprint, she met Drew's eye. He just sneered at Willa and ran faster, his team veering down a different path.

That was over an hour ago. They haven't seen Drew's team since. They've passed others every now and then, charging in the opposite direction or gathered in harried, bickering groups around a map in the middle of a trail. The rest of the time there has been just the seven of them, storming over hills, their only company the birds and an occasional living thing shuffling through the undergrowth to avoid them.

As they charge up a final stretch of hill, the bottom of Willa's feet feel bruised. They are no longer running, though. They started the game at a sprint, desperate to get the advantage, but couldn't sustain it.

The third marker is a purple plastic triangle nailed to a white post, just like the others have been, with numbers stamped on it. The girls high-five while Eva marks the number down in her notebook. Willa digs in her bag for the trail mix, and they wash it down with gulping slugs of water.

Willa pulls her T-shirt from her stomach and flaps it, looking around at the girls, transformed from their usual photo-readiness into these sweaty, determined creatures. This is when they show that other, ruthless part of themselves. This is when Willa feels closest to them. When they're competing. When there is a thing she can and wants to have in common with them.

As soon as her lungs give her permission to speak, she turns to Holly. "Where's the next one?"

Holly splits her neat auburn ponytail and yanks it tighter. And without even looking at the map, she recites, "Four hundred metres south-southwest until we meet trail six, then down a few hundred more towards the creek."

"Did someone say downhill?" Ling grins. "Woo!"

Willa nods at them. "Okay, ready?"

Eva moans quietly, and Amira bends over and pulls a face, but she nods. Willa turns on her heels, ignores her aching legs, and leads them along the trail.

~ ~ ~

They are still tracing the crest of the hill when pounding footsteps round the corner. It's Drew's group, led by a tall boy with a buzz cut. They, too, have slowed to a walk. But when he sees them coming, he begins to jog.

"Three down, three to go," the buzz cut hoots, flipping them the finger as he strides past.

"So what? Same here!" Ling yells as the rest of the group charge past, grinning and catcalling. "Dickheads," she mutters, pushing her thick fringe from her face. She goes to shout something at their disappearing forms.

Willa grabs her arm. "Don't."

Ling frowns but obeys.

"Don't tell them how far we've come," Willa tells her. "Now they know we're even."

Ling slaps her own forehead. "God, sorry. That was dumb."

"It's okay," Willa tells her. It isn't, but it's done. And Willa can't exactly tell anyone off for not doing the right thing. Not when she was the one who led them to this impasse in the game.

Twenty minutes later, they're jogging downhill, eyes on the prize of the fourth marker. Willa's step slows when she sees someone moving in the distance. She plucks the map from Holly's hand and stares at it as she walks. No other team should be crossing their paths at this point.

"Hey, stop," she hisses, and ducks behind a rock. Even though she doesn't know why yet, her instincts tell her to hide. The girls obediently gather behind her. "Stay here for a sec."

She yanks on her grey jumper to hide the stark white of her T-shirt and creeps out to the cover of a tree. Somewhere in the gully, shadowy figures dash from tree to tree, taking cover every now and then. She leans out to get a better look. Squinting, she recognises them immediately, the buzz cut and a skinny ginger from Drew's team.

Every now and then, one of them turns, looking up the hill, as if they're expecting to see something coming.

"Holly, come here. But stay low."

Holly shuffles in behind her. Willa points through the shrubbery and passes her the map. "Where are they going?"

"Nowhere they *should* be going. That only leads up to our next marker and then to the east perimeter. The only team that should be anywhere near here would be the green team."

"Hey, Eva!" Willa hisses. "Who's on the green team?"

Eva checks the cross list she started to make, unasked, at the start of the game as the teams were given their trails. This girl is all kinds of Virgo, and Willa has never been more grateful. "Those weird ones from the old cabins. The ones who always look depressed."

Willa nods. They saw them way back, sitting on a rock, staring at their map, already looking dejected. She stares at the two boys as they move through the gully and lets out a slow breath. Because she knows exactly what they're doing.

She turns to the girls. "We keep low and quiet, okay? Stay behind me."

They nod and set off just below the crest. When they're close to where their marker should be, Willa leaves them behind a rock and creeps slowly down the hill, moving from one tree trunk to another. She brushes past a bush, and a bird flies up into the trees, squawking loudly.

Her heart skips a beat. She is suddenly arrested by the feeling that she is in some tense, dangerous action film scenario. Feeling silly, she shakes it off and dashes to the cover of a tree so she can look for them.

And there they are.

Below her, the ginger boy is kicking something while the blonde watches with his arms folded. Ginger brings his foot down hard. The sound of splintering wood tears at the air, and she sees a flash of purple as the marker hits the ground. Buzz Cut immediately moves in and kicks dirt and leaves over it. Willa bristles.

When they're done, the boys take off at a sprint up the hill, and she marches back to get the girls, rigid with rage.

CHAPTER 49

Willa swipes the leaves and dirt from the marker, and stands it up against a tree. Eva automatically writes down the number.

Holly's eyes widen. "Those guys did that?"

"Seriously?" Ling shakes her head. "That is low."

There's outrage all round. Not Willa, though. She's already done with that. She's trying to find a plan.

"But why do they want to sabotage us?" Eva shakes her head. "Why not just try and win?"

"I guess they got worried because they know we're even now."

Willa avoids her eye, but Ling lets out a little moan anyway. "I am so sorry, you guys. I really am."

"Don't worry, hon." Amira throws an arm around her shoulder. "We've got this." She looks at Willa. "Haven't we?"

They all turn to Willa.

Willa thinks fast. Well, mostly she's testing her moral compass against her desire to win, because she already knows in her gut what they need to do. She shakes away any slivers of guilt. Because it's not like Drew's team doesn't deserve it, after throwing her team under a bus to get revenge on Finn's friends. After getting the whole camp punished for Drew's thieving. After this petty little act of cheating.

She puts her hands on her hips and looks around at them. "Who's the strongest runner?"

Maria holds up a hand. "Regional long distance last year."

"Then you're with me." Willa turns to Holly. "You and the others finish the course, okay? As fast as you can."

"Okay," she says slowly, looking quizzically at Willa.

"What are you guys going to do?" Eva asks before Holly can.

"Exactly what he did to us."

Amira cackles and then makes a show of *tsk-tsking*. "Naughty Willa."

Willa shrugs. "I don't like cheating, but he did it first. So while you guys finish the course, Maria and I will go straight for his last marker. If we go across country, we should get there ahead of him, right Holly?"

Holly consults the map and nods. "For sure. But we only have one map and one compass, and the hills can throw you off direction pretty easily. How will we all know where to go?"

Willa frowns, stopped in flight.

"Damn," Ling hisses, driving her runners into the ground. The mood shifts from high to low in seconds.

That's when Willa decides she'll do it anyway, but alone. She'll just memorise the map as well as she can. That way, if she gets lost or caught, they can blame it on her. She's just about to say so when Amira dances on the spot.

"Hang on, I've got you covered." She digs around in the front pocket of her knapsack and pulls out a phone. The girls hoot. Then she glances at the screen and frowns. "It's only got a little bit of charge left, though."

Eva shakes her head. "Mir, I am *so* happy you can't live a day without talking to that boyfriend right now."

Amira tosses her a mock dirty look and turns to Willa. She has a sweat streak of mascara smeared under her eye. "We'll take a snap of the map and then you can take this with you."

"Thanks." Willa knows they're moving deeper into trouble territory, adding contraband electronics to their list of broken rules. But she doesn't care. She's doing this for them.

Holly holds out the map for Amira to take a picture. "I'm still worried about the hills throwing you off."

Amira clicks her fingers and points at the phone, grinning. "Sorted. I'm pretty sure it's got a compass app. I used it once in a club to find a guy from Tinder." She rolls her eyes. "He thought he was being cute."

They all laugh as Willa takes the phone and tucks it into the pocket of her cut-offs. Thanks goodness for Gandry girls and their high-end gadgets.

Once Holly has mapped out their route, following the creek to the final marker and back over another hill to meet the girls, Willa nods at Maria. She looks so super fit that Willa hopes she can keep up with her. Then she pushes the doubt back.

She opens her bag and passes the girls the extra bottle of water. "If you see other teams, hide so they don't notice you're missing anyone, okay? Especially if you see Drew's team. Our trails shouldn't cross again, but he might be doing the same thing to other groups. We'll see you at the last marker as soon as we can."

"Stuff 'em up good," Eva says in her weary, worldly voice.

Willa has to smile as they take off into the bush, the girls calling out hissed encouragements at their backs.

~ ~ ~

The scrub seems to sprint past in a kaleidoscope of greens as Willa pounds along at Maria's heels. At first, she flew high on the idea of revenge and the win, but now her legs are nothing but tender strips of muscle pain, and there is that special burn on her heels that tells her that blisters are forming. Maria is a machine, tramping steadily over the rough terrain like it's a paved road, and Willa has to fight to stay on pace with her.

It's taken them longer than she thought it would. Mostly because they've had to keep crisscrossing the creek, finding the bank with the thinnest scrub. And still Willa's arms are scratched and grazed. Sometimes they've even had to use the creek itself, stepping from stone to stone like she did with Finn did the other day. Willa's stomach floats loose for a moment as she remembers Finn's lips on hers as they sat on their rock. But she pushes it away and keeps moving, intent on the prize, a small blue piece of plastic hidden somewhere in this scrub.

CHAPTER 50

Willa spots the marker standing at attention between two trees. They hide behind a bush, keeping a silent, breathless watch for incomings. All is quiet except for the screech and call of arguing birds. Then, just as they are about to inch closer, there's a shout somewhere at the top of the hill. Willa's heartbeat only slows when she realises the sound is moving away from them, not closer.

As she contemplates the marker, Willa's stuck, because she doesn't want to do what they did and destroy property. Instead, she drags a broken branch to the post, and together they arrange it so it looks like it has simply fallen onto the marker. They'll find it eventually, but it should slow them down for a while.

She is desperately kicking leaf litter over the drag marks when she hears voices again. They're coming down the hill this time.

"Quick," she hisses and bolts up the other side of the gully, putting distance between them and the sound. They duck between bushes and hide.

They've taken too long. They need to get back to the girls. She whips out the phone, and her heart stops beating for a moment when she sees the battery sign flashing. She opens the map, tries to ingrain the terrain into her mind, and then flicks over to the compass. Southwest to the hilltop and trail four, and then four hundred metres south. She recites it like a mantra in her head and then turns off the phone, hoping it will save that last bit of juice. The voices are arguing, but she can't hear what they are saying.

Willa grabs Maria's sleeve, and they set off, keeping low. As soon as she thinks they're far enough away, she stands up, taking one last look behind her. As she peers through the trees, she can't see if they've found it. What she does see is Drew, about thirty metres up the opposite hill, standing among some ferns and looking right back at her. Willa's heart lurches to her throat, but she just stares at him, keeping her face perfectly still. Then she turns and strides away without looking back.

~ ~ ~

They dash up the side of the valley so fast Willa feels like her lungs are going to the shred themselves into pieces. Even Maria's panting loudly by the time they reach the top.

"We can't stop," Willa gasps. "They're too close."

Maria nods, stoic, and keeps running along the dirt trail.

Willa pulls out the phone as she runs and tries to turn it on. The screen stays resolutely blank. She clenches her jaw, thrusts the phone into her pocket, and focuses on re-creating the map in her mind. She veers off down the other side of the hill in the direction she prays they are supposed to be going.

On the path downhill, Willa has that out-of-control feeling like on a bike, when you stop pedalling and let the wheels and the wind take you along. It's like her feet can't keep up with the gravitational thrust of her body, and she's scared she's going to fall or snap an ankle on a rock. But she doesn't stop. She cannot stop.

She's flying between trees when she hears the hissed call. "Willa!"

She brakes so hard it hurts and then looks to her left, scanning the green. A hand waves from behind a thick belt of ferns. The girls spring up, grinning.

Holly's eyes are wide. "Did you do it?"

Willa nods.

Eva shrieks and jumps in the air. Willa's never seen her so excited about anything.

"Yes!" Amira lifts her hands to high-five her, and it takes everything Willa has left to raise her arm in return.

"Drew saw me," she pants, clutching her roiling stomach.

Maria's eyes widen. "Really?"

"Yep. You were already running, but he saw me."

"Who cares?" Amira says. "He did the same to us. He can't exactly go crying to the teachers now."

"Let's hope not." Eva looks out into the bushes. "It also means they might have figured out what you're doing and found the marker."

Willa nods. "True. We better move."

Holly waves the map. "The good news is our last stretch is much shorter than theirs."

Instead of shouting a hallelujah at the heavens like she wants to, Willa summons every last morsel of energy she has left. "Let's do this."

They are off again, storming through the bush in a tight cluster. And in this moment, they're her kindred.

CHAPTER 51

As they plunge through the last few hundred metres, Willa starts to fill with doubt. What if Drew has somehow beaten them? Her rational brain knows it's probably not possible, but still. Then there's the other fear: what if someone else has already won? What if while they were totally focused on beating Drew, someone else powered through? Her stomach tightens.

Her fears are assuaged when they sprint into the clearing where they will all camp tonight, before heading back tomorrow. It's empty except for a cluster of teachers by the fire circle and some bored-looking kids who faked injuries. The Gandry girls huddle together, catching their breath.

Willa can't stop shifting from side to side, opening and closing her hands through the wait. Will they get away with it? It will be her responsibility if Drew's team rats them out. And she'll own it. It was her idea and her doing, so she won't let the girls go down for it. But the pride that runs thick through her also means she won't tell on Drew either. Even if that means she comes out of this looking like the low creature *he* is while he wins.

Preparing herself for the worst, she runs through the story she'll tell in her head, how, stupid and overly hungry for a win, she slipped away from the group to sabotage Drew's team without telling them. She'll tell the girls to say she made some other excuse for leaving them. She's imagining the shock on Mr Wiseman's face as she, group leader, is cast as the villain when voices drift out of the scrub.

Willa's heart slows and speeds up again. And once again, she finds herself locking gazes with Drew as he sprints into the clearing. It's their destiny for today, apparently. His eyes narrow as Willa fights to stop hers from widening. He glares but says nothing.

It's the ginger boy who reacts loudest. He curses and kicks a stick out of his path. It skitters toward the creek.

"Language!" A teacher jabs a warning finger at him

Ginger glares at Drew, but Drew gives him the slightest shake of his head.

Willa fights a smile. She is now ninety-nine per cent certain they're going to be okay.

~ ~ ~

One by one, other groups rush into the campsite.

"Who won?" a kid asks as more teams appear in the clearing.

"Gandry," someone says.

Of *course*," she hears one kid mutter.

Willa's split between pride and resentment. If only he knew what it took. Every part of her body aches, and she can feel the burn of her heel, bloodied and glued to her sock.

Eva fidgets beside Willa, eyes glued to Drew. "Do you think he'll tell?"

"I think if he was going to, he would have already."

"Good."

"He really can't afford to look bad again."

Amira swipes her fingers under her eyes, cleaning her smeared make-up. "Yeah, Ice Cream-gate kinda ruined his rep. He doesn't need this kind of social suicide now."

"He'll get revenge sometime," Willa says, folding her arms. "Somehow."

"Probably."

Eva rakes her fingers through her ponytail, smoothing it back to its usual pristine form. "Is it terrible that I don't feel even the slightest bit guilty about cheating?"

"Nope." Amira leans her arm on Eva's shoulder. "Think about it. We were so far ahead it was probably always down to us or Drew's group. It's not like we cheated anyone else. *And* we spared everyone from having to put up with the ego parade after Drew won."

Eva snickers. "True."

"What about that blonde girl's group? Finn? They could have caught up," Ling says. "That hot boy runs every morning, and they're all really smart. They'd figure out the compass bit really fast."

There's an instant hum in Willa's ears at the sound of Finn's name.

Maria peers around the clearing, hand on hip. "They can't be that good, because they're not even back yet. I think they might be the only ones *not* back."

Willa looks around at the kids clustered around in packs. It's true. And one minute she was quietly full of her win, and now she is full of Finn. Where is she? Soon the teachers start asking the same question. It's ten minutes before the game is supposed to officially end. It takes all her willpower not to keep turning and checking that they are not coming down the path.

They're all sent to set up their tents and gather firewood while the teachers discuss what to do if Finn's group doesn't make it in time. Before they've decided, someone yells out, "They're back!" in a faux horror movie voice.

Willa nearly drops the tent pole as she spins around. There's Finn, looking fed up and tired as she trudges the last stretch of trail, the blue-haired girl limping besides her.

~ ~ ~

Willa stays close to her team during dinner but watches Finn whenever she thinks she can get away with it. She's sitting on the other side of the fire, next to the blue-haired girl whose ankle is now steeped in a bucket of ice-cold creek water. Finn brings her food and drinks, helping her even though she looks exhausted. There's a warmth in Willa at witnessing Finn's kindness. Maybe it's nostalgia, because she knows what it is like to be in its beam.

That was what made her first notice Finn. Her combination of grit and sweet has a charm most people wouldn't get away with. Tonight, though, Willa can see something grating at Finn's calm. Like maybe nothing went to plan for her today.

They all gorge on the hot, salty stew that's dished out in heaping bowlfuls. Usually the Gandry girls are all cosmopolitan, grazing restraint, but even dainty Eva is shovelling food down by the spoonful.

Maria runs her finger over the edge of the bowl and licks it. "So what will we ask for? For the prize?"

They all look at Willa.

"Whatever we can get toward making industry."

Amira tips her head toward Drew and his group. "So we won't need him?"

"Exactly. But he'll still be beholden to us for food."

Amira's eyes grow wider. "That's awesome. You're awesome."

Eva frowns, because she's always the one to think of details first. "But who will we trade with instead? We need to keep the economy steady."

"I have some ideas," Willa tells her.

"Cool," she says simply and goes back to her food.

Satisfaction ripples through Willa. It's such a strange thing to be so utterly trusted. These girls will never know how close Willa came to dropping the ball. Because she has found her way again.

"I can't believe we just did that. I mean…" Ling looks around the group with a sly smile. "We're us, so I can. But still, it's cool."

They all trade self-satisfied looks. And Willa's heart leaps a little. Because she's made a Gandry girl admit her love of the win out loud. This has to be a first.

CHAPTER 52

Willa loves that space between bedtime and sleep. Because that's when she's free to be the dreamer she secretly is. Amira's latest obsession is Chinese horoscopes. The other day she informed Willa that she's double fire, born in both the year and the sign of the flame. Amira wasn't surprised.

Willa is. Sometimes she feels like she's air, pretending to be fire. But what would she know?

All she knows is that tonight she's the blissful owner of her own tent. She's shared a room all her life. Been subject to every shift and snore and snuffle her sister has made in her dreamtime since they were little. Willa's comforted nightmares, begged her sister to go to sleep, and even played tooth fairy to save Nan a trip upstairs. Tonight is a rare gift of solitude.

She stretches out, fully dressed, her body flooded with weariness. All she's managed is to wash her face in the icy creek water and tend to her blisters. Around her, kids giggle and rustle and call loudly from tent to tent, but still, she's drifting inches from sleep when she hears the sound of the tent zipper. Her head lurches from the pillow.

"Hey, it's just me." Finn is no more than a shadowy outline in the light drifting through the gap.

Willa just blinks, her heart thumping still.

"I asked The Hulk if I can sleep in here. Amy's snoring."

"Oh." Because that's all Willa can think of to say. She pulls herself up on her elbows and dazedly watches Finn crawl in, sleeping bag under her arm. As she gets closer, Willa can see her hair is sticking out of her hoodie at gravity-defying angles.

She suddenly stops in her tracks. "You don't mind, do you?"

"What do *you* think?" Solitude be damned.

Finn grins as she wriggles into her bag and settles on her side next to her.

"Is Amy *really* snoring?" Willa asks.

"I promise. Like an actual wild creature. The Hulk listened for half a second from outside the tent and let me flee. It must be the painkillers."

"What happened to her?"

"Twisted it. Right after Brian dropped our map in the creek, which was after Hana and Craig insisted we take a thousand rest breaks." Finn rolls her eyes. "My team is high in brain power, but some of us are not exactly God's gift to physical fitness. Today sucked. Royally."

"I'm sorry."

Finn gives her a shrewd look. "It didn't suck for you, though."

"No." Parts of it did, though. Willa wishes she could tell her everything that happened, but she can't.

They lie there, blinking at each other in the faint light. Outside, the night rings with laughter and play fights and punchlines, but inside, there's only the hushed sound of their slow breaths. Willa concentrates on absorbing Finn right up close, on making her beautifully familiar. That cute nose and that slightly pouted mouth that turns so easily to a smile. Her sweet smatter of freckles.

"It's very annoying," Finn suddenly whispers.

"What?"

"I want to hate you for winning, but you're also the only person I want to be around."

Willa nods. This is the very problem of them.

Finn's smile turns to a frown.

"What's wrong?"

She kicks Willa through their sleeping bags. "You *never* kiss me first. You did that one time, but you never did again."

"I think I'm still getting used to the idea that you could want me to." Nerves fizz through Willa's insides. She doesn't know how to tell Finn that she's still getting used to saying these things out loud. That this is all so terrifyingly new.

Finn kicks her again. "I want you to." And when Willa retreats, kiss bestowed, Finn's eyes are shining. "Better."

162

Willa pushes Finn's hood back, running her fingers through her hair. Finn stares at her, lips parted, watchful. Then they're kissing again, and Finn's arm is snaking around Willa's waist, pulling her close. Willa does as it bids, ignoring her aching limbs. Couldn't do anything else. As their sleeping bags are pushed back, Willa's hand slinks under the bottom of Finn's hoodie, fingers gliding the soft stretch of her lower back. Finn inhales sharply and pushes in closer until there's no air between them. And as their kiss turns fierce, Willa fingers trace Finn's spine up to her neck. There's a small, throaty sound as Finn curls under her touch. Willa can barely fathom how easy it is to create this need in each other.

They become a chaos of sensation. And in the mess of hunting out each others' terrains, jumpers and T-shirts are tossed aside. Before Willa knows it, they're pushed skin to skin, fingers dancing around the clasps of bras, daring but not quite daring. But then something changes, and instead of accelerating beyond this blissful kiss plateau, they seem to slow again. And then they're sliding backwards, hands drifting to the safer topographies of backs and hair. Kisses stall and stop.

Then they're staring at each other in the faint light washing through the canvas. Finn's got her teeth clamped on her bottom lip, and there's that crease by her eye that Willa wants to kiss away, because she's already learned it means Finn's hurt or worried or something that doesn't make her feel good.

"I'm sorry," Finn whispers.

Willa's stomach flips as she tries desperately to read her expression, to understand this sudden ceasefire. "What for?"

"I mean, I just…I don't want to go so fast."

"Hey, don't be sorry," Willa whispers hurriedly. She has no idea how they got here so quickly. "We don't have to do anything." Willa smooths her finger across the furrow by her eyes. "Have you done it before?"

"Once. With a guy. You?"

"Just once." She likes knowing Finn's no more experienced than her, that they're both rookies at this. She finally asks the question she's been too shy to ask. "Have you only liked guys?"

"No. I like *people.*"

"So do I." Willa grins. "They just happen to be girls."

Finn chuckles, but her expression turns contemplative. She touches a finger to Willa's bottom lip. "I like *you*."

It takes Willa a moment to find air.

"And it's not because I haven't slept with a girl before that I don't want to yet," Finn says in a rush. "I mean, I want to. You're…" She shakes her head. "Just not now—not yet."

And before Willa can tell Finn that she doesn't have to explain anything, Finn tells her *that* story, the one with the girl who liked the boy who seemed to like her just as much. And then, smitten, she slept with him. And before she knew it, he started to treat her like crap. Made her feel less. That one. Everyone knows it. Even Willa knows it. She's got one of those stories about a girl.

Finn tells her she's nervous of repeating history, of rushing in that fast and that far again. Willa already knows there's no way she'd ever do something like that to Finn. No way she'd want to. But Willa also knows it doesn't matter if *she* knows that. What matters is that Finn doesn't. And telling her won't help Finn to know. Words are useless like that, sometimes.

And Finn doesn't know that Willa already feels like a spoiled princess with what she has. She thinks of the soft drag of Finn's finger along her arm the other day. How just that small touch felt so big because, finally, here is someone who wants to touch her like that and who Willa wants to have touch her like that. This coincidence of attraction seems miraculous enough to her. She could live on that morsel of touch for days, weeks, months. Even now she possesses the exquisite knowledge of being pressed to Finn's almost-bare torso, or the sound of her breath catching in her throat as Willa kisses it. Willa is still just as content to lie here and just *be* next to her. To prove it, she sits up and pulls on her T-shirt. Then she passes Finn's to her.

Finn smiles, in a way that tells Willa she's done everything exactly right for once. And she's radiant with this knowledge. She's made so many stupid mistakes with Finn by being her raw, blunt self. Now that she's found this place with her, she wants so badly to stay.

Finn curls into her side. Willa automatically slides an arm around her shoulders and presses her nose to her hair. Already they fit together like they've lain this way every single night of their lives. Outside, the campsite is nearly silent. Finn pushes her lips against Willa's.

"Goodnight," she whispers.

Willa smiles into the darkness. "Oh, so still with the kissing, then?"

"All the kissing, Will."

She thrills at the way Finn says "Will". Like it's inevitable that she'd shorten her name. And Willa knows she could hear her call her that over and over and never once tire of it.

~ ~ ~

When she surfaces in the morning to Finn's arm slung over her side and the slow beat of her sleeping breath on her neck, Willa squeezes her eyes shut again, riding a surge of bliss. Is there a better way to wake up? If there is, she's never known it.

They drift through the early morning noise in a sleepy snuggle. Willa's starting to hear teachers' voices cajoling people out of tents when she's shoved into waking by the sound of her name and the tent zipper lifting. Finn automatically rolls away, pulling her pillow with her.

Eva's hair is already pulled back into a neat braid. She smiles and then, seeing Finn, raises an eyebrow. "Oh, hi."

Willa's face turns hot. "Her friend was snoring last night."

"Incredibly loudly," Finn mutters from under her sleeping bag.

"Fun." Eva says dryly. "Amira asked me to get her phone."

"Oh, right. Here." Willa digs it from her bag. "It's dead. I hope she has a charger back at camp."

"Whatever. It was worth it." Eva gives Willa a conspiratorial look.

The minute she pulls the zipper down, Finn rolls back to face her. She shuffles right in, pressing her cheek to Willa's collarbone. "You're all over this Camp Nowhere contraband now, aren't you? I thought you were a good girl," she teases sleepily. "What were you doing with a phone this time?"

"Never mind."

CHAPTER 53

"Hey Amira, I'm going to need you to do something."

Amira looks up, wide-eyed, her make-up back to casual perfection now that they're within easy reach of mirrors again. "Me?"

"Yes, you."

Willa can see Eva glance up in her periphery, curious. Probably wondering what Amira can do that she couldn't. Eva thrives on being the capable and dependable one. That's her thing. But Willa needs Amira's particular brand of inveigling charm for this one.

"Sure. What is it?"

"I need you to find out which teams Finn is making deals with."

Amira raises a perfectly sculpted eyebrow. "Me? Shouldn't you? I mean, you actually talk to her sometimes. I don't even know her."

Willa prays the small flush of heat that washes through her isn't enough to stain her skin. "You won't be talking to Finn."

"Oh." Amira frowns.

Eva taps her pen against her book. "She wants you to play spy, not go ask outright."

"Oh, *right*." Amira slaps her forehead. "Sorry."

"And she's sending you because the boys love you, and she's hoping they'll spill if it's you asking questions."

Willa turns to Eva. "Thank you for translating."

"Guys? Did…Willa…just…crack…a joke?" Ling stares, open-mouthed at Willa. "Watch it, or they'll take your job away when we get back to school. Gandry's academic leader cannot be having a sense of humour."

"I consider myself warned." Willa turns to Amira. "Just chat to a few people. See what you can find out."

"Guys, she means," Holly adds.

"Don't worry, I'm down. I know my powers." Amira flicks her hair over her shoulder. "And I love them."

"Thanks." Willa could never imagine possessing that kind of confidence. She hunches over her book, feeling her muscles flinch from yesterday's epic run. She's still tired. Guilty too. It's such a wrenching leap, going from waking this morning with Finn curled around her to preparing to spy on her. But Willa has no choice. And Finn would probably do the same if she had to. Maybe she already has.

"Well, good afternoon, ladies."

Willa looks up and immediately returns her eyes to the page, smothering a sigh. *Really? Now?* She doesn't have time for this.

"Oh look, everyone. It's Drew." Amira says it in the flattest voice she can muster.

He smiles around at them all, his hands at rest on the edge of the table like he's running a meeting. "What are we up to over here? Planning some more ways to cheat?"

"Oh, I think that's more your thing." Holly smiles beatifically at him. "We were just learning from the best."

"Whatever you say. So, what advantage did you choose? A super mall for your capital? Some finishing schools for your uneducated people?"

"Oh, wow." Eva looks around at them, eyes wide. "Look how cleverly he's trying to pick on our girly, private-school status? Because we couldn't possibly be interested in anything but clothes and table manners. Dude, our school has ranked higher than yours academically for the past sixteen years. In fact, the only thing you've done consistently better than us in is cricket. Because we don't play it. Gus told us we don't have to tell anyone what our advantage is until tomorrow." She flaps a hand at him. "Now, shoo."

He turns to Willa, as if Eva didn't even speak. "There are going to be a few changes you'll need to know about. We might need to chat."

"And we will," Willa replies calmly. The best way to react to him, she's decided, is by *not* reacting to him. "Tomorrow. In our scheduled meeting time." She looks back at her work.

Everyone ignores him. Willa almost feels sorry for him. *Almost.* Why does he keep trying so hard to make everyone's life hell? It only makes people hate him more.

"Well." She can feel him losing his grip on the moment as he stands there. "I'll, uh, be seeing you tomorrow, then."

"See you." She doesn't even look up. But there's the smallest clench in her gut. What's he planning now? She really needs to get her ducks in a row.

"Amira," she says after he's gone, "you need to do this today, okay? I need to know before that meeting."

"Oh, don't you worry, babe. I'll get it done."

CHAPTER 54

Amira leans forward, spreading her fingers on the table. "Okay, so Stefan told me that it's that guy Leon and his group." She turns to Eva. "You know, I think you should tap that."

Eva's brows furrow. "What, Leon?"

"Yup."

"Me? Why?"

"He's got that geek charm thing going on. And he's really chill. I feel like you'd be a match." She turns. "Or maybe you, Ling-o."

Ling doesn't even lift her head from the page. "I'm sorted, thanks."

"Then you, Eva. He's single. I checked."

"Not in my name, I hope."

"Uh, somehow I don't think Willa's going to want us hooking up with the enemy," Maria says.

Willa very deliberately keeps her eyes fixed on her page.

"But imagine if they fell for each other?" Amira says. "And it would be this whole forbidden love thing, like *West Side Story*. I saw it on stage in London. Totally retro amazing."

"Oh, wow." Ling shakes her head. "You're going to liken Eva hooking up with Leon to a fifties urban race war?"

Eva throws her hands up in the air. "Guys, it doesn't matter, because I'm not hooking up with anyone at this stupid camp. What would we do? See one of Gus's slide shows together? Go for a dinner date in the picnic area?"

Willa sighs. "Guys. Amira, what did you find out?"

"Sorry. Anyway, Leon's made some deal with Finn over water."

Willa nods. She figured that was how Finn was strengthening her assets.

"And then she's got something similar going on with that mixed group from the old huts, but I didn't get details."

"Thanks."

"No sweat. I'll spy any time. Squeezing that info was way more fun than writing this economics paper."

"How'd you do it, anyway?" Maria asks.

"How did I do it?" Amira looks affronted. "Why Maria, I shamefully and insincerely flirted with Stefan until he told me stuff. Even if it makes me sick to my stomach because he goes out with that Emma girl from his group and guys are shits and predictable and it always works. Even though now he thinks I'm some bimbo, when I got a ninety-eight in Psych last term. Which is why I know how to extract info from his daft brain."

Willa smiles with the others, but really she's thinking, *wow*. That's three more marks than she got in Psych. She shakes off the add-water-and-stir competitiveness and pores over the map. "If Finn's got the mixed group and Leon's group, who's left?" she asks Eva.

"There's the group that have the wood huts."

"And the green group from yesterday, right?"

Eva nods. "The ones who never smile."

"Those guys are weird." Holly taps her pen on her front tooth. "I call them Glumtown."

"I need to set up meetings with them," Willa says. "They both trade with Drew, right?"

"Yup." Eva flips through her meticulous notes. "They both buy food from him. And the wood huts group sell timber back to him."

The bell rings, and the girls start talking evening plans. As if there's that many options. Willa knows they'll mostly end up lying around on the porch, chatting and keeping one eye on everyone else. The same thing they do every night. And maybe if Willa's lucky, she'll with get a moment alone with Finn.

The thought makes her tingle. It dies quickly, though, when she contemplates the page of notes in front of her.

"What are you going to do tonight?" Eva asks as she shuts her notebook.

Willa blinks. People don't usually ask her that question. "Probably come back here and try to figure out what those guys have and what they need."

"I'll help."

"It's okay. You don't need to give up your free time."

"And you don't always have to do everything, you know."

Willa blinks at her.

"You seem like you're used to doing everything on your own. And I'm just saying you don't have to. I'm your deputy, and I'll help you." She rolls her eyes. "Besides, I'm now avoiding Amira 'til she gets this stupid Leon idea out of her brain."

Willa smiles awkwardly at her. "Okay. Well, I'll be here after dinner."

"So will I, then. We'll find a carrot to dangle in front of… What did Ling call the green group?"

"Glumtown."

Eva chuckles. "I have to admit, it's fitting. See you."

Willa packs up her books and stacks them in her bag, still shaken by Eva's gentle jab. She's not used to Gandry girls *seeing* her. Not beyond the surface "you play your role, I'll play mine" social order stuff. But there's been a definitely a change in the dynamic since the race yesterday.

Eva's observation chafes a little too. She never thought she was doing something wrong by trying to do things on her own. That's just the way she knows how to get things done. In the past couple of years, as Nan's body has begun to let her down, Willa's only known the lonely scramble of days, of frantically trying to meet responsibilities. Of figuring out how to balance her homework and job with remembering which nights the recycling goes out. Or learning to distract a grumpy kid who doesn't want to be at the supermarket into behaving. Or learning the dance of helping Nan in every way she needs while letting her keep her sense of autonomy.

To get all that done, Willa *has* to stay in control. Because otherwise, the balls will fall, and then where will they all be?

CHAPTER 55

Willa holds her shoulders perfectly straight as she stalks away from Drew's table. She will not betray even an ounce of the anger that is currently coursing through her body. No way. Not that the news she just received is surprising. Not one bit. Still, it's hard not to feel the rage when he meets her expectations.

Eva's silent too. She doesn't say a word until they drop down into their chairs. "He's not even pretending there's an economic precedent to this," she mutters. "He's just doing it to get revenge."

"Of course he is." Willa replies, more calmly than she feels. She has to be the voice of reason right now. "And we knew it would happen."

Amira frowns. "What did Ratboy do now?"

"Upped food prices," Eva mutters.

Willa glares at her books. He upped food prices even though Willa did as he asked and didn't take Finn's group in. "By a lot."

"Are we going to be okay?" Eva looks worried for the first time.

Willa nods, even though she's not entirely sure. "We just need to start trading elsewhere. We're talking to the other two groups later, remember."

"But can he just make things worse if we do that?"

"Probably. But what else can we do?"

No one answers.

CHAPTER 56

Damir from the wood huts is an easy sell. He's got this car dealer "happy doing business with you" manner but no apparent clue about how to do business. From what Willa has seen so far, his group has just been coasting along on what they've got. Which is all well and good for survival but isn't much good for finding things to say for the written component of the game.

This is probably why he's quick to snap up this new partnership like she offered him a piece of gum. Glumtown is harder to crack, though. Mark, their leader, a pasty guy with acne, just stares blankly as Willa talks him through her idea.

Willa stares at the constellation of whiteheads on his neck and says, "See, with the three territories aligned, we'd be able to trade as a collective."

"But we get our food from Drew." He folds his arms. "So do you."

"And you still can. We're not stopping you from doing anything you're already doing. We'd just be forming a co-operative for the sale of our goods to him to ensure better and fairer prices. And in doing so, you'd get the protection of our numbers."

"But what do we need protecting from? We just do our own thing."

Willa thinks quick. "Well, would you be okay if there's another drought? What if it affects your plantations? Or fires? What if you have nothing to sell for the food?" she asks, hoping her scaremongering will penetrate his thick indifference. "We do. More than you, anyway."

He doesn't respond, but she can see the seed's been planted. He looks at his deputy, a small skinny girl called Avi.

What do you think?" Mark asks Avi.

She doesn't answer straight away.

"Besides," Willa reminds them, "the teachers like it when we take some risks."

Avi gestures to Mark, and they go stand a few feet away and talk quietly.

Avi does most of the talking as they stand there, leaned in, serious. Avi's Indian too, but real Indian. Both parents and a culture. Willa just shrugged on the day of the getting-to-know-you game, when Avi asked how she ended up with a name like Willa. Just like she has so many times when she is picked out by other Indian kids and shows herself clueless. But how can she explain that she has no idea why her mother named her Willa? How can she explain she knows nothing about the part of her history that lays claim to her skin colour?

Her Indian-ness is something that is stamped on her, not something she holds inside. Lost along with her mother, irretrievable and unknowable. When she was a kid, it used to embarrass her when people asked her about it and she couldn't say. Like she was failing at something. Later, it was annoying. And now, it's still strange to think that some of her blood resides in a place she cannot know.

Finally, they come back to Willa. "Alright," Mark says. "It can't hurt."

Willa gives him a tight smile and holds out a sheaf of papers. "Great. Here's what we're proposing."

CHAPTER 57

"That rat bastard," Eva hisses. She's got Drew's latest report clutched in her hand like it's a set of bad test results.

Willa looks up, dreading whatever Eva's got to say. She's feeling edgy enough after reading the report from Finn's group about their alliance and their mills and their markets. She's embarrassed by the pettiness of her jealousy, but it's all so freaking inspired. Part of her just wants to sit back and admire Finn's ingenuity, but the other part of her wants to cry. Because Finn's getting stronger every day while Willa is flailing *again*. All she ever seems to be doing is trying to keep her group's head above water. "What's Drew done now?" she asks warily.

Eva just shakes her head. "I can't believe it."

"What, Eva?" Willa asks, louder this time. But she just shakes her head again. Clicking her tongue, Willa leans forward and plucks it from her grasp. Eva's holding it so tightly, the page rips a little.

"Sorry, he's planning to use his military. To stop the alliance," Eva finally says as Willa skims the report. "First he's going to take over Damir and Glummer's territories and then us."

"That's ridiculous." Willa stares at the page, but nothing goes in.

"Well, it's not like he's never been ridiculous, is it?"

"True." Willa sighs.

Will he ever give up trying to torture them in excessively stupid ways? This guy redefines loose cannon. She looks around at the girls, suddenly transformed from mid-morning distracted to wide-eyed and serious. A sudden military threat *is* kind of a mood killer. Even Amira looks tense as she chews gum furiously and taps her pen on the table in time with it.

Holly puts her hand over the pen and turns back to Willa. "Can we fight this?"

Willa stares at the piece of paper in her hand. "Probably not on our own. His military is way more advanced than ours, and we haven't exactly been focused on ours because we've been too worried about food and trade."

"Yeah, but it's not like we thought anyone would try and randomly invade us, did we?" Eva mutters.

Before Willa can answer, the bell rings for the end-of-morning session.

"Meet after lunch?" Eva says.

Holly shakes her head. "We've got kitchen clean-up, remember?"

There's a collective groan.

Willa scrapes her books into a pile. "Tonight after dinner, then. I need some time to think, anyway."

They pack up their things, all of them mutter-plotting painful Drew deaths. Outside, the first thing she sees as she squints into the bright sunlight is Mark, arms folded, waiting for her. He's clearly read the briefs too.

'Thanks a lot," he mumbles before she can say a word.

"Hey, we—"

He holds up his hand to stop her. "You said we'd be *better* protected if we joined you. So how the hell did we end up facing an army?"

"Just idle threats," she assures him even though she has no idea how serious Drew is. "We'll figure this out."

"You better," he tells her. "You got us into this. You *have* to get us out of it."

"I will. I swear."

He stalks away, letting her promise drift into the air.

CHAPTER 58

As soon as she's done with kitchen duty, Willa hurries up the creek to their spot.

Finn's already hunched on the rock, poring over a page of messy handwriting, her sketchbook by her side. Willa drops onto the rock behind her and wraps her arms around her waist.

"Hello." She presses her cheek against the sun-warmed bliss that is the back of Finn's plaid shirt.

"Mm, hi," Finn murmurs happily.

And Willa is instantly transformed from kitchen weary to a feeling like being suspended in a slick of warm syrup. Drew's threats disappear. The long day of study vanishes. Her anger at Mark and Glumtown is gone. The hot, stinking kitchen is no longer. Now there's just the two of them on a rock in the sunshine and Finn being happy she's here. "What are you reading?"

"Letter from Dad. A really long story about a bike and a wallaby." She folds it up. "Really just an excuse to check in and see if I'm talking to him yet."

"And are you?"

"I don't know. Probably. I guess it's not totally fair to be angry at him."

Willa remembers how she used to get mad at her dad when he came to visit. First because she didn't know him, and it was forced and strange, and then because just when she'd gotten used to him, he'd leave again.

Finn tucks the letter into the front pocket of her knapsack and then leans back into her arms. They sit there, the creek rushing around them.

"Hey, can I ask you something?" Finn asks, pulling Willa's arms tighter around her.

"Mhm."

"Have you told anyone here about us?"

"No." Who would she tell? "Have you?"

Finn shakes her head. "I feel like it could be weird with my teammates and the whole game thing, if they knew."

Willa nods. "Me too."

Finn threads her fingers between Willa's and squeezes her hand. "So should we keep it on the down low?"

"Probably." Willa doesn't know how to articulate the fact that she would probably have done that anyway. That she's not in the habit of having people know her heart.

"As long as you know that I'm not hiding us for any other reason." Finn shuffles around to face her. Her eyes are shining. "I mean, why would I hide *you*?"

Willa can't imagine Finn wanting to hide anything. She's too brave and honest and too *her* to care about that kind of thing. She picks up Finn's hand and kisses it. "Tell me something."

"Like what?"

"I don't know. Something about you. When did you first start drawing?"

"I paint more than I draw, actually. But it's a bit hard to carry paint everywhere here. Besides, my art teacher wants me to practice pencil and ink sketching."

"What do you paint?"

"The world. But kind of…different. Colourful. My best friend, Dan, he says it's like a fantasy version of reality. I don't really know how to explain it."

"Will you show me one day?"

"Of course." She picks up Willa's hand and kisses it.

Willa doesn't have a creative bone in her body. If she did, she'd like to play music. Maybe something plaintive and dramatic like violin or cello. "Tell me something else," she demands, suddenly ravenous. "Tell me lots of things about you. "

"Um, okay. I like movies that make me sad. I've lived in the same house all my life. We have two dogs. I get annoyed when people are mean. Dan and I are trying to watch every single film that ever won the best film Oscar. Hmm, what else?" She chews on her lip and then laughs. "I think, right now, my mum will be extra fine if I'm dating a girl, because she's a vice principal at that school where they caught that huge group of guys selling up-skirt pics, and she's kind of hating on teenage boys right now. I love plain margherita pizza and Tim Tams—but not at the same time. I have a half-sister, Anna." She suddenly chuckles. "And the last piece of sisterly advice she gave me was that I should get myself a toy," she leans closer and grins slyly, "if you know what I mean." Then she laughs with delight as Willa's mouth falls open.

Willa flushes furiously at her own prudishness. But she wasn't expecting *that* bit of information to follow Tim Tams. "Really?"

"Yep. She was totally serious about it. She says every girl needs to know what she likes for herself first. Not let someone else decide for her. Or something like that. I don't know if it's because she's a gynaecologist or just because she's her, but she has zero issues with talking about that stuff. Or asking questions. I had to get used to it pretty quick." She shakes her head and laughs. "I am also insane about recycling, my favourite colour is terracotta, and I love wombats."

Willa shakes her head, still trying to leave the toy thing behind. She manages to stutter, "Wombats?"

"They're cute and grumpy, and they do whatever they want."

"And these are redeeming qualities?"

"In a wombat, yes." She reaches out and takes Willa's hands, yanking her closer. "Okay, is that enough? Because I think I need to kiss you now."

Willa laughs, because that was more than enough. They sink onto their rock, wallowing in a series of slow, indulgent kisses before tipping their faces to the sun and dozing.

Finn turns and nuzzles her shoulder. "Hey, is your family religious?"

"No, not really. Nan's kind of churchy. But now I think it's more a social thing. She never makes us go. You?"

"Definitely not. Mum refuses even to discuss it, and Dad says there are bigger things to worry about than whether there's an invisible entity in the sky."

"Like what?"

"Like equality. Like ending violence. Like making sure all lives matter. He says his religion is giving a crap, because the worse thing people can do is not care."

Willa smiles. "Sounds like he kind of rubbed off on you."

"Yeah, I think it's my religion now too. And I'm okay with that."

"You should be." Willa kisses the side of her head.

"What about you? What do you believe in?"

"I don't know. I mean, I guess I believe in those things, equality, and nonviolence, when I think about it. But I also see some of them as…inevitabilities. I'm not sure if people will ever see each other as equal." Willa thinks of all the history books she's been devouring this year, and how the only way things ever seem to happen is with violence. "And I wonder if there'll always be some kind of conflict. Violence is wrong, but it seems kind of innate too."

"Well, that's pessimistic."

"It's not that I wouldn't want it to change. I just think there's always going to be people who'll use whatever means they can to get power. To get what they want."

Finn frowns. Willa knows she's not completely satisfied with that answer, but that's the only one she has.

Willa picks up Finn's wrist and checks her watch. Her stomach sinks. The afternoon is disappearing fast, and she really shouldn't be here, indulging in Finn time. She should be figuring out how to get her group out of the mess they're in.

She sits up. "I need to get back and do some work."

"Okay." As Finn packs up her bag, her eyes dart toward Willa, then away, and then back again. She looks like a sparrow, uncertain if it's the right moment to dive for a crumb.

Willa's instantly wary. "What?" Finn stands, chewing her lip. She doesn't speak. Willa stands too. "What is it?"

"I know we're not supposed to talk about the game, and I know I'm breaking all our rules," Finn says in a rush, "but I just want to say that I heard what Drew's doing to you guys. And I know he's out to get you, for whatever reason."

Word flies at lightning speed around this camp, that's for sure.

And Willa can't look at Finn for a moment. Because she hates not being able to tell her why he's so bent on making her life hell. But Finn, relentless, grabs Willa's hand and pulls on it until she returns her gaze. "You could join us, you know."

Willa just stares at her.

Finn nods. "You *should* join us. All of you. I was thinking, if we all formed an alliance, there's no way he could pull any of this crap. We'd be too big. Too powerful."

Willa can't answer. She's still stuck in speechless.

Finn steps forward, radiant with her idea. "Think about it: between all of us, we could keep everyone in trade and food and production, and he wouldn't *matter*."

Willa nods slowly, her brain turning over the ins and outs of the idea before she's even sure she wants to. "And with that kind of manpower, our military could be bigger than his, which might scare him off."

"Exactly." She tugs on Willa's hand. "What do you think?"

Willa tips her head and stares at her for a moment. "But why would you want to do this? You don't need us to help you win."

Finn gives her a baffled look. "So? Anyway, why *not* do this? He's being crazy, and we can stop him. Besides, the more of us there are, the more resources we have. We could create something really incredible. Anyway, I'm just saying, the offer's there. I know I could convince the others."

And when Willa still says nothing, Finn drops her hand. "Think about it. Let's get back."

Willa follows her along the creek, lost in a tumultuous silence. But already the drumming in her blood is telling her that this is what she has to do. Because this is all they have to get them out of this mess. And to get the people she has dragged into this mess with her out too.

CHAPTER 59

Willa looks around at them all, her palms pressed to the table. Is she really about to do this?

She practically has to shove the words out. "Finn's suggested we all form an alliance. Our groups with theirs. To protect us all from Drew."

Eva frowns. "When did that happen?"

"She mentioned it after lunch." Willa hopes she lets it slide.

She does. "So, what do you think?"

"I think we'd better do it." She clocks Amira and Holly's reactions. They're wide-eyed but intrigued. "If the terms are right."

"And if we form an alliance, we can start trading with them?" Holly asks.

"Exactly. And with that kind of collective manpower, Drew will have to back down."

"What do you mean by the terms being right?" Amira asks.

"I mean how much autonomy we'd maintain as a territory. How things would be decided. Who would be in charge, that kind of thing. I'm going to talk to Damir and Mark." She turns to Eva. "Coming?"

Eva nods and grabs up her notebook.

Willa gazes around the room until she spots Finn hunched over her work at a table with her team. Gathering up her pride, she strides over.

Finn's eyes widen slightly at the sight of Willa, but she quickly replaces it with a warm smile. "Hey guys."

"Hi." Willa focuses on keeping her voice steady. It's so hard to play normal in public with Finn. Hard with all these feelings pressed up against her. "I was hoping we could set up a meeting later." She doesn't want to say more in case Finn hasn't consulted with her group about it yet.

Finn catches on straight away. "Of course. We can meet in an hour?"

"Sure."

And as Willa walks away, relief mingles with bitterness. Because she wishes it didn't have to come to this, to this need for rescue. Because Willa's never needed rescuing before. Not once in her life. She's made sure of it.

As if she knows what Willa's thinking, Eva says quietly, "Remember, this will be just as beneficial to them as it is to us. There are opportunities for trade, expansion, protection. We won't exactly be hiding under their coattails, you know."

"I know." But it still feels like they will be.

CHAPTER 60

Willa checks her watch. Fifteen minutes until bedtime. She thrusts her hand in her pockets, wishing they'd all hurry.

Next to her, Finn is dug deep inside a giant blue hoodie. She's crunching on an apple and talking to Jessie and the big boy, Craig. They're busy losing themselves in the familiar, some story about one of the kids back at their school. Willa can't focus, because she's still stuck in her doubt. Even now that it's all decided and official, it terrifies her a little, the idea of relinquishing her control to a larger group.

By the time everyone materialises out of the shadows, there are thirteen of them. Six leaders, six deputies, and Craig, who Finn nominated as chair of the meeting. They all stand in a tight circle. Willa can feel the energy coming off them all. Even Mark and Avi from Glumtown are antsy. It's kind of exciting, she has to admit. This plotting in darkness. This unexpected alliance. Everyone so full of its Shakespearean potential.

And Willa knows she should be grateful that everyone agreed to it. It took some convincing with Mark, already burnt once by joining forces. And then there was the fear that Finn's groups wouldn't want to take them. But now, feeling this buzz in the air, she knows their acquiescence is maybe more about the renegade, clandestine nature of this coup. No one saw this twist coming, and that's the fun of it.

Craig steps forward, his hands deep in his pockets. "Okay, so all parties have agreed to the formation of an alliance. The alliance will facilitate military protection, trade agreements, and resource sharing among the six teams where possible. Now we need to vote on the head. This is the person who will run meetings and orchestrate decision-making."

He pulls out a stack of paper slips and a bunch of pencils from his pocket. "This is how it's going to roll. You only vote for one of the six leaders, and you can't vote for your own team, okay?"

There are a few murmurs, but everyone nods.

"The person with the most votes leads the alliance. The person who comes second is deputy. Put your own name at the top and then the person you're voting for below."

Willa takes a slip of paper, writes her name on it, and then pauses. She looks around at everyone, stopping with Finn. Because she always must stop at Finn. She's already scribbling, her blonde hair falling forward, hiding her face.

Willa surrenders to the inevitable and scrawls Finn's name under hers.

It seems to take Craig an eternity to count the votes as he hunches over the picnic table, sorting slips. The second hand of Willa's watch creeps closer to nine.

"Hurry up, dude," Damir grumbles. "We've got about three seconds 'til bed bell."

"Sh, always gotta do two counts. It's a thing." Finally, Craig trudges over to them. "Our leader's Willa. Finn's deputy."

There's only a quiet murmur, like no one's surprised. Except Willa.

Eva chuckles and nudges her. "Well, ain't that a win for girl power?"

Finn turns to Willa with a smile. "Congratulations."

Willa smiles, but she barely hears her. She's too busy forcing herself not to visibly reel. She was sure it would be Finn. "Thanks."

And as people offer their congratulations before rushing back to wherever they sleep, Willa realises that they've chosen her because they only know what they can see, the things they have seen Willa *do*. Like scaling a rock face when no one else wanted to. Like winning The Great Hunt. Like publicly telling Drew off for getting them all punished. This is what they've based their choices on. They don't know the quiet but just as powerful things Finn has achieved, like scraping her team out of trouble with her ideas or being such a visionary with her mills and her marketplaces. Or caring about what happens to everyone in this ultimately selfish game. And even though Willa's relieved to maintain the control that being leader will give her, she still feels like she's cheated.

By the time she pulls herself together, nearly everyone has left. She turns to Eva. "I'll meet you at the cabins, okay?"

The three of them are up ahead, walking fast. "Hey, Finn!" she calls.

Finn turns and jogs back to her. "Hey. Everything okay?"

"I just wanted to say, uh, I'm sorry, I guess?"

Finn frowns. "What? Because they voted for you?"

"And I now realise that sounds super weird." Willa shrugs and forces herself to meet Finn's eye. "I just...I honestly thought it would be you."

"And I thought it would be you. People really respect you, you know, Willa."

"Yeah, but people really *like* you."

"They like you too. They just don't know you."

"I guess."

"Anyway, I don't care who leads. I'm just glad we're all going to work together and beat that idiot."

The wind musses her bangs as she talks. Willa combs them down affectionately. This girl. But before she can say anything, the bedtime siren splits the night.

"You deserve it, Willa," Finn whispers. She kisses her. "You do."

But Willa's not thinking about that anymore. She's thinking about what she did to deserve to have a girl like Finn want to kiss her.

CHAPTER 61

"Eva, I'm telling you, go for Leon. He's cool. I chatted to him during that game yesterday. He's also—total bonus—not an asshole. If not him, then that guy Jessie from Finn's team."

Willa yanks her attention away from her book at the sound of Finn's name. She can't help it. It's like she's programmed to respond to any mention of her.

It's Amira, hounding Eva again. Eva rolls her eyes and swats at Amira with her book. "Mir, stop! Yes, I agree. They are acceptable specimens of the male species, but you're forgetting something."

"What? You need them to be masterful lovers?" Amira purrs. "I could find out."

Eva's eyes widen in horror. Amira cackles and throws herself down on the bed. She wraps an arm around Eva's waist, still laughing. "Not like that. I just mean by reputation."

Eva swats at Amira again. "You're forgetting that I am happily single and plan to stay that way at least until summer."

"But why?"

"Because, unlike you, I don't see the need to be perennially coupled up."

"I don't need a guy either. I just like them."

Eva affectionately boops her nose. "I know you do, honey. But I'm one of those girls who needs my alone time." She tips her head to one side. "That Jessie kid *is* cute. A geek, but a slick geek."

Willa listens to them talk and wonders how they know these things. Not stuff about guys, but about what they want in a relationship. Willa barely has a clue. How can she when she's never really had one until now?

Willa didn't even figure out she was gay on her own. It was her grandmother who told her. Sort of. She was thirteen, and it was summer, one of those hot nights where they had all the doors and windows open, praying for a breeze or some rain or any kind of relief. They were chopping tomatoes for salad when Nan swiped the plump red segments from the board into the bowl and announced in her matter-of-fact Nan way that Willa didn't have to like boys if she didn't want to. That some girls don't.

In the moment, Willa just felt her face turn hot and said nothing. But later that night, under cover of the dark, she admitted to herself that her grandmother might be onto something. The first part, anyway. All the girls around her seemed to have departed for the desperate, second-guessing land of "does he?" and "will he?", while she stubbornly stayed put, bewildered. But even as she slowly realised she definitely did like girls, she still didn't do a single thing about it. Because she didn't know what she was supposed to do about it.

Kelly and Maida had lots of ideas when she finally ran Nan's hypothesis by them. They wanted to take her to gay cafés or to a group, or find her someone online. But like everything she doesn't want or isn't ready for, Willa resisted with busyness. With homework and housework and sibling responsibilities. She evaded it all the way to Freya. And then—because of Freya—ever since.

It was Freya who made the first move, champagne drunk. Willa was too choked by her own wanting. By the possibility of rejection that might come with committing her crush to fact. So it's still incredible to Willa that she kissed Finn first. And she still cannot explain her boldness that night. Or her ability to improvise. Because every time they kiss or curl their limbs together now, it stuns Willa that she knows what to do, that she instinctively knows how to take part in these acts of being with someone. But she also wishes she knew more, because she feels like she's teetering on the brink of getting something wrong.

But it's not just the inexperience that makes her feel so naïve when the Gandry girls talk like this. Because now that she's finally decided to tune in, Willa's seeing more and more gaps between her and other girls. Like the way they're so self-aware, the way they so easily make statements like "I am" and "I believe". Finn and Maida do it too. Where do they get such a keen sense of themselves? Willa feels like she's barely figured out how to get enough sleep sometimes, let alone know how to make these proclamations. And as for what kind of girl she is, she's not even sure how to go about knowing. As far as Willa knows, she is what she does. Isn't that enough?

CHAPTER 62

Willa's being an astronaut, moon-stepping between sun-bleached rocks, going happily nowhere. Just squinting her eyes against the hot sun and focusing on finding the next dry place to put her foot. It's blissful, enforced living in the moment.

Behind her, Finn's sketching the ripples in the water. Willa's book lies on the rock, unopened. It's trying to call out to Willa, but for once she's ignoring it. It's been an epic morning of discussion, debate, and planning with the new alliance leaders, and she wants to leave the brainwork behind for a moment.

She saw the exact moment Drew found out about the alliance. Willa was waiting for it, watching him intently from her table. And she saw the exact moment he read the brief. There was a flash of shock in his eyes, then a frown, and then a hasty return to his default sneer. But it was too late. She saw the ripples inside him. He didn't say anything, though. Waited until the blond boy pointed it out. Only then did he respond with a nonchalant shrug, like this new alliance is a mosquito he'll simply swat away.

But she doesn't want to think about that anymore. Not now that she's turned around and drunk in the sight of Finn in the sunshine, her mouth squeezed into that cute little frown she gets when she's drawing. All Willa wants to do is be next to her.

And when Willa does stretch out beside her, Finn's eyes don't part with the page, but she smiles as if to say she knows Willa's there, and she likes it. Then she reaches for her. First her fingers land gently on Willa's thigh, where the sun is already baking the denim. She doesn't stop drawing, though. Willa's eyes drift closed. The sun's glare burns white against her eyelids as she feels Finn place her palm flat against her belly.

What she likes most is the way Finn's touch is so reflex. She's not necessarily thinking about it, but Willa is here, and so Finn touches her. There's something beautiful about that.

Then Willa's dozing again, bathing in the caress as Finn's thumb idly strokes her belly, smoothing the hem of her T-shirt at the place where it meets her jeans. Then, like it was meant to be, her thumb is slipping underneath, stroking the exposed skin. How can the world be sweetened just by sunshine and the pad of a thumb swept over skin? When Finn's fingers chase her thumb and her whole hand slides underneath to span the stretch of Willa's belly, she is completely captive.

She opens her eyes to a rustle, and to the sight of Finn swiping the sketchbook from her lap. Then she shifts forward onto her knees, moving her face close to Willa's, a cat's-got-the-cream smile on her face. Willa is filled with this molten feeling. Because it is with Finn she remembers she's a girl, a girl with flesh and feelings. She knows in an abstract way that she's supposed to be pretty—desirable, somehow. But she doesn't feel it until she's with Finn, until she's pinned under her gaze.

Finn's fingers trace the rise from Willa's belly up to the base of her ribs and back again. And once more, Willa's eyes are forced shut against the thrill of her delicious little expedition. When she opens them again, Finn's leaning in, her kisses all nip and tease.

Every part of Willa is humming. She's just about to pull Finn down to her when the sounds of laughter and footsteps punch through the still afternoon air and they're wrenched from this dreamy nowhere. Finn looks around them, eyes wide, as Willa yanks her T-shirt down. By the time she's pulled herself up to sitting, Finn's already found the source. Willa follows her gaze to the far side of the creek, and her stomach thuds.

It's a couple of Drew's minions, in tanks tops and runners, clearly back from a run off grounds. She can tell they saw. Can read it in the sudden silence that dropped between them as if weighted. In the way they don't greet Willa and Finn but continue to walk, their eyes flicking toward them and darting away just as quickly, as they make small smirks of their silent mouths.

"Something tells me we're about to make headlines," Finn mutters.

"Probably."

"Hey?"

"Mm?"

"You're not embarrassed having people know you're with me, are you?"

Willa can see the hurt forming in Finn's eyes already. She grabs Finn's hand and squeezes it. "Of course not. I hate the thought of people gossiping about us, but I'm not embarrassed."

"Good." Finn picks up her sketchbook. "I'm definitely not looking forward to my team's interrogation when they find out, though."

Willa stares at Finn's painstaking sketch of the creek. As usual, she's perfectly rendered what she's witnessed, translating the rush and whorl of water onto paper. "Just because they know doesn't make it their business," she reminds her. "This is ours. Not theirs."

"I know." Finn gives her a slow smile, but that crease is still carving its space next to her eyes.

Surprised by this small show of vulnerability from her warrior girl, Willa wraps her arms around her. "Don't worry. We can still come and hide from the world up here."

"I wish we could stay here now." Finn squeezes her tighter. So tight she can barely breathe.

"Me too. But we should go. We don't want to be gossip fodder *and* in trouble."

CHAPTER 63

By lunchtime, it's obvious the news has spread through the camp like wildfire. People stop talking momentarily as Willa passes on her way to the dining hall, watching, like this new knowledge somehow *means* something. She assumes her best poker face, and stares straight ahead like she always does, even as the blood roars in her ears.

She wants to look for Finn, to see how she's coping, but she doesn't dare. Then she finds herself near her in the line for food. Keeping her eyes fixed on the notebook in her hands, Willa pretends not to notice. For the first time ever, Willa wishes one of the Gandry girls were with her, distracting her with chatter.

"Oh my God, our alliance has two mommies!" It's Amy, saying "mommies" in a twee American accent. She claps her hands gleefully. "This place finally has a power couple."

Finn doesn't dignify Amy's ridiculousness with a reply. Just stares at the food on offer.

"But I thought you were with Matt Jenner last semester?" Craig says.

"So?" Finn says, plucking an orange from the bowl.

"So, uh…"

Finn sighs. "Listen, I'm perfectly happy to help you out with difficult concepts. Like that time that I explained anaerobic respiration to you, but I do not have the time or the energy to explain really basic stuff. Especially when the meaning is in the actual word. *Bi*sexuality. Hear that? *Bi*."

Sorry." He sounds sheepish. "Got it."

"Good." Finn immediately moves onto another subject. And as awkward as Willa feels right now, she has to smile at Finn's little takedown. Because Finn's already told her how she used to worry about this stuff. Used to think she had to decide: guys or girls. That you couldn't be stuck in between desires like she was. Then she realised she wasn't stuck anywhere. There was nowhere to be stuck.

But Finn also told Willa that she's learned that not everybody sees it like that. Willa's never even thought about this stuff before. Never had to. Maybe she's lucky.

When Willa joins her table, the Gandry girls are all twinkle-eyed significant looks. She tries to pretend she's too busy enjoying her meal to notice, but it's hard to do when it's a claggy, pallid pasta salad, limp greens, and a half-stale bread roll.

Luckily, Eva saves the day. "I guess we find out what Drew's going to do about the alliance later. Think he'll back down?"

Willa stabs at her pasta. "I hope so, but I really don't know."

"Maybe he's too distracted by news of *another* alliance right now," Amira teases. "Just like the rest of us."

The table stills.

"Leave her alone, Mir," Eva finally says when Willa doesn't fill the silence. "What Willa does is her own business. And maybe she doesn't want to discuss it here. Or with you."

"*I know that*, Eva." Amira gives her a withering look and turns to Willa. "But, you know, it is nice to know that you're human. *And* that you have good taste. That Finn's a cutie."

And this time, Willa cannot stem her blush.

193

CHAPTER 64

Drew's team's gossip-mongering doesn't seem to have achieved much, except earning Finn and Willa a whole lot of intrigued stares. No one seems too upset by the news or what it means for the game. They're curious, yes, but bothered, no. And that must make Drew even more frustrated, because his latest brief makes it clear what he's going to do— which is not change a thing. He's just widened the territory he's planning to invade.

Willa's stomach churns as she reads, sure everyone will blame her for dragging them into her group's problems. But no one's saying anything about that when they sit around, discussing the brief after dinner. They're too stuck on being stunned by Drew's latest move.

"Is this guy stupid?" Jessie shakes his head.

"Uh, clearly." Leon plonks down onto a beanbag. "Instead of just playing nice so his people can eat, he's going to sic his military onto the rest of the world." He shakes his head. "What a waste."

"How much of a threat is he, anyway?" Damir asks.

"In numbers, we've definitely got the edge," Willa says. "But in terms of technology, he does. For starters, they've got an air force, so his military would be more mobile *and* more precise."

"So we have to stop him from being at least one of those things, right?" Finn says. "Mobile or precise?"

"I guess."

The bedtime siren bellows, making them all jump.

Jessie shoves his books into his bag. "Well, we have to do something fast. Next week's the end of the game. We've basically got the weekend and Monday to come up with something to stop him."

"We'll think of something." Willa tries to look more confident than she feels. "We will. Everybody put their minds to it, and come to me with any ideas."

CHAPTER 65

By Saturday, they still don't have a plan. Willa's worried, but it's hard to think when you have jobs to do all morning and then you're forced to hike up yet another steep incline. Why must there always be hills involved in their activities?

She and Finn stroll back from a stolen half hour at the creek. Even though they grudgingly traded their usual furious kissing session for brainstorming, they've still got nothing.

No one pays them much attention. It's funny, because yesterday the camp was aflame with revelation of an unexpected hook-up, but now they're old news. Willa's definitely got a reason to love the three-minute attention span around here. Now, thanks to the alliance and the gossip, people *expect* to see them together. Maybe Drew's group did them a favour.

On the oval, a game of kick-to-kick is in full flight. They lean on the fence and watch. A small, skinny girl from Finn's group takes a mark and screams in shock at the sight of the red, oval ball in her hands. Finn laughs and yells, "Go Zaki!"

Zaki's return kick is a mess. The ball comes off the side of her foot and skitters across the grass in the direction of no one. "I hate this," she screeches. "Can we play real football?" She drops to the grass, laughing hysterically. "I kill at football!"

"I'm thinking more of a defensive, backline role for her in this game," Finn says with a laugh.

Willa smiles, even though she has no idea what Finn's talking about. She's never watched a game of Australian Rules in her life. Still, she stands next to her, watching instead of going to do her homework. Because she's never just stood beside someone like this. Not a someone who is possibly becoming her girlfriend. Even though the thought of publicly touching Finn still makes her face flame, this small platonic act of being side-by-side is blissful.

"Hey, Finn! Willa!" It's Jessie coming at them at a run. He starts talking the minute he gets to them. "Hey, I've been thinking and thinking, and I might have an idea for how we can deal with Drew's offence."

Before he can go on, the siren goes. He groans. "I am *so* sick of the sound of that thing!"

Willa's got to agree.

"Can we meet after dinner?" he asks. "I'm on serving tonight."

"Sure," Willa says.

Finn groans. "I'm on clean-up, so I'll be at least an hour or two. I'll come find you after, though."

"Okay, well, I'm going to dish up some swill." Jessie rolls his eyes. "See you in the rec hall after."

CHAPTER 66

By the time Finn gets to the hall, the others are long gone. Only Willa and Jessie are left in the hall, busily making lists.

Finn's hair is lank, and her face is pink from the kitchen steam. She drops into the seat next to Willa and sighs. "That sucked. Okay, so what's happening?"

"We're all over it." Jessie waves a hand over all their notes and lists. "The plan's in place, and everyone will have their sections to work through on Monday so we can submit Tuesday."

"We just need to work out the finer points now," Willa says.

Finn sits back and sighs, letting her arms hang at her side. "Wow, cool. So what are we doing?"

"What do you know about the Leningrad Siege?" Jessie asks.

Finn shrugs and wipes her damp forehead. "That it happened in Leningrad? Don't ask me where Leningrad is, though."

"I was reading about it last holidays." Jessie leans in. "So, in the Second World War, when the Germans invaded Russia, they wanted to conquer Leningrad first. But Hitler didn't want to waste resources on fighting a war in a city he didn't actually want, so they decided that instead, they'd just completely surround the city, starve the population out, and then conquer it once it was weakened by hunger."

"Whoa." Finn pulls a face. "War is so…" She shakes her head.

"I know, right? Now, the Russians escaped in the end because they had troops battling from the outside, too, and they made exits. But as long as we completely close off the perimeter and surround them before they know what's happ—"

Finn's eyes widen. "Hang on, you're saying we should do this?"

He blinks at her slowly and then grins. "Well, yeah, that would be why I'm describing the Leningrad Siege to you."

"You want to repeat an inhuman act that Hitler and his army orchestrated?" Finn says slowly, an eyebrow firmly raised. "*Hitler?*"

"Well, that's just one example. They do it in *Game of Thrones* all the time too. Surround the castles." His grin hangs there for a moment but dissolves under Finn's glare.

Willa tenses. She wasn't expecting this. She thought Finn would be relieved they'd found a solution.

Finn's eyebrow is still hiked in disbelief. "And you think everyone is going to be on board with this?"

"Actually, we already held a vote," Willa says. "So yes, I do."

"But I wasn't here. Doesn't my vote count?"

Willa instinctively goes to grab Finn's hand to pacify her, but then stops herself. "Of course it does. We were just in a hurry. If the vote tied, we were going to use yours to decide it. But it wasn't."

"So that's it. We're doing it?"

"Yeah," Jessie says, looking as bewildered as Willa feels. "That was the vote."

Finn turns back to Willa. "And you *want* to do this?"

"It doesn't matter. We *have* to do it. We don't have the resources to fight a war against them, but with our combined military population and maybe some enforced conscription, we could easily block them from moving against us."

Finn folds her arms over her chest. "I hate this."

"It's the most logical solution we have."

"Logical?" She pulls a face. "I don't care about logical. You two are suggesting we starve a population to death. A population who have no say in the idiot choices their leader makes. That's barbaric."

"Hey, relax." Willa notes the way Finn's nostrils flare at the "relax" and quickly changes tack, speaking more softly. "But we're not actually starving anyone. It's just a game."

"So? It's a game modelled on the real world. And I'm sorry if I'm no more comfortable with being metaphorically inhumane than I am with being literally inhumane."

Frustration flickers through Willa. "But we want to beat Drew, don't we? I thought that's what we were trying to do."

"Of course. But not like *this*." Finn's expression returns to that place between disbelief and anger. "Why do you have to be so brutal about it?"

"I'm being practical."

"Yeah, well, your practical solution is brutal."

Willa tries to curb her irritation with a slow, steadying breath. "And you're acting like I'm some kind of murderous dictator."

"Well you're acting like one," Finn retorts. "We formed this alliance for our protection, not to create a bigger, scarier army."

"Actually, that was a part of it," Jessie says before Willa can.

"You know what I mean," Finn snaps. Then she sighs, and her strident tone withers into something weary and defeated. "We weren't supposed to actually use it."

"It's not like Drew wouldn't do the same if our army moved on him," Willa reminds her.

Finn holds up her hands. "Well, first, our army would never have moved on him, because we're not power-hungry idiots. And secondly, that's exactly what I mean. Since when did you want to be like him?"

Willa succumbs to her anger, glaring. "I *don't* want to be like him."

"Could've fooled me."

Willa gives her an icy stare. She still really doesn't understand why this is such a big deal. It's only a game. Besides, they don't have time for this. She turns back to her books.

"I'm sorry if that's the way you feel about it, because it's what we're doing. Everyone voted. We have no other options, and we really need to get to work." She picks up her pen.

Finn pushes her chair back. "Well, I don't want to be a part of this option." She points at Jessie. "If he's so happy with his solution, he can be your deputy. I'm out." She marches out of the hall.

Willa clenches her jaw as she watches the door slam shut behind Finn. A few people in the corner start whispering.

Stinging, Willa stares down at the page in front of her so she doesn't have to know if they're looking at her.

When she finally looks up and meets Jessie's eye, he attempts an awkward grin. "I guess she didn't like my idea."

She presses her pen into her notepad and frowns. "It doesn't matter if she likes it, it's what needs to be done. Let's work."

She leans back over her notes and continues her list. But even as she scribbles, there's a tug of something telling her to examine what just passed between them. But she shoves it away. There's no time.

CHAPTER 67

Finn doesn't meet her in the morning.

Willa stalks away from the oval, hardening against the hurt. What does Finn want her to do? The end goal is to not let Drew win, so that's what they're doing. Besides, Willa has a responsibility to her own team, too. She can't let them lose.

All morning, even from a distance, Willa can see the anger still burning bright in Finn. It's in the set of her shoulders and in her drawn, distracted expression. It's in the way she's so intently not looking around her, just in case—Willa is sure—she catches Willa's eye.

This is what stings most. Being ignored. Freya did it to her a lot when they were friends. Punishments meted out for some perceived wrongdoing. And Willa would have to wait it out until she came back, often within hours, too craving of attention to keep it up for long. But this is different. Because this is not a game. Finn doesn't do things just for attention.

And for the second time since arriving on this camp, Willa cannot see a way. Even if she wanted to change their plan, there's no time. And she knows Finn is not going to back down. Willa knows this because she knows that she wouldn't back down either. This is a compromise Willa cannot and Finn will not make.

The afternoon and evening yield the same silence. After dinner, Willa sits on her bunk as the girls come and go, going through her notes for a Geography assignment. But she can't lose herself in her work. Not with her feelings rubbing raw like this.

After lights out, she lies in bed, wide-eyed and assaulted by an unfamiliar ache, almost wishing she could go back to the cold, cleansing truth of her aloneness. She thinks about her dad on his boat, happier in his salt-encrusted silence, as far from land and people and their confusing ways as he can get. Maybe she's like him. Maybe she'd be better off like that.

CHAPTER 68

It's misery that accompanies her into waking, and it muddies the purity of her anger. Because inside it she finds the simple truth: she misses Finn. Already. Doesn't even know how she'll get through another day without talking to her. Maybe Willa's not so much like her dad after all.

And that's how Willa finds herself making a beeline for her the first moment she spies her alone—before she's even decided she's going to do it or what she's going to say.

Finn's on the grass outside the rec hall, reading. When she sees Willa coming, her expression doesn't change, sending a trickle of hope through Willa.

Willa clutches her books to her chest, and whispers, "I'm sorry." She doesn't even know exactly what she's being sorry for. It's just the need to make things okay that sends the words to her lips.

Finn's eyes seem to soften for a second. Then she tips her head to one side and stares up at her. "Are you still doing it? The siege?"

Willa nods.

"Well, I still don't want anything to do with it."

"But we have to do *something*."

"I know that, Will. And you already know I don't want to."

"I do." Willa's throat aches. Why did she have to call her *Will* now? Misery overwhelms her. She feels stupid and weak for it. If she'd thought before she spoke, she already knew Finn wouldn't budge. Willa was just clinging to the hope that while the game version of them falls apart, the version of them that clings to each other on a rock in the sunshine could still be allowed to exist.

She chews on her lip and stands there dumbly, helpless to the next move. Why does she never know how to say things? Is this another thing mothers teach girls and she missed out on it? Or is she just bad at it?

Finn stands up, closing her book. "You know, *you're* the person who told me it's no use having ideals if I wasn't going to fight for them. Remember?"

Willa stares down at her books and nods. Because she does remember. She remembers the flinch of Finn's anger that day. Remembers fighting the internal duel of liking this girl so much and knowing she was making herself impossible to like for the sake of the game. And here they are again, crammed in another tight space.

"You know, Willa, I spent the first half of this camp being some weird non-version of myself. And it was kind of hard to get the me I know back again. I'm not losing it or doing something I'd never do for the sake of a game and getting one over some idiot. I'm not."

Willa presses her lips into a tight, stinging line and nods. Because she knows she can't ask Finn to do that. So she has to let her walk away.

CHAPTER 69

Willa's nibbling her sandwich on the porch with some of the girls and staring out into space when one of the kids from Glumtown runs over.

"Hey, Willa, Gus said to come up to the office after kitchen duty. You're getting a call at two."

Willa freezes, her sandwich halfway between her mouth and plate. "Who's calling?"

"How should I know? He just said to tell you." The girl dashes up the steps, calling for someone else.

And there it is, the instant churn of fear. Something's happened at home. She knows it. Her sandwich drops to her plate.

"Hey, don't worry," Eva says. "If it was serious, they'd call you up straight away. Don't stress."

"Yeah." Ling says, inspecting her apple. "When that girl from the mixed group's dad went to hospital, Gus came and got her himself."

Willa follows the logic but can't stem the tide of fear and questions. She runs through the litany of things she's already imagined could go wrong before she was convinced to come here. Is Nan sick again? Did something happen to Riley or Jack at school? Her heart skips a beat when she thinks of Jack. Poor Jack. She hopes it isn't those little bullies again. Or is something up with her dad?

Eva nudges her. "Come on. Let's go start clean up. It'll make the time go faster."

Amira groans. "Will it?"

"For *Willa*, you selfish wench," Eva says.

Willa stands at the dishwasher, working on autopilot, trying to drown out the din of her fears with the roar of the machine. As soon as her watch says five to two, she leaves without saying a word. She jogs up the path, the cold breeze batting the steam-dampened fabric of her T-shirt.

When she knocks, an elderly woman with a coiffed, maroon helmet of hair peers through the screen door of the fibro building. "Willa?" She opens the door and beckons her into the brown-carpeted office block "I'm Lorina, Gus's mum. You need to call…" She peers at a piece of paper for way too long. "Kelly." She waves at a phone at the edge of the large desk and passes Willa the slip. "You can ring on that phone, love."

"Th-thanks." Willa starts dialling the number before she's even sitting in the chair. The moment Kelly picks up, she asks, "Hey, what's wrong?"

"Hey, Will!" Kelly yells cheerfully into the phone. The sounds of cars and people talking fills up the background.

"Kell, what's happened?"

"Oh, hey, chill, it's okay."

"How would I know that? All I got was a message to call you."

"Sorry. Didn't mean to scare you."

"Well, you did."

"I just called because Nan's friend just found out she has to go back home."

"Why?"

"Her daughter's in hospital."

Willa is rushed by relief. It's not Nan or the kids. Then it's swiftly replaced with guilt. "Is she going to be okay?"

"No idea. But the problem now is Jack and Riley. Nan's been sick. Nothing major, just a bad cold. But I'm not sure she's up to it."

"I'll come home."

"You don't need to."

But Willa's already making plans. "I'll find out if there's a bus or something, and I'll come home tonight. Or maybe your brother can—"

"Jesus, Will, *chill*," Kelly says again. "You don't need to come home. We'll sort it out. I just thought you'd want to know."

"Of course I want to know. And I'll come home, I said."

"And I'm saying you don't need to. Stop being an idiot."

Willa frowns, but she feels a twinge of comfort too. Only Kelly would call her an idiot.

She's about to snap back when Kelly interrupts, speaking slowly. "Will, I need you to breathe and listen. Give me a couple of hours. Let me see what we can work out before you do anything drastic, okay?"

Willa draws in a slow, grudging breath. Kelly's the only person she'd trust with this. Fierce, fun, old-before-her-time Kelly. "Alright."

"Good. Call me in a few hours. At about five?"

"Okay," Willa says in a small voice, as the homesickness escalates from twinge to ache. Maybe going home wouldn't be so bad.

"Okay. Talk then." And she's gone. Willa stares at the receiver in her hand. She has three hours to wait, now.

"Everything okay, love?" Lorina peers over the computer while her fingers continue to storm across the keypad.

"I think so. May I come back and call later?" she asks in her politest voice.

"Of course. I'll be here. Just pop back in."

CHAPTER 70

It's like this day was designed to torture Willa. Because the ways in which it has sucked have been both specific and cruel. She stares at the name she has drawn from Gus's hat for the afternoon activities. "Drew," she says dully.

He waves from his table. "Howdy, partner."

The girls give her sympathetic looks. Resigned to this painful fate, she waits for everyone else to draw their partners and avoids all eye contact. Like everything else, news of Willa's out-of-hours phone call has gotten around fast, and she's already tired of catching curious glances.

As she waits for Drew to come over to her (she will *not* go to him), she can't stop herself from sneaking a glance in the direction of Finn's table. The moment their eyes meet, Finn looks away. But Willa catches the concern in her gaze. Finn was checking she's okay. And that little look makes Willa ache a little. Finn still cares what happens to her.

Ruining the moment in that way only he knows how, Drew drops down on the bench next to her. "Afternoon," he says with a grin.

Willa simply nods as she examines the piles of coloured paper and pencils that a teacher drops in front of them.

He *tsk-tsks* at her. "Hey, don't be like that. Let's just leave the game behind, shall we? Enjoy the moment?"

"I'm not being *like* anything," she says calmly. "It's just hard to enjoy the moment when I don't particularly enjoy you."

He chuckles. "That's right. You enjoy the ladies, don't you? My bad."

"*That's* not..." she starts to say but then forces her mouth shut. She's giving him too much energy. The best way to drive an attention whore like Drew crazy is to starve him, she reminds herself.

Gus turns the projector on, and Willa very deliberately turns from Drew to listen.

"Okay, guys, time for a bit of reflection on our personal values." Gus points to a list of coloured words listed on the PowerPoint. "I want you to use the slips of paper on your table and make four choices for each colour. For example, where it says 'four personal possessions you can't live without' in blue, write down the four personal possessions you think you can't live without on your four slips of blue paper, one on each. Where it says four significant memories in green, do the same on green and so on. And remember, they don't have to be four happiest memories or people or places, they just have to be important, for whatever reason. Okay." He drums on the table. "Get to it."

Willa gathers her slips of paper and stares at the list, chewing her lip. She decides to start with her four people. Because that's the easiest. Her arm curves around her slips as she carefully prints out their names: *Jack, Riley, Gran, Kelly*. She wonders if she should feel bad for putting Kelly down instead of her dad, but swipes the feeling away. Kelly's the one sorting out Willa's life right now. Not her father. He's nowhere to be found.

She moves onto the rest of the list. Some things come easily. For significant places, she instantly writes down Nan's house. Then the river they camped by that time. For possessions, she puts the collage Jack painstakingly made for her, and the beautiful shirt that Kelly and Maida bought together for her birthday. For memories, she puts the one of her mother at the mangrove forest, and that time, after they'd moved to Nan's, when she realised her dad wasn't coming back. For goals, she scribbles down travel, then her dream PhD in international relations and her bigger dream job at the UN. Then, stuck, she quickly scribbles in *helping people* and goes back and finishes all her slips. She bites down on her lip as she puts down the rock by the creek as one of her four places.

"So, who's Riley?"

Willa jumps. She'd forgotten about Drew. "My little sister," she says dully.

He reaches past her and rifles through her slips. "What about Kelly?"

"A friend."

Drew waggles an eyebrow. "She hot?"

Willa pushes the rest of her slips back into little piles, hiding them. "She would be none of your business," she says calmly.

"Okay!" Gus shouts, drumming on the table again. "Everybody finished?"

There's a murmur and some groans as people rush to scribble out slips.

"Good!" he shouts, ignoring the protests. "Now, I want you to look at all your slips and remove five of them. And in doing so, it will mean those five things will have never existed in your life. Go." He slaps the table. "Make good choices."

Willa frowns as she spreads her slips out again. She quickly removes most possessions, and then the memory of Jack's birth. Because she still has Jack.

"That wasn't so hard, right?" Gus cries. "Good. Now take another five away. Remember, they never existed."

Willa weighs her options, and then finds herself giving up some more memories, her shirt, and her dream to travel. Next to her, Drew's casually flicking slips into a messy pile like it's a no-brainer.

"Guess what I'm going to ask you to do now?" Gus grins. Someone moans.

"That's right, he says gleefully. "Another five! Until you are down to the last five things you simply, simply cannot let go of."

Ten coloured slips taunt Willa as she tries to mentally triage her life. It feels impossible. But Willa's never not finished anything just because it seems impossible. So, one by one, each choice hurting more than it should, she slowly pulls something from her pile. That memory of her mother at the beach, her dream job, Kelly, her PhD— they all disappear, no longer part of Willa's survival pyramid.

And then there were five. In those final five strips, she sees her life set out before her. Most of it's predictable. Riley and Jack and Nan, of course. And the house, which Nan always says will be theirs one day. The house that will keep them together for as long as Riley and Jack need her. It's the final slip that surprises her most: helping people. Because if you'd asked Willa twenty minutes ago if this would have been in her final five choices, she would never have guessed. But when she thought about it, she realised it's the umbrella that covers her PhD and her dream job, *and* her desire to keep Riley and Jack safe, so she kept it.

"Poor old Kelly had to go, did she?"

Willa reads the handout. "We're supposed to compare our five choices and then answer these reflection questions for each other now."

He leans right over her, peering at her slips. He smells of too much aftershave and wood smoke. "A house, some names and helping people?" He wrinkles his nose. "How earnest."

"What did you choose?"

He lounges back in his chair and flaps a hand at the slips in front of him, inviting her to look.

"Mansion, guitar, car, to rule the world and future hot model." She pulls a face. "There's nobody from your actual life in this list?"

"They can be replaced," he says blithely.

"Even your family?"

He flicks at a slip. It coasts across the table. "You didn't expect me to take this crap seriously, did you?"

Willa reads the questions on the handout. They're all about why they made the difficult choices they did and what it says about what they value in life. There's no point even going through them if Drew didn't do it properly. Besides, there's no way she's spilling her guts to him. That would be hard enough to do with someone she actually liked. She pushes her slips together and turns them facedown.

Then she eyes him, suddenly curious. He's got his eyes shut, pretending to nap. "Why were you chosen to be here?"

"Eh?" He opens one eye and shrugs. "No idea."

"Really? Most kids are here because they're top in a subject or school or sports captain or something. There must be some reason."

He opens his eyes and gives her a withering look, like she's ruining his precious nap time. "I *am* top in something," he says in a dull voice. "A couple of things, actually. I kill at anything to do with numbers."

She gives him a dubious look, but feels her ego flinch at the same time. Could this idiot be smarter than her?

He folds his arms. "And guess what being crazy smart has taught me?"

"What?"

"That this stuff is crap and meaningless, and none of it is going to determine if we're tomorrow's leaders. It's just something to occupy us for a while so the teachers can focus on the dumb kids before we start VCE." He leans forward. "And frankly, being here is marginally more entertaining than being at school, so I agreed to come. You're probably here because you think it will look good on your resumé later or something. And you're right, because if there's one thing people get sucked into, it's the appearance of making an effort."

He smirks and then points at her pile of slips. "And of course, *helping people.*" He shuts his eyes again. "But hey, it's nice you want to help. Sweet."

It takes everything she has not to react. He *really* doesn't care. At the back of her mind, she'd always figured there was something making him tick, some reason he needs so much attention and makes such dumb decisions to get it. But now she knows it's just the fact of being too smart for his own good, with the dangerous symptoms of boredom to show for it. He's advancing an army on them because he doesn't give a crap what happens, and he needs a way to amuse himself.

This little epiphany makes Willa feel strangely calm. She points at his scraps of paper.

"You know what? If you only get those things you left at the end, and you're going to have a pretty miserable life. Because the worst thing a person can do is not give a crap." Her throat clenches at those familiar words but holds his gaze. "Some advice, though: try not to take too many people who actually *do* care down with you."

He stares at her for a moment, then cocks some finger guns at her. "Thanks for the advice, hon, but I'll be just fine. As long as there are people like you and your little girlfriend to fix my messes, we'll all be okay. It's a win-win, isn't it? I stave off boredom, and you get to feel good about yourselves. Everybody's happy, right?"

"I don't know." Willa folds her arms. "*Are* you happy?"

She turns and stalks away before she has to hear another lie from his mouth.

CHAPTER 71

At five, Willa dashes back to the office. Lorina's still typing, like Willa never left. "Hey, it's me," she says when Kelly picks up. "Is everything okay?"

"Completely sorted, my love," Kelly says cheerfully. "I should be someone's PA one day. I'd kick ass. The neighbours across the road are taking Jack for the week. I think he might be secretly stoked to have a week with his bestie and twenty-four-hour access to a PlayStation. Riles is staying at Brittany's tonight, and then either Maida or I are going to stay with her and Nan all week, so there's someone around. We've got you covered, Will."

Guilt begins to instantly chip at Willa's relief. "But I don't want to wreck your week with having to look after Riles. She can be such a—"

"Oh don't you worry about that. I can handle Little Miss Riley Jane. It's just a matter of whether she can handle me. And I love Nan. You know it."

A warmth rushes her. "Thank you."

"Don't thank me," Kelly says, all gruff. "We love you, stupid, and you'd totally do the same for either of us."

"I would."

"So, you let us take care of here, and you stay where you are and kick some ass. *Are you kicking ass, by the way?*"

"Maybe."

"Okay, well, are you having fun?"

The question just drags her back to the problem of Finn. Willa wishes she could sit down with Kelly and workshop it all. But Willa can't say a word right now. Not when Kelly doesn't even know Finn exists. And definitely not when Gus's mother is busily online shopping for chemist products just two feet away from her.

"It's okay," she finally says. "I'm learning a lot, I guess."

"Our geek girl's got to love that, right?" There's a sudden shuffle and a mutter at the other end of the phone before Kelly's voice returns. "Princess Riley needs to talk to you before you go. See you, babe."

"Okay. Bye." Willa smiles as she hears Riley's muffled protest at the 'princess'. A week with Kelly might be good for her.

The next thing she knows, her sister is chattering down the phone. "Hey, Will, I miss you. Kelly says I have to watch the *The Bachelor* instead of *Modern Family*. Can you tell her I *cannot* miss the finale?"

CHAPTER 72

Willa walks out of the dark little office and keeps walking. Past the rec hall, where kids are lounging on the wooden porch. Past the games of football and basketball on the oval and courts. Past the kids lining the fences, watching, and past the cabins, where the rest of them snooze and chat. And she doesn't stop until she's reached the creek and stepped slowly from stone to stone until she's back in their spot.

She drops onto their rock and shocks herself with the instant surrender to tears. She swipes at her face and stares suspiciously at the damp on the back of her hand. What is she crying for? Everything's okay now.

So why does she feel like this? It's as if the silent panic she felt as she waited to speak to Kelly has shaken something loose. All her fears about leaving them for this camp were storming back.

Everybody said it would be okay, but Willa wasn't sure. All she could think about was what would happen if something went wrong at the house or Riley or Jack needed something? Nan can cook and do light cleaning. She can also dole out hugs and her old-lady, "behave like a lady/gentleman" advice. But she can't manage the constant loads of washing and vacuuming and shopping it takes to keep a house of four running. And what if something happened to her while Willa was gone? If she got hurt or sick again? And if anything happened to Nan? What would happen to them? Her brother and sister don't need any more disruption or uncertainty in their lives.

It wasn't until one of Nan's old students offered to come and stay at the house that Willa even considered coming to camp. But still, she worried. And she's become so used to worrying about them all, it's hard to just let go of that.

And she's carried it like a background guilt since she got here, one that ate at her when Riley sent that letter, begging her to call, and then again as she waited to speak to Kelly. It was the fear that if she snapped the thread she's been forced to hold so tightly, that everything would unravel.

And maybe, just maybe, it's just as unsettling that nothing has gone wrong now that she has let it go. Where does that leave her?

She wipes her face with the bottom of her T-shirt and stares miserably into the rush of water. Willa doesn't usually do feeling sorry for herself. There's no time for that. Ever. But she's letting herself have it today. Because there's the other mess looming large, too: the fact she has no idea how to solve the problem of Finn. Of them. Because while Willa knows everything that she has ever read in a textbook, when it comes to the simplicity of two people being together, she's learning she knows *nothing*.

She rests her chin on her knees and faces down the question that's swirled at the edges of her mind all day: what if Finn is done with her? Her total radio silence seems to say she is. And the only reason Willa knows that they're not entirely finished yet is that Finn would say it out loud and to her face. But that could still be coming.

She came so close to having something that was just hers. Something amazing.

Willa hauls in a breath and dwells in her misery for another minute. Then, sick of herself, she washes her face in the cold creek water and returns to camp.

Because it's time to work. They have to keep going if they're going to win. She joins the others in the rec room and throws herself into it.

CHAPTER 73

Willa has five more precious minutes of internet time. She could probably trade them for gold bullion around these parts, but decides to check her e-mail instead. Not that there'll be anything exciting. Just some school announcements and maybe a short, whining message or a kitten GIF from Riles.

There's something from Finn. The sounds in the rec hall fade. She inches the cursor across the inbox and clicks, giving in to her curiosity.

The message is empty. So is the subject line. There's just a link.

She clicks again. The page is a frenzy of black-and-white images and text. The first thing her eyes lock on is a black-and-white photo of a wide-eyed girl in a headscarf standing among a group of children. She frowns. Why is Finn sending this? It's only then that she takes in the text. It's an article from the anniversary of the Siege of Leningrad. About the diary that was found, written by a little girl who watched her family members starve to death, one by one, and marked their deaths in her journal while she, too, wasted away. Willa reads the whole article, her stomach tying itself into knots, hoping for a happy ending. But of course there isn't. She was evacuated from the city at the end of the siege, only to die of tuberculosis alone in an orphanage.

Willa barely breathes as she scrolls past the pictures of gaunt, starving citizens of the city, her eyes skimming over the awful litany of the little girl's dead. She's never been so happy to hear the bedtime warning siren. She shuts down the computer, but the images are still there. Finn's definitely made her point.

Willa feels like she's withering inside after this day.

"Hey, are you alright?" Eva asks as they trudge down the steps.

"I'm fine." She walks a little faster, but Eva just matches her pace.

"Honestly, Willa, you don't seem like it."

Willa frowns at her, but Eva just looks back calmly as if to say she knows she's breaking some unspoken rule but doesn't care.

"It's just been a long day, I guess," Willa finally says.

"Was everything okay at home?"

"It is now."

"Good." Eva stays silent until the others, up ahead, veer off to the cabins. "Finn's pretty mad about what we're doing, isn't she?"

Everyone must know about the fight by now. It's spectacularly obvious they haven't really spoken to each other since Finn slammed the door of the rec hall the other night. Willa wishes she could go back to a time when she wasn't even close to being a worthy subject of gossip. When the reward for scrutiny was Finn, Willa could ignore it. But now it's just another hurt, raw and exposing.

"I don't get it. I thought she was all about beating Drew?" Eva says. "I thought everyone was on board with that one."

"She is." Before she can decide what she wants to tell Eva, she's doing it. "She's upset because she hates the idea of a siege. She thinks it's inhumane, even if it isn't real. She's got pretty strong opinions about stuff like that."

"I can respect that. What does *she* want to do?"

"I don't know. She's barely spoken to me since we decided."

"Oh. That's not good."

"We were supposed to be keeping us separate from the game." Willa is almost shocked by her sudden willingness to share, but she cannot stem the flood now.

Eva smiles wryly at her. "Yeah, that was never going to work."

"I guess. I don't know what to do now."

"Maybe you should just ask her what *she* wants to do. At least it's a way to get her to talk to you again."

"Maybe."

There's a silence, until Eva turns to her again. "You know, I was kind of surprised you two were into each other."

Willa grudges a smile. "I think quite a few people were."

"You're both such strong personalities, but you're completely different."

"I think that's what attracted us." She folds her arms and glances at Eva, shy. "We're really different, but we get each other—get *it*, you know?"

"I do, actually." She gives Willa a wry grin. "You know, even though I was surprised, I had already guessed about you two."

Heat washes over Willa's face. "How?"

"That time she came to the cabin after curfew. That morning in the tent after the game. You just kept popping up together. And I already had my suspicions about you."

"Why?"

"Can I ask you something?" Eva asks instead of answering.

"I guess."

"Did something happen with you and Freya Williams?"

Willa's face is burning now. "Sort of. How did you know?" She stops next to the fence that borders the oval. This is not a conversation she wants to carry to the cabins. They sit, backs against the fence, facing the sun. "Does everyone know?" Willa asks.

"No, don't worry. I used to be friends with Freya a long time ago, until I wasn't. I know what a user she can be. And I saw how she latched onto you when you came to Gandry. And you looked kind of devastated after she left. I guess I figured it was more."

"It was." Willa plays with her loose shoelace instead of meeting her eye. "For me, anyway."

"And let me guess, she made the most of your attention?"

"Yeah." It's enough feeling awful about Finn tonight. Willa doesn't need the added assault of thinking about Freya.

"Hey, do you know Maria?"

"Yeah?"

"Did you know she's gay?"

"No." The only time Willa's ever spent with Maria was during the Great Hunt, sprinting through the bush in silence.

"Well, she is. We might have made out at a party last year. I get stupid on champagne." Eva gives her a wry smile. "It was fun, but I'm into guys. Now she's going out with Steph D'Urso."

"I didn't know." Willa always wondered if there were other girls at her school. Statistically, she knew it was likely, but how would she find out?

"Well, why would you? You hardly know any of us. You barely even speak to us."

"I didn't really think anyone noticed."

"Of course we notice. You've been at our school nearly a year, and you've barely said boo to anyone unless it's about schoolwork."

Willa doesn't know how to explain that the idea of walking in and finding common ground, of negotiating their complex, foreign social terrain, was too daunting. That it seemed easier to go without friends. Willa still remembers that first day at Gandry, exchanging green checks for a royal blue blazer, feeling unarmed and terrified in this shiny, new world without her smartest-kid reputation and her best friends.

"Amira and I were wondering if you'd be different on this camp."

"You were?" Willa can't even imagine them talking about her. She's too boring.

"And I guess you are. I mean, we're actually having a conversation." She gives her a sly smile.

"I'm sorry. I don't mean to be rude."

"I don't think anyone thinks you're rude. People just don't know what to make of you. You're this weird combination of quiet, tough, genius girl. And we know nothing about you." She leans against the fence. "You're allowed to keep to yourself, Willa, but you should also know we're not that bad. I know you probably have other people in your life, but, you know, if you ever, like, wanted to make a friend at school, we're nice people. Mostly."

Willa smiles weakly, awash with guilt. "I do know that."

"Good."

They lapse into silence.

Willa finally turns and eyes Eva. "Hey, can I ask you something?"

"Why not?" Eva says dreamily as she stares up at the sky.

"Do you think what we're doing is wrong? The siege?"

"I don't love it. I can understand why Finn freaked. It's kind of a gross act."

Willa nods, feeling the crawl of dread. Because maybe after seeing that website, and after that conversation with Drew yesterday, maybe she should care about this more too. Not just for Finn, but for herself. Because isn't caring the difference between people like Finn and people like Drew? For the first time in her life, Willa's realising she may have to pick a side.

But what's she supposed to do if on one side there's winning, like they set out to do, and on the other side there's doing the right thing and helping Finn not sacrifice her ideals? How is she meant to choose between these finely sharpened points?

"But remember, Drew's act was gross first." Eva says. "And I don't really see another option."

Willa's relieved that Eva gets it. If it were Kelly, she'd say it was just a game and who cares. But Eva knows everything that's riding on it.

"But just because you and I can't think of one doesn't mean there isn't one." Eva pushes herself off the fence and turns to her. "You should talk to Finn. Maybe she's had an idea. Remember that thing I told you—about how you don't have to take responsibility for everything? I know you like to be in control, but sometimes you have to flinch, you know? Sometimes there's something worth surrendering for." She smiles. "I'm talking about Finn now."

Willa chews on her lip, gathering her courage. She's said so much to Eva tonight, what's a little more oversharing? "You know, I've never had a girlfriend. Or anything but that mess with Freya. I don't even know *how* to be in a relationship. I definitely don't know how to fix one."

"Have you and Finn broken up?"

"I don't know. N-not yet."

"Then you do know how to be in one. And as for fixing them, all I know is…well, you know all that stuff our parents and magazines and the movies spout about compromise?"

"Yeah?"

"I think it might be very, annoyingly true."

Willa picks up her books and sighs. "I wasn't expecting Finn to get so upset. And I wasn't really thinking about whether I thought what we're doing was right or wrong. I was just focusing on trying to win. For Gandry."

"Eh, it might do us good not to win everything for once," Eva says breezily. "Rumour has it we're too full of ourselves." She grins. "I mean, I'd still prefer we did, but I'm open to trying new things."

"*Apparently,*" Willa teases. "Come on. We better go."

Eva stares at her, a look of mock shock on her face. "Did you just make *another* joke, Willa? About my party pash with Maria?" She trails Willa down the path to their cabin. "Because that would be your second funny in, like, a week. I might have to tell the others, you know."

CHAPTER 74

Finn stops mid-step when she realises Willa is the only person in the picnic area. She doesn't walk away, though.

"I thought we were all meeting." Her tone is terse.

"Hey." Willa jumps off the table. "I'm sorry. I didn't know how else to get you here. Please stay and talk to me." When Finn doesn't answer immediately, she clasps her wrist. "Please?"

It feels like the longest moment in the world. She finally gives Willa a tight nod, and they sit on the scarred surface of the table. Willa takes a deep breath. Because if there's one thing she has to get right, it's this.

"See," she says slowly, "when I actually think about it, I don't love the idea of what we're doing either. I was just trying to find a solution. I think I'm so used to having to solve everything that I just go on automatic. See a problem, fix it, you know? I wasn't really thinking about what it meant. But when I do, I don't like the idea of a siege either. And I definitely don't want to be like Drew."

Finn's staring out to the scrub where the birds are noisily settling in for the night. Willa knows she's listening, though.

"But the thing is," she continues. "I can't think of another way. Not in the time we have left. Not if we want to win. I have no idea what to do now. And for the record, I have never said that out loud in my life."

Finn almost smiles. *Almost.* "I bet you haven't."

"If I thought we had time, I'd say let's try and come up with something else, but we don't."

Finn's eyes brighten. "We have tonight."

"But whatever we come up with, we'd have to write up another plan, do all the work—"

"So? We're a squad of all-out geeks. We kill at all that."

Willa smiles back at her. How can she not? When Finn looks at her like this, all stubborn, tenacious hope? And now that she's staring into the face of Finn's relentless optimism, Willa knows like she's known nothing else in her life that Finn's never going to stop being that way. It's Willa who is going to have to surrender on this one, who is going to have to learn how to surrender if they are to get past this. So this is that compromise thing.

"Will, how close was the vote?" Finn asks. "When Jessie suggested the siege?"

"Pretty close," Willa admits.

"And you and Jessie were both into the plan when you told them about it, right?"

"Yeah."

"Did anyone else say anything?"

Willa thinks back to that quick, urgent meeting in the rec hall. "Not really."

"See, I wish you'd waited for me. I know you were going to count my vote if you needed it, but you didn't let me have a voice before we voted, either. To try to convince everyone to look for something different. That's not fair."

Shame assaults Willa. She didn't even think about it.

"I'm so sorry. I honestly didn't consider that you'd hate the idea so much. I just thought you'd be happy we'd found a solution. I wasn't trying to silence you or anything."

Finn breaks a small twig into pieces, flinging each section into the grass. When she finally meets Willa's eye, she says in this quiet voice, "I guess we don't know each other that well yet."

That "yet" makes Willa's heart skip a beat. She gives Finn a hopeful smile. "I'm learning."

The return smile is tiny, but it's there. Finn flings the last piece of twig away and sighs.

"I just feel like we can do better than this. That we're better than this."

Willa thinks of the endless discussion and argument this will mean and fights a sigh. She owes Finn this. "Alright. Let's get everyone together. If we can come up with something tonight, then we'll do it. But if we don't, we'll *have* to stick with the plan. Tomorrow's the last day."

Finn's tiger eyes are shining. "Then we better come up with something, then. Where will we meet? And when? We've got activities after dinner."

"After lights out, I guess. I'll figure out a place."

Finn smiles. Properly this time. "My, aren't we breaking a lot of rules tonight?"

Willa's heart lurches. Finn's teasing her. This is a good thing. And if breaking rules makes Finn smile at her again, she'd break a thousand more right now if she could.

"Okay, I'm going to round up whoever I can find." Finn springs from the tabletop and charges off, her arms swinging by her sides. Then she stops, turns on her heel, and dashes back to Willa. And the next thing she knows, Finn's got her hands planted on her shoulders. Her face is grave. "I'm sorry I stopped talking to you."

"I'm sorry I didn't let you have a say."

"I'll have it tonight."

"I wish I was like you," Willa says quietly. "So certain."

Finn's smile is pure radiance. She drops a swift, fervent kiss on Willa's lips. "I missed you," she whispers before taking off into the night.

Willa watches her disappear around a corner and lets out a slow breath. Eva was totally right. Some things are worth flinching for.

CHAPTER 75

The cabin stinks of chicken Twisties and a whole lot of people cooped up in one teeny space. Willa leans against the brick, enjoying the subtle press of Finn's leg by hers as they sit jammed between bunks in a spare cabin.

They've been in here for half an hour since Finn said her piece, discussing what to do by torchlight and taking turns on teacher watch. The options so far are to siege or not to siege. There are a few who'd like not to, but problem is, no one has yet come up with an alternative.

Amy wrinkles her nose. "I mean, starving them out? It *is* kind of intense." She nudges Finn's foot. "Remember those heady, innocent days we were just trading food and trying to find a bed to sleep in? When Brian thought we could prostitute ourselves?"

"Unfortunately, I do."

"We wouldn't have to do this if Drew wasn't such a militant asshole," Leon grumbles.

Eva laughs and passes him the chips. He grins at her and takes them, but only to offer them to her again. She takes one and smiles at him.

Are they flirting? Willa wonders if Amira has finally convinced Eva to go there with Leon. These are the kinds of things Willa would never have even noticed before this camp.

Finn elbows her "What are you grinning about?"

"Nothing."

She gives Willa a curious look but says nothing.

"Come on, guys, we need a plan," Damir says. "Something Drew can't beat."

"Drew is such a giant douchebag," Amy says.

"Yeah, I think we've pretty much covered that," Finn says. "Drew's a douche. Case closed. Can we just focus on what to do?"

Amy salutes her. "Yes'm."

"Come on. Ideas, people," Amira says, although all she's contributed so far is the Twisties.

Everybody stops talking for a minute, and the sound in the cabin is reduced to the rustle of chip bags and the shuffle of rearranged limbs as they think.

Finally, Mark groans and drops his head back against the brick. "It's impossible. How am I supposed to think of a way to counter such a diabolically stupid idea? It's almost like we need one as stupid of our own."

Eva sighs loudly. "I know, right?"

"I can't believe anyone on his team didn't point out how nuts it is." Craig shakes his head. "Or how hard Gus and the teachers are going to come down on them in the academic part. I mean, they can't all be as idiotic as him, can they?"

"Wouldn't they have stopped him if they were a few IQ points up on him?" Amira asks.

Willa remembers her conversation with Drew earlier. Chances are he's much smarter than all of them. At schoolwork, anyway. Not that school smart means life smart. Willa knows that. Otherwise she'd be doing a lot better, wouldn't she?

Finn suddenly sits up. "That's it!"

"That's what?" Amy asks.

"That's it," she says again, eyes gleaming. "They can't all be that stupid. But they have no choice because he's the king, remember?" She turns to Willa, as if no one else is there. "I know what we're going to do."

"What?"

"We're going to gently encourage his team to utilise their no-confidence vote."

"How are we going to do that?" Willa had forgotten about that option.

"We intimidate them into it."

"How?"

Finn grins at her. "That's where you come in."

"Me?"

226

But Finn isn't listening. She's already turning back to the group. "Okay, so here's what we'd have to do."

~ ~ ~

Willa frowns as she watches everyone clear the stifling little space to sneak back to their cabins. There are so many ways this plan could fail them. So many ways *she* could fail them, given her part. When they are the only ones left, she turns to Finn. "If this doesn't work, will you be really upset?"

"Yes." A smile breaks over Finn's face. "But you won't let it fail, because you're Willa."

"Well this is only happening because *you're* Finn." Willa wraps her arms around her waist. "I missed you too," she whispers, "a *lot*."

Finn just holds her tighter. They stand in this sweetly suffocating clutch until Finn pulls away. "We'd better go. We'll wreck the whole thing if we get caught. See you in a few hours?"

Willa nods, but she lingers a moment to watch Finn walk away. Just to drink in the buoyance of Finn's step now that she's righted the troubles of the world. And Willa's suddenly captured by a memory from when she was a kid. Nan gave her two dollars to bet on a horse in the Melbourne Cup. Willa picked a horse called Brave Idealist, just because she liked the lofty romance of the name. She still does. And she'd bet on Finn right now.

CHAPTER 76

They gather in a loose, sleep-deprived group under the trees, someone setting off an eruption of yawns every now and then. Willa stands next to Finn, still electric with the knowledge that standing next to her is an option again. They exchange small smiles, but Willa can tell Finn's edgy from the way she taps her foot against the dirt and her hands are shoved deep in her pockets.

Willa's not. Instead there's this calm steadily stitching its way through her. And she knows it's their faith in her to execute this part of the plan making her feel like that. Or Finn's faith, anyway.

"Just do your straight-backed, chin-up, stare thing," Finn instructed her as they walked up the hill. "They'll listen to you. It's impossible not to. You're intimidating as hell when you're like that."

Willa may have elbowed her at the time, but she's planning on doing exactly what Finn says.

Everyone perks up at the sound of footsteps. It's Amira, striding up the path, looking disgustingly morning fresh compared to the rest of them in her crisp tee and artfully messy side braid. She marches right up to Willa with a grin. "That was the weirdest early morning task I've been given, but they're coming."

"You sure?"

"I flirted. Trust me. They'll be here."

Amy frowns. "Don't you feel super creepy using your sexuality to get stuff?"

Amira's eyes flash. "I don't know, don't you feel super judge-y thinking you're better than me because of it? I bet you're a slut-shamer too." Then she turns back to Willa. "About ten minutes."

In exactly ten minutes, they hear footsteps. It's the blond deputy Finn told Amira to target, and another one with curly brown hair.

Willa draws in a slow breath. It's time.

When the guys see the group waiting for them, their steps slow. The blond glares at Amira. "What the hell's going on?"

"Someone needed a chat with you."

He's about to say something when Willa steps forward. "I don't think we've met," she says in a calm, clear voice. She holds out her hand. "I'm Willa."

"I know exactly who you are." He doesn't take her hand.

"But I don't know who you are," she says, still holding it out. "Your leader makes so much noise that it's hard to hear the rest of you."

He reluctantly takes it. "Cameron," he mutters.

"Nice to meet you, Cameron." She turns to the other guy. "And?"

"Simon." His shake is firmer than Cameron's.

She takes a step back, folds her arms over her chest, and stands tall, harnessing all the command she can find, just like Finn said to.

"She's brought *that* Willa," she hears someone mutter behind her. Someone else shushes them.

"I was wondering," she says slowly. "If you'd like to hear what our plan is to stop your military advance?"

Cameron pulls a face. "Why would you tell us that?"

"That's not what I asked. I asked if you wanted to know what it was."

"Go right ahead." Simon shoots Cameron an amused look.

"Okay." She turns and paces in front of them, her arms folded over each other. "So, while your army is mobilising in the centre, the military from six other territories are moving rapidly toward your borders. By the time you try and move, we'll have you surrounded. And we'll have you surrounded so closely and so quickly you won't even be able to use your air force without sacrificing population."

Cameron frowns and goes to say something, but Willa continues. "With all food trade cut, we've estimated your population can survive on food stores for maybe one month. Then your citizens and your army will slowly starve while we, supplied by our territories from the outside, wait you out until you're too weak to fight. Then we'll invade. That's what will happen."

"Right, sounds awesome," Cameron says, sarcastic. "Again, gotta ask, why are you telling us? Because now that we know, we can just go and change our plan."

"Change your plan to what, exactly? Oh, and do you know you have about two hours to write it all up and submit it? Two hours where we're supposed to eat breakfast, clean cabins, and do our morning walk?"

Simon crosses his arms, feigning indifference, but she sees his gaze sweep casually down to his watch.

That's when she decides to move in. She turns to Cameron, the deputy. "Can I ask you a question, Cameron? Do you, personally, want to do well in the game?"

Cameron shrugs. "Of course."

"And do you want to get a good report from this?"

"Yeah."

"Do you think Drew does?"

He shrugs again.

"And do you think Gus and the teachers will think moving your military against all the other territories was a solid plan? Or even vaguely justifiable? In fact, do you honestly think any of Drew's recent decisions will look good on paper?"

Simon lets out an exasperated breath. "I have a question too. It's the same one as his. Why are we talking about this?"

Willa looks him up and down. "So you know your options."

He scoffs. "But it doesn't sound like we have any."

"Actually, as far as I see it, you have two." She begins to pace again. "You can starve in the siege and let all your people slowly die for no good reason other than your leader's a bored, petty dictator who just *loves* power. *Or* you can utilise your no-confidence, vote him out and take charge." She watches his eyes flicker at that thought. "And you would be welcome to join our alliance and start trading with us again. You and your people can eat, and maybe even prosper. Think about it. We could all win. Or you could lose."

Finn steps forward, holding up a sheaf of papers. "And, bonus, if you do decide to join us, your homework's already done." She waves the paper at them. "The agreement is all here, written up for you."

Willa takes the papers and passes them to Cameron with a smile. "We'll leave the decision with you."

He slowly grasps the papers, meeting her gaze for a fleeting moment. She can see the cogs turning already. "But what's the catch?" he says.

"There is absolutely no catch," Willa assures him. "Read it and you'll see. We will ally with you in exactly the way we have with everyone else here, and foster the same mutually beneficial trade agreements. But only if you vote him out. It's up to you."

Cameron stares at the sheaf of papers in his hand. He looks at Simon. Willa can't quite read the look passed between them, but she's sure they'll be at least having a conversation about it.

Finally, he holds up the agreement. "We'll think about it." They turn and walk away through the scrub.

As soon as they are out of sight, the clearing erupts into claps and cheers.

"You were *amazing*, Willa." Leon shakes his head.

"Yeah, you were," Amy agrees. "Do you have any idea how terrifying you are?"

Amira turns on her. "Do you have any idea how obnoxious *you* are?" She slips an arm through Willa's. "Don't listen to her."

Willa bites down on a smile at Amira's kneejerk Gandry defence of her.

"Yeah, I actually do know how obnoxious I am. That's what keeps me on the right side of charming." Amy turns to Willa. "I totally meant it as a compliment. I mean, you're so tall and hot and, like, stone cold when you want to be. I wish I could turn it on like that. I can only do angry chipmunk."

Even Amira has to laugh.

They trudge, wearily triumphant, to breakfast. "Amy really did mean that as a compliment," Finn tells her as they trail the group. "About you being terrifying."

"I can't help how I am."

Finn elbows her. "How you are is amazing, anyway. A little salty at first, maybe, but..." she laughs at Willa's expression. "well, I won't tell you the names my teammates used to call you."

"What kind of names?" Willa narrows her eyes.

"Don't worry. Some of them were very complimentary, including a high approval rating for your legs and your sass levels."

Willa's eyes widen. "What did they say about my legs?"

Finn just cackles and dashes up the steps to the dining hall. At the top, she turns and grins. "They *are* hot legs." And she gives them a thorough, teasing up and down before she turns and strides into the hall.

CHAPTER 77

Willa's staring at the clock when a hand clutches her arm so hard it hurts. "Ouch, *what?*"

Eva gestures at the door with her chin, where the boys from Drew's team are slinking in.

"Sorry," Cameron mutters at Gus as they make their way to their table.

"Drew's not with them," Eva hisses, still digging her fingers into her forearm.

Willa nods, shaking her claws off and inspecting the marks on her skin.

"Sorry," Eva mutters. "But that's got to be a good thing, right?"

"I hope so." Willa looks across to Finn's table. Finn is looking right back at her. They exchange hopeful smiles.

~ ~ ~

Leon holds his can of drink up in the flickering firelight. "Well, we did it."

"Eleventh-hour strategy too." Jessie knocks his can against Leon's. "It's official: we are an epic alliance."

"We are." Amy says. "Awesome idea, Finn."

"Awesome execution, Willa," Finn says.

Willa smiles shyly as she digs her chin into her collar against the cold.

"Yes." Amira nods. "Truly awesome execution, Willa. If I ever need to interrogate someone, you're my girl."

"Thanks, I think."

"You know, this camping spot isn't so bad," Eva says, looking around their small campsite. "You've got a fire and the creek. It's pretty."

"Yeah, but we also sleep in cold tents on the rock-hard ground," Amy tells her.

"Okay, well there is that." Eva sits up. "Hang on. The game's over, isn't it? Why can't you move back to the cabins?"

Amy sits up. "We probably can." She turns to Finn, who nods.

"They probably won't let us tonight, but tomorrow night, maybe?" she says.

Amy grabs Finn's arm. "We are *so* asking."

"Yes, Amy, we'll ask," Finn says patiently." And you can finally stop whining."

Amy pulls a mock-offended face. "Whatever do you mean?"

Finn just looks blankly at her. Then her face crumples into a yawn. "I'm so glad the game is done, though. It was kind of stressful at the end."

Willa meets her eyes, and they smile their relief at each other. Relief at it being over. Relief at being *them* again.

Amy catches the look. "Aw, our two mommies have made up."

"Not funny, Ames," Finn mutters.

"Sorry." But Willa can tell she's not sorry one bit.

Jessie throws a log into the fire. Sparks skitter up into the darkness. "So, camp's about done. Apparently we're officially future leaders now."

"Pfft." Eva smirks, waving a hand at the landscape. "Future leaders of nowhere."

"Eh, as long as we're its leaders and Drew isn't."

"Nah, he's future nothing of nowhere."

"Whoa, hang on a minute," Amy suddenly yells.

Finn jumps in her seat. "Jesus, what?"

"We're not asking to move back into a cabin." She stands up.

Finn looks as confused as everyone else. "Uh, okay then," she says slowly. "Then what are we doing?"

CHAPTER 78

They advance like an army. A ragtag, loud, and wildly disorganised army, with Amy at its head. The ever-growing group charges across the oval, people laughing and hooting, high on anticipation.

Less invested in Operation Mansion Storm, Willa, Finn and Craig bring up the rear. They walk sedately like weary, resigned adults dragged along for supervision.

"I thought you'd rather stab yourself in the eye with a fork than go to this place?" Finn says to Craig with a grin.

"This is different."

When they get to the lawn of the big old house, the pack pounds up the stairs and inside. By the time Willa and Finn make it inside the living room, kids are already making themselves at home, throwing themselves down on the sofas that line the edge of the room, heckling the occupants.

The mansion boys are taking the invasion well, though. They just grin and shrug and dude-bro their way around the teasing, giving it right back. Willa suspects it's got something to do with the size of the female population currently invading their space.

"Welcome," Cameron says, coming up to the three of them like they're the honoured guests. He sweeps his arm out like he's a game show host, showing off the prize, "Welcome to our humble abode."

"So, where's the Xbox hiding?" Craig rubs his hands together.

"That's why you came," Finn says, rolling her eyes.

Cameron laughs. "Dude, we have nothing. Not even a TV. Other than the size and, you know, being indoors, this place has nothing. Beds, sofas, a table, and chairs. It's all smoke and mirrors, my friend."

"Damn."

"What do you like to play?"

They start talking games. And when they get going, they sound just like Jack and his friend Tyler back home, lost in game world, talking like it's real. Willa feels a small pang, remembering she's going to see him soon. She's going to see them all. This camp has been amazing in some ways, but she can't wait to get home. She's about to ask Finn what she's missed most when Amy bounds over, Zaki and Hana in tow.

"I think I could be quite comfortable here!" Amy grins evilly and turns to Finn. "I want to see the upstairs. Coming?"

"Why not?" As she sets off, Willa feels a tug on her wrist. It makes her grin. It looks like she's coming too. She trots up the dark stairway behind them.

At the top, Amy heads straight for a room with its door wide open and the lights on. "Not bad," she says, turning in a slow circle.

Willa walks in behind them, curious. The room is biggish, with dusty wooden floors, white walls, and two single beds pressed to the edges. There's a dude mess of clothes and toiletries flung all over the floor between them, and two long windows stand at attention at the end of the room, looking out into the darkness. There's no other furniture except a wooden trunk in the corner. As spare as it is, this would be a nice room to wake up in, Willa thinks, when the morning sun is hitting it just right.

"They still have to share," Hana says, hands on hips. "I thought it was going to be like the Hilton."

"Yeah, gotta say I expected a bit more luxury from this place." Amy stalks out.

"I love her, but she's such a spoiled brat," Finn says to Willa as the girls follow Amy out.

Willa doesn't answer. Instead she stealths a quick kiss. Finn's eyes widen, but Willa just grins and darts out of the room. As she follows the others into the hallway, she feels the small teasing dig of Finn's finger into the small of her back. And suddenly Willa is engulfed in this bright, exquisite feeling. How did she not know about this feeling? She wants to turn around and fold her arms around Finn, but she doesn't dare.

Amy's standing in front of a closed door. "So, what do you think is behind door number two?" Before anyone can respond, she turns the handle and shoves it open. "Well, hello there!"

Drew is slouched across a bed, book in hand. He sits up, shaking his head, glaring. "No way. Get lost."

"Don't think so." Amy practically skips into the room. "Lucky you. Scored a single room. Perks of being leader, huh?" Then she covers her mouth, mock contrite. "Oops, my bad. *Former* leader."

Willa leans against doorjamb, curious about how he'll deal with this. She's barely seen him since the deal was made and his group turned on him. She can feel Finn at her shoulder, watching too.

"What are you doing?" he asks as Hana and Zaki waltz in behind her. They begin to strut around, inspecting the room. Zaki points and giggles at a pair of boxers hanging off the edge of the lone chair.

"Get out of my room."

"Ah, see, that's where you're wrong," Amy tells him. "It's everyone's room now."

"Seriously, you need to leave." He tries to go for a weary, sick-of-the-children tone, but Willa can see his usual attempt at indifference dissolving.

"Nope." Amy blithely picks up each of the books sitting on the trunk next to his bed. She examines the covers like she's in a bookshop or library, casually browsing. "Hmm, didn't pick you for a sci-fi geek."

He jumps off the bed, swiping a hand through his hair. "I mean it. Get out."

"And I told you, it's not your room anymore. In fact, *I* might sleep here tonight. Looks comfy." She jumps into the spot he's just abandoned, making a show of tucking her hands behind her head and wriggling. "I mean, you owe me at least that. You're the reason I had to sleep in a tent. I hope you like sleeping bags and the cold, hard ground."

"Actually, that was my fault," Finn pipes up. "I drew the wildcard."

"Don't help, Finn," Amy says.

"Sorry."

Willa smothers a laugh. Finn's so honest she doesn't know when to shut the hell up.

"Anyway," Amy continues, "if he's not the reason I ended up in a tent, he *is* the reason I stayed in it so long. So now I'm here."

"We're all here." Hana hauls up the window, peering out into the night. The sound of laughter floats up from the porch.

Willa watches him decide how to react. To see if he can find a way through or out of this. "I'd really appreciate it if you could piss off," he says, smiling.

"You can keep saying it," Amy says, like she's talking to a kid, "but it won't happen."

Finn shakes her head and backs out of the doorway like she's had enough. Willa stays, curious about how he's going to react. She can see rage agitating at the perimeter, wanting out. But she can also see the fight for control, his need to retreat to the safety of that smirk. But the anger is pushed way too hard against him.

He explodes. "For fuck's sake!" He kicks his backpack across the room. It slides over the dusty wood, stopping at Zaki's feet. She jumps and giggles, hand over her mouth.

"Look, you won the game!" he shouts. "You got your prize. Let me have some freaking peace until this stupid social experiment of a camp is over and I can go home."

"Drew, are you sad because you're a failed experiment?" Amy asks, while Hana and Zaki jump on the bed with her, a united, giggling front.

He just mutters something and shoves past Willa. The girls on the bed fall in a heap, cackling as he storms down the stairs.

"Happy now. Ames?" Finn asks, coming back into the room. "He's definitely pissed."

"You don't say?" Amy flings her arms in the air. "I'm positively delighted." She sniffs the doona and wrinkles her nose. "But I'm not really sleeping in here. I might catch Drew."

"You're such a child," Finn says fondly. "Somehow I don't think the Hulk is going to let us sleep anywhere we want, anyway."

"True," Amy sighs.

"Hey, Finn, do you remember that guy, Costa, from Year 10?" Hana asks.

"That guy whose dad who yelled at the vice principal?"

"Yeah, him." She launches into some high-speed story chock full of names and places and asides. Willa listens for a minute but then drifts away. She wanders the length of the hallway. It's more of the same: sparsely furnished, wood-floored rooms littered with careless boys' belongings.

She trots down the stairs, away from the living room, which is packed now that word's gotten around that the mansion is for the taking. Out the back, the hall opens out into a dining room with a huge wooden table and chairs covered with the detritus of abandoned homework. Behind is an old kitchen, crowded with nooks and crannies and small cupboards that Willa can imagine stocked with food for hungry farmers. Meaty stews and solid, buttery cakes designed to fuel, not impress. Beyond, there's an old laundry with a giant stone sink and nothing else, still somehow smelling of damp clothing.

Amy's right. The house is much less impressive than it looks. Really it's just a large, old testament to utilitarianism. She pushes open the wooden door leading outside and finds herself on the porch.

She's hit with a flurry of familiar. Because this is the very spot where she and Finn sat that night. The night Willa pulled all her bravery from somewhere and kissed the girl. She can't help smiling as she steps outside, even as she remembers that nausea she felt as she walked away from this house that night, not knowing whether to be hopeful or humiliated or both.

When she turns to trace the journey back around, she finds herself meeting her destiny again: she's face-to-face with Drew.

"What do you want?" he mutters, his mess of curls falling forward as he hunches on the bench.

"Nothing. I didn't know you were out here." She rests her arms on the railings, staring out into the night, strangely unwilling to leave. Finally, she turns to examine him. He doesn't look angry *or* self-satisfied any more. He just looks over it. "Are you okay?"

He pulls in his chin and scoffs. "Of course I am."

Willa turns right around, pressing her back to the railing. "Is it hard, pretending all the time?"

"I don't know," he fires back. "Is it hard being such a goody-two-shoes all the time?"

"No, not really."

He fires off a grunt of a laugh. "Anyway, I'm fine. Except there's some chick in my bed, and not in the good way. But other than that, I'm all good."

"No you're not. You're upset because your friends betrayed you."

"How would you know how I feel?"

"Because anyone would feel like that. Even if I didn't care about winning or school or the game, I'd care if my friends were willing to turn on me. And besides, you wouldn't be sitting here by yourself with that look on your face if you felt fine."

"Maybe I just dislike your company."

She shrugs, as if to say "fair enough", and stares back out into the moonlit view, all leafy shapes and shadows.

"Besides, those guys aren't my friends. They're just people I go to school with."

That's exactly how she used to think. "Don't you get afraid you'll end up alone? With this whole not caring thing?"

"That's my problem, isn't it?"

"I'm just saying maybe you should rethink it."

He snickers. "Thanks. I'll take your highly earnest advice on board."

"Good," she says, pretending to miss his sarcasm.

"And I suppose you're feeling pretty great? Got the girl and the win."

"*She* got the win. And maybe I care less about that than I did at the start."

"Aw," he coos. "Ice maiden had a learning experience. Gus would be so happy."

"I did," she agrees. Who cares what he knows about her at this point? She's never going to see him again after this camp. Not if she can help it.

"Why are you even talking to me?"

"I don't know." And she really doesn't. Maybe it's those recognisable fragments of herself. The ways that they are both alone and the ways that they have been wilfully alone. He's still wilful. She's learning not to be. And she's learning it's worth it too. But she can't make him see that.

"I'm going back in. You should come in too."

"Why?" he sneers. "So I can make it all better?"

"Everyone will probably just pretend it never happened if you do. Except maybe Amy."

"Yeah, I'll give that a miss."

She watches him folding back in on himself. He's right. Why is she trying so hard? It's not her job to make him a better person. She's got enough work to do on herself. "Okay, see you, then," she says lightly.

He doesn't answer.

Willa slowly traces the porch back around to the front, feeling light and unhurried. When she finally makes her way to the front steps, some of her Gandry girls are sitting out there under the porch light. Finn and Amy and the rest of their group are there now, too. Music pulses out of the open window, and the sounds of laughter and footsteps spill out along with it. She tunes in to the chatter as she moves closer.

"What? You have to wear your blazer all day, even in summer?" Hana pulls a face. "That's actual cruelty."

"When we're on the street we do," Eva says. "That's an up-itself inner-Eastern school for you."

"Our school's so loose, it's barely a private," Finn says. She automatically wriggles over on the bench, making room for Willa. "Our Year 12s only have to wear the uniform jumper."

"Lucky them," Amira sighs. "I'm a prisoner to blue check for another two years."

"Where have you been?" Finn asks as Willa sits down beside her.

Willa just shrugs. She'll tell her about it later.

"Take pity, my friend. Our dresses have purple stripes," Hana tells her, pulling a face.

"Don't forget the white Peter Pan collar," Zaki adds with a shake of her head.

As the chat drifts around them, Willa feels the soft slide of Finn's fingers taking hold of hers on the wooden bench between them. She stiffens and then softens. Because why fight it? Instead she just squeezes Finn's hand and leans against the cool brick of the house. And Finn's only answer is to shift slightly closer until her shoulder is a sweet press against Willa's arm. A warmth radiates through Willa as she listens to the conversation, tethered to this night and to this girl.

Finn

CHAPTER 79

"Not going to lie, guys. This is a first. We've never had *all* territories end up on the same team." Gus grins and plucks at his beard. "You bunch of peace-loving hippies."

People laugh. Finn has to. If only Gus knew how close it came to being the opposite. Or maybe he does know and is pretending it never happened.

"Anyway," he drums on the table lightly, recapturing their attention, "this game has never been about who gains territorial dominance. It's about *how* you play the game. That's why every year, as well as handing out the academic prize to the team with the highest standard of report writing and research, we hand out another prize."

Finn glances over at the Gandry table, where the academic trophy already sits in front of Willa. Of course. Over on Glumtown's table is the cleanest cabin prize, handed out at the start of the night. Who knew they had that up their sleeve?

"At every camp, the major prize is given to the team that shows the most resourcefulness, research and initiative in creating and maintaining their territory." He looks around the room. "It was easy this time. Because at every camp, there's also a group that is dealt the worst hand, the wild card. They are given no territory and no resources, and they have to figure out a way to survive. Some find sanctuary, some eke out a means to eat, and others never really manage. I've seen wild-card groups trade food—*actual food*—for shelter. And I've never seen that group win this prize."

Amy nudges her, but Finn studiously ignores her, even as her pulse quickens.

"That is, until now," Gus says. "Because this time around, this particular wild-card group not only found a way to survive, they found a way to flourish. All while roughing it in tents."

"Only because Finn wouldn't let us do anything else," Amy mutters. Everyone at their table laughs. Even Finn, while she's busy kicking Amy under the table.

"This group developed a solid strategy for survival *and* to improve their lot and maintain independence. That's why this time around, Finn Harlow and her group take the all-camp prize for a fantastic show of innovation and enterprise. Well done."

He drums on the table again, bringing on a thunder of applause. "Come on, Finn."

Her cheeks burn as she traipses up to the front of the hall. She hears Amy whooping behind her, and a sneaked glance shows the Gandry girls all clapping and whistling. Finn cannot smother her smile as she takes the trophy from Gus.

"Well done, kiddo," he says. "Terrific work."

"Thanks," she mumbles and dashes back to her seat, still blushing.

She sits down hurriedly as Gus speaks about the things they supposedly learned at this camp. He sounds just like that suit from the first day. She examines the trophy. It is just a small rectangle on top of another rectangle, with a small gold-ish plate. Boringly un-kitsch. No one will even notice it among the sport prizes in the cabinet at school. It doesn't matter, though, because *Finn* knows. And as much as she doesn't want to admit it, she's proud of this one. Of winning at this camp that she thought she'd hate. Of her gorgeous, idiot teammates for finally pulling it together. Of herself. Because she made it happen. *That* Finn is back.

She spies Willa watching her through the crowd, and Finn sends her a sly smile. Because it was a little bit Willa too. Beautiful, forceful Willa, who made Finn fight for herself. Willa, who pushed her so hard, but who, in the end, bent for her too.

When Gus is finally done talking, the teachers pass fizzy drinks and boxes of ice creams between the tables. A cheapskate celebration, but people dive for them. Amy rips an ice cream from the box and screams, "Finally! Why so freaking tight?"

The hall erupts into laughter and echoing taunts.

"They must have restocked them," Craig says, tearing open the wrapper, "after Drew's raid."

Hana hands an ice cream to Zaki. "I have this image of a giant, walk-in freezer in the middle of the bush somewhere, powered by a generator and guarded by men with weaponry."

Jessie chuckles. "I wouldn't put it past Gussy. Hey, did they ever bust Drew?"

Finn shakes her head. "Don't think so. I guess we can give him that win."

"Yeah, but that's all he gets," Zaki says, grinning. She holds up her ice cream. "To us."

Finn holds hers up with the rest and joins the chorus. "To us."

CHAPTER 80

In the thready early morning sunlight, they make their way up the creek one last time, their rock-jumping journey practically muscle memory now.

Lying on the cool surface of the rock with Willa's fingers threaded through hers, Finn stares up into the towering dome of eucalypts. She loves this place.

She turns on her side and sifts her fingers through Willa's hair, hanging loose for once. Willa's face is sleepy-cute, and for the zillionth time, Finn is arrested by how lovely she is. But it's more than that. It's the feeling she gets, the one she knew was missing with Jessie, that strange cocktail of flutter and gravity. Finn gets it just looking at Willa. Has been getting it since that kiss on the hill two weeks ago. It's a mammoth overdose of intense and terrifying and wonderful, and she wouldn't give it up for anything.

Willa gives her a small, sweet smile, and Finn is suddenly covetous with knowing that there's a Willa for her—the one that smiles like this—and a Willa for everyone else.

Willa swipes a fingertip over her nose. "You've grown some freckles."

"Really?" Like Finn needs more freckles. "Are you sure they weren't already there?"

"Trust me. I've spent a lot of time staring at you. They're new."

"Boo."

"Sh. They're cute." Willa picks up her hand and kisses her fingers lightly. "Last day. Can you believe it?"

"No." She really can't. It feels like a forever they've been here. Long enough for this place to seem like her only reality, anyway.

"I was thinking about all the stuff that Gus and that suit were talking about on the first day." Willa plays absently with the cords that dangle from Finn's hoodie. "Do you feel like you learned anything on this camp? Like, about yourself?"

Finn draws in a breath, thinking. "I guess I feel more like I got something back. What I'd lost before I came here, if that makes sense?"

"It does."

"What about you?"

"I learned things."

"Like what?"

"I learned I really like my teammates."

"Well that's probably lucky, seeing as you go to school with them every day."

Willa smiles, but turns serious again. "But I think I learned more from you than from the game."

"From me?"

"I learned I need to maybe figure out what I want and what I believe, not just what I think I should be doing. Stop ticking boxes for a minute, you know?"

Finn nods and presses a swift kiss on her. "I get it."

"And I learned you're one of the most amazing humans I know."

Finn buries her face in Willa's neck, surfing a tidal wave of happy. "Shush."

"No."

"I have something for you." Finn sits up and pulls her portrait of Willa from the oval out of her bag. "I figured I'll be able to draw more pictures of you."

Willa holds the picture gingerly. When she looks up, her face is a curl of doubt. "What happens when we get back to Melbourne?"

"It'll be awesome. Think about it: we won't have to sneak off to be alone. And we can do geek things together. Hang out properly." Finn knows that isn't exactly what Willa is asking, but it's a better answer. Because now Willa knows that, in Finn's mind, it's a given that they'll be seeing each other. And that the only person who could stop this inevitability is Willa herself.

"I have to be home a lot. To look after everyone, and—"

"Hey, it's okay. I know you have a lot to do, with your brother and sister and everything. As long as we can sneak some time."

"As much as I can possibly get. I promise. I'm going to miss being up here, though."

"Me too." Finn drops her head onto Willa's shoulder. Willa's fingers curl over her neck, and the contented silence that drops between them is filled with everything Finn will miss: the sound of the creek tumbling between rocks. The impatient peals of the bell birds, heard but never seen. That addictive stink of wet earth and eucalyptus and rotting wood. The musky warmth of Willa's skin.

She lets out a slow, awed breath. How can it be that the girl she wasn't even sure she could want in her life a couple of weeks ago has somehow become one of the most important and good things in it? How does that happen?

"Come on. It's time," Willa says, standing and pulling her up.

Finn stands there a moment, feasting on Willa's smile, thinking that maybe there's no answer to her question. Maybe it just happens. She takes Willa's hand and leads her into the streaming sunlight.

Willa

CHAPTER 81

The car park is a catastrophe of kids and luggage and parents in beeping cars. While Willa stands there, waiting to get onto the bus, the air fills with shouted goodbyes and swiftly dealt parting shots. She returns Mark's wave as he flings his backpack into the underbelly of his school van and grins. Then, inevitably, she searches the rubble for Finn. She doesn't have to hunt for long, because Finn's coming at her, bag under one arm, phone clutched in the other. She's busily typing something as she strides across the gravel.

Willa grins as she comes to a stop in front of her. "You didn't waste any time."

Finn hugs her phone to her chest and shuts her eyes. "Ah, sweet technology. I've missed it so much."

"You have?"

"God, yes. I've got, like, an epic list of things I need to Google the crap out of. And I'm going to need at least a few solid hours of social media catch-up before I can face school again."

Willa had no idea Finn was so into that stuff. She loves that she's still got all this real-world Finn knowledge to gather up. She feels like a greedy magpie, collecting up silver bits. There's still so much to know.

"Speaking of, I just realised that I need your number," Finn says. "You won't just…be on the oval every morning."

Willa obediently recites it.

"I just messaged you." Finn's smile is all tease, and Willa pings with anticipation at seeing it even while she is still standing right in front of her. Finn tucks her phone into the pocket of her shirt and bounces on her toes. "Hey, so Dad's bought me a ticket to fly over to Hobart and hang out with him next Saturday."

"That's good. That means you're talking to him again?"

"I guess." Finn shrugs. "Anyway, I know the week will be frantic, getting back into school and everything, but do you think we could meet up on Friday night? Before I go?"

Melbourne. The real world. Weird. Melbourne with Finn in it. Amazing. Willa chews her lip, assessing her chances. "I want to. It's just, I might have to look after Riley and Jack, though, depending on Nan."

"Can you just bring them? We could take them to the movies or something."

Willa pulls a face. "Really?"

"Sure. Why not? If you have them, you have them."

Again, all Willa can think is, *this girl.* This girl who doesn't mind her little brother and sister tagging along if it means seeing her. This girl who makes her smile like she's never going to stop. Like she's smiling right now. "Okay."

"Good." Finn steps a little closer. "So," she says quietly, biting down on a smile, "how do you feel about me kissing you right now? Full, unabashed public display of affection?"

There goes another one of those thumps in Willa's chest. It's so sweetly thunderous she doesn't respond. Instead she steps in and kisses Finn first.

"Ooh hot!" It's Amira, of course, hooting as she jumps on the bus.

Willa ignores her. She grabs Finn's hand and squeezes it. "See you soon?"

"Speak to you sooner." Finn rises on her tiptoes and kisses her again. "Bye, Will," she whispers. And then she's gone.

Still smiling, Willa climbs onto the bus. She throws her bags with the rest of the luggage on the front seats, and inches down the narrow aisle. Eva's already chatting on her phone in a middle row. She smiles and moves her jacket and her book from the seat next to her as if to make room.

Willa hesitates and then drops down next to her. Because she's all out of resistance. It can't hurt to have one friend at Gandry, right? She waits impatiently for her phone to wake as the bus engines grumble into being.

Finn's text, when it finally appears, is a kiss emoji, followed by *yes, I'm gross and being only faintly ironic. Expect more of this.* Willa grins.

The bus grinds into gear and begins to inch along the dirt track behind the others, finally passing under that stupid sign directing them to *Live, learn, lead* and out into the bush.

Eva drops her phone into her lap and sighs. "Goodbye, Future Leaders camp." She turns and grins. "Where Willa Brookes learned it's okay to follow sometimes."

"And goodbye, future leaders camp, where Willa Brookes learned that Eva Hawkins is way more of a smart ass than she seems."

Eva just laughs and elbows her.

Willa's phone vibrates in her hand. It's Kelly this time.

I'm bringing the sibs over to meet your bus. Keep me posted on ETA.
They're insanely excited to see you.

Willa punches out a rapid reply.

Thanks. I can't wait to see you guys, too.

She replies straight away.

So, are you officially anointed a future leader? Should I bow when I see
you or something?

I don't know. Possibly. I do know I met the most incredible girl.

Willa sits back against the leather seat, grinning as she imagines the expression on Kelly's face.

Another text. Finn again. Amy's fallen asleep before they even hit the highway, and Finn would most definitely prefer Willa was the one drooling on her shoulder right now. Willa smiles, her heart suddenly full.

So this is what it is like to have a someone.

END BOOK ONE

THE STORY CONTINUES IN

All the Ways to Here
(COMING IN AUTUMN 2017)

About Emily O'Beirne

Thirteen-year-old Emily woke up one morning with a sudden itch to write her first novel. All day, she sat through her classes, feverishly scribbling away (her rare silence probably a cherished respite for her teachers). And by the time the last bell rang, she had penned fifteen handwritten pages of angsty drivel, replete with blood-red sunsets, moody saxophone music playing somewhere far off in the night, and abandoned whiskey bottles rolling across tables. Needless to say, that singular literary accomplishment is buried in a box somewhere, ready for her later amusement.

From Melbourne, Australia, Emily was recently granted her PhD. She works part-time in academia, where she hates marking papers but loves working with her students. She also loves where she lives but travels as much as possible and tends to harbour crushes on cities more than on people.

CONNECT WITH EMILY:

Website: www.emilyobeirne.com

Other Books from Ylva Publishing

www.ylva-publishing.com

Here's the Thing

Emily O'Beirne

ISBN: 978-3-95533-728-5
Length: 182 pages (65,600 words)

When Zel is forced to move to Sydney for a year for her dad's job, she has to leave her best friend/epic crush and their unfinished subway project behind in New York City. Zel tells herself she'll just wait it out until she can get back. But as she finds new friends and a new life in Sydney, she must figure out how to move on while leaving no one behind.

The Space Between

Michelle L. Teichman

ISBN: 978-3-95533-581-6
Length: 280 pages (92,000 words)

Life is easy for Harper, the most popular girl in her grade, until she meets Sarah, a friendless loner who only cares about art. Inexplicably, Harper can't stop thinking about her.

Unsure of her feelings for Harper, Sarah is afraid to act on what her heart is telling her. She can't believe Harper feels the same.

Can Harper and Sarah find a way to be together, or will fear keep them apart forever?

The Light of the World

Ellen Simpson

ISBN: 978-3-95533-507-6
Length: 357 pages (107,000 words)

Confronted with a mystery upon her grandmother's death, Eva delves into the rich and complicated history of a woman who hid far more than a long-lost-love from the world. Darkness is lurking behind every corner, and someone is looking for the key to her grandmother's secrets; the light of the world.

Ex-Wives of Dracula

Georgette Kaplan

ISBN: 978-3-95533-410-9
Length: 338 pages (122,000 words)

Mindy's best friend, Lucia, is a vampire. Every second Mindy spends with her she's in danger of becoming dinner. But Lucia needs help. To keep her alive they need fresh blood, and to cure her they have to kill her sire. So why is it that Nosferatu, the cops, and the chance of becoming an unwilling blood donor don't scare Mindy half as much as the way she feels when Lucia looks at her?

Coming from Ylva Publishing

www.ylva-publishing.com

Pieces

G Benson

Orphaned Carmen is sixteen, newly homeless and will do almost anything to survive and keep her and her kid brother safe, together, and out of foster care. Ollie, also sixteen, has a life that's all about parents, school pressure, friends and dreams of summer. The two fall into each other's orbit, and one kiss changes everything. Ollie is captivated ... but then Carmen vanishes. When they cross paths months later, everything is different.

A young adult queer romance that looks at what we're prepared to sacrifice for those we care about.

All the Ways to Here

Emily O'Beirne

In this sequel to *Future Leaders of Nowhere*, Finn and Willa come home from camp to find everything is different. Even as they grow more sure of their feelings for each other, everything around them feels less certain.

When Finn gets involved in a new community project, she's forced to question where her priorities lie at school. Meanwhile, her dad has moved interstate, her mother is miserable, and her home feels like a ghost town.

Willa's discovering how to navigate the terrains of romance and new school friendships when an accident at home reminds her just how tenuous her family situation is. Suddenly, even with her dad in town, she's shouldering more responsibility than ever.

As they try to navigate these new worlds together, Finn's learning she has to figure out what she wants, and Willa how to ask for what she needs.

Future Leaders of Nowhere
© 2017 by Emily O'Beirne

ISBN: 978-3-95533-821-3

Also available as e-book.

Published by Ylva Publishing, legal entity of Ylva Verlag, e.Kfr.

Ylva Verlag, e.Kfr.
Owner: Astrid Ohletz
Am Kirschgarten 2
65830 Kriftel
Germany

www.ylva-publishing.com

First edition: 2017

Credits
Edited by Astrid Ohletz & Michelle Aguilar
Proofread by Lee Winter
Cover Design by Adam Lloyd
Font Design by flou (www.behance.net/flou) / typeface cutepunk
Print Layout by Allen at eB Format